Praise for the novels of Hester Fox

"*The Witch of Willow Hall* offers a fascinating location, a great plot with history and twists, and characters that live and breathe. I love the novel, and will be looking forward to all new works by this talented author!"

—Heather Graham, *New York Times* bestselling author

"Beautifully written, skillfully plotted, and filled with quiet terror… Perfect for fans of Simone St. James and Kate Morton."

—Anna Lee Huber, bestselling author, on *The Witch of Willow Hall*

"*The Witch of Willow Hall* will cast a spell over every reader."

—Lisa Hall, author of *Tell Me No Lies*

"Steeped in gothic eeriness, it's spine-tingling and very atmospheric."

—Nicola Cornick, *USA TODAY* bestselling author, on *The Witch of Willow Hall*

"Fox spins a satisfying debut yarn that includes witchcraft, tragedy, and love… The inclusion of gothic elements adds a visceral feel that fans of historical fiction with a dash of the supernatural will enjoy."

—*Publishers Weekly* on *The Witch of Willow Hall*

"A Gothic romance with the flavor of Edgar Allan Poe, this is also a suspenseful mystery novel…highly recommended."

—*Historical Novel Society* on *The Widow of Pale Harbor*

"Sophy is a strong gothic heroine."

—*Publishers Weekly* on *The Widow of Pale Harbor*

Also by Hester Fox

The Witch of Willow Hall
The Widow of Pale Harbor
The Orphan of Cemetery Hill

A LULLABY FOR WITCHES

HESTER FOX

GRAYDON
HOUSE

GRAYDON
HOUSE®

Recycling programs
for this product may
not exist in your area.

ISBN-13: 978-1-525-80469-4

A Lullaby for Witches

This is a work of fiction. Names, characters, places and incidents are either the product
of the author's imagination or are used fictitiously. Any resemblance to actual persons,
living or dead, businesses, companies, events or locales is entirely coincidental.

This edition published by arrangement with Harlequin Books S.A.

Graydon House
22 Adelaide St. West, 41st Floor
Toronto, Ontario M5H 4E3, Canada
www.GraydonHouseBooks.com
www.BookClubbish.com

Printed in Italy by Grafica Veneta

For the lost, the forgotten and all those denied the chance to tell their own story.

A
LULLABY
FOR
WITCHES

PROLOGUE

Margaret

I WAS BEAUTIFUL in the summer of 1876. The rocky Tynemouth coast was an easy place to be beautiful, though, with a fresh salt breeze that brought roses to my cheeks and sun that warmed my long hair, shooting the chestnut brown through with rich veins of copper. It was enough to make me forget—or at least, not care—that I was an outsider, a curiosity who left whispers in my wake when I walked through the muddy streets of our coastal town.

Do I miss being beautiful? Of course. But it's the being found beautiful by others that I miss the most. It was the ambrosia that made an otherwise solitary life bearable. And it was being found beautiful by one man in particular, Jack Pryce, that I miss the most.

He would come to find me out behind my family's house as I helped our maid hang the laundry on the lines or weeded my rocky garden. He always brought me a little gift, whether it was a toffee wrapped in wax paper from his parents' shop, or just a little green flower he had plucked because it reminded him of my eyes. Something that told me I was special, that those stories around town of him stepping out with the Clerkenwell girl weren't true.

"There she is," he would say, coming up with his hands in his pockets and crooked grin on his full lips. "My lovely wildflower." He called me this, he said, on account of my insistence on going without shoes on warm days when the grass was soft and lush. Whatever little chore I was doing would soon be forgotten as I led him out of sight of the house. With my back against a tree and his hands traveling under and up my skirts, we found euphoria in a panting tangle of limbs and hoarsely whispered promises. Heavy sea mists mingling with sweat in hair (his), the taste of berry-sweet lips (mine), the gut-deep knowing that he must love me. He must. He must. He must.

But like all things, summer came to an end, and autumn swept in with her cruel winds and killing frosts. Jack came less and less often, claiming first that it was work at the shop, then that he could no longer be seen with the girl who was rumored to practice witchcraft and worship at the altar of the moon on clear nights. Finally, on a day where the rain fell in icy sheets and even the screeching cries of the gulls could not compete with the howling wind, I realized he was not coming back.

Time moves differently now. Then, it was measured in church bells and birthdays, clock strokes and town harvest dances. It was measured in the monthly flow of my courses, until they stopped coming and my belly grew distended and full. Now—or perhaps it is better to say "here"—time is a fluid thing, like water that flows in all directions, finding and filling every crack and empty place, like my womb and my heart.

I did not want to give the babe up, though I knew it could only bring heartache and pain to my family. A mother's heart is a stubborn thing, and no sooner had I felt the first stirrings of life within me, than I knew I would do anything in the world to protect my little one.

It was folly, I know that now. A woman like me could never hope to bring a child into this cruel world, could never hope that the honey-sweet words of a man like Jack Pryce carried any weight. What irony that I should not realize such simple truths until it was too late. Should not realize them until my blood ran icy in my veins and my broken heart stopped beating. Until the man I thought had loved me stood over my body, staring down as the life ran out of me like a streambed running dry. Until I was dead and cold and no longer so very beautiful.

1

Augusta

"HELLO?" AUGUSTA THREW her keys on the table and slung her bag onto one of the kitchen chairs. As usual, a precarious stack of plates had taken over the sink, and the remnants of a Chinese food dinner sat out on the table. Sighing, she covered the leftovers with plastic wrap, stuck them in the fridge and followed the sounds of video games to the living room.

"I'm home," she said tersely to the two guys hunched over their gaming consoles.

Doug barely glanced up, but her boyfriend, Chris, threw her a quick glance over his shoulder.

"Hey, we're just finishing up." Turning back, he continued mashing keys on the game controller, shaking his dark fringe from his eyes and muttering colorful insults at his opponent.

Chris and Doug weren't the best housemates. Sure, they paid their share of the rent on time, but the house was constantly a mess, and video games took priority over household chores.

She supposed that's what she got for living with her boyfriend and allowing his unemployed brother to move in with them.

"Well, I guess I'll be in my room if you need me," Augusta said, too exhausted to pick a fight about the mess in the kitchen.

"You can stay and watch," Chris said without turning back around.

She'd had a long, hard day. Between the air-conditioning being broken at work and discovering she only had ninety-eight dollars in her bank account after paying her cell phone bill, she wasn't in the mood to watch Chris and Doug massacre each other with bazookas. She grabbed an apple from the kitchen, and went back to the room she shared with Chris, closing the door against the sounds of gunfire and explosions. Outside, the occasional car passed by in a sweep of headlights and somewhere down the street a dog barked. Loneliness curled around her as she sat at her laptop and began cycling through her bookmarked job listing sites.

Her job giving tours at the Old City Jail in Salem was all right; she got to work in a historic building, it was close enough that she could walk to work, and the polyester uniform was only a slightly nauseating shade of green. But it wasn't challenging, and she wasn't using her degree in museum studies for which she'd worked so hard. Not to mention the student debt she was still paying off. The worst was dealing with the public, though. Some of the people that showed up on her tours were engaged in her talks, but mostly the jail attracted cruise tourists who hadn't realized that it was a guided tour and were more interested in snapping a quick picture for Instagram than learning about the history. The other day she'd really had to remind a full-grown man that he couldn't bring an ice cream cone into the house, and then had to clean up said ice cream cone when he'd smuggled it inside anyway and dropped it. And the witches! Just because they were in Salem, everyone who came through the door assumed that there would be history about the witches, never mind that the jail didn't even date from the same century as the witch trials. Most days she came home tired, irritable and unfulfilled.

From the other room came an excited shout as Chris blew up Doug's home base. Augusta turned her music up. Most of the listings on the museum job sites were for fundraising or grant writing, the sliver of the museum world where all the money was. She knew she shouldn't be choosy, the millennial voice of reason in her head telling her that she was lucky to have a job at all. But Chris, with his computer engineering degree, actually had companies courting *him*, and his job at a Boston tech firm came with a yearly salary and benefits.

She was just about to close her laptop when a new listing popped up. Harlowe House in Tynemouth was looking for a collections manager to work alongside their curator. As she scanned the listing, her heart started to beat faster. She wasn't familiar with the property, but a quick search showed that it was part of a trust dedicated to the history and legacy of a seafaring family from the nineteenth century. She ticked off the qualifications in her head—an advanced degree in art history, museum studies or anthropology, and at least five years of experience. She would have to fudge the years, but other than that, it was made for her. She bookmarked the listing, making a mental note to update her CV in the morning.

The door swung open and Chris came in, plopping himself on the bed beside her. Tall, with an athletic build and dark hair that was perpetually in need of a trim, he was wearing a faded band shirt and gym shorts. "We're going to order subs. What do you want?"

"Didn't you just get Chinese food?" she asked.

"That was lunch."

Augusta did a quick inventory in her head of what she'd eaten that day, how many calories she was up to, and how much money she could afford. After she'd fished ten dollars out of her purse, Chris wandered back out to the living room, leaving her alone.

She picked up a book, but it didn't hold her interest, and soon she was lost scrolling through her phone and playing some stupid game where you had to match up jewels to clear the board. A thrilling Saturday night if there ever was one.

In both college and grad school, Augusta had had a vibrant, tight-knit group of friends. She'd always been a homebody, so there weren't lots of wild nights out at clubs, but they'd still had fairly regular get-togethers. Lunches and trips to museums, stuff like that. So what had happened in the last few years?

Her mind knew what had happened, but her heart refused to face the truth. Chris had happened.

She had been with him ever since her dad died. She'd run into Chris, her old high school boyfriend, at the memorial. He'd been a familiar face, and she'd clung to him like a life raft amid the turmoil of putting her life back together without her father. It had been clear early on that beyond some shared history, they didn't have much in common, but he was steady, and Augusta had craved steady. A year passed, then two, then three, and four. She had invested so much time in the relationship, sacrificed so many friends, that at some point it felt like admitting defeat to break up. For his part, Chris seemed content with the status quo, and so five years later, here they were.

That night, after Chris had rolled over and was lightly snoring, Augusta lay awake, thinking of the job listing. The words *Harlowe House, Harlowe House, Harlowe House* ran through her mind like the beat of a drum. A signal of hope, a promise of something better.

Work the next day was eight hours of pure, unair-conditioned torture. They were understaffed that day—weren't they always?—which meant Augusta was giving tours back-to-back, with little time to even go to the bathroom or grab a drink of water, never mind to hop on her laptop and fill out an application for the Harlowe House job. As busy and stressful as it could be sometimes, working at the Old Jail at least kept her busy, kept her mind from wandering and dwelling on all the unknowns and shortcomings in her life. Maybe it would be easier just to stay. It wasn't her dream job, but at least she knew the routine and got along with most of the other tour guides. Dream jobs were for kids with trust funds and safety nets. Nothing would be worse than taking the risk of applying to a new job and then not getting it. If she was stuck here, then at least she wanted to be able to pretend that it was her own choice. It was the easy way out, but that was what was at the heart of it: if she was honest with herself about why she was playing it safe with her job, then what else in her life might she be forced to reexamine? Losing her dad and missing two semesters of school because of depression and starting over at twenty-two had been hard enough. Did she have it in her to make the leap and start again?

"Jesus, you look like you're making Sophie's choice over here," a voice said, drawing Augusta out of her thoughts.

She looked up to find two of the other guides, Maureen and Vin. If she was going to be interrupted and interrogated by her coworkers, at least it was by the only two who she considered anything close to friends.

Maureen slid into the seat across from her at the circular lunch table, flicking her long black hair out of her face, while Vin examined the plate of muffins someone had brought in, finally choosing one. Maureen had light brown skin, penetrating dark eyes, and her full lips were perpetually pulled up at one corner in a crafty smile, as if she were plotting something.

"So?" Maureen asked expectantly. "What are you looking at?"

If anyone else had demanded to know, Augusta probably would have made something up to avoid having to get into a deep conversation, but Maureen had a way of getting Augusta to spill all her secrets. Maybe it was the genuine curiosity that lurked beneath her shrewd gaze, or that Augusta always found herself wanting to impress the cool girl with the dark eyeliner and green streaks in her hair.

"Just this job I found online. I'm thinking about applying."

Maureen shared a look with Vin, who was popping muffin pieces into his mouth while he tipped his chair back, feet on the table.

"Finally!" Maureen exclaimed. "We've been wondering when you were going to start looking around for something better than this."

She hadn't been aware that her coworkers ever talked about her, let alone were concerned with her career. "You were?"

Vin finished chewing. Deeply tanned and freckled, Vin had a mass of dark curls that were only barely tamed into a pompadour for work, though he was forever running his hand through them, threatening to send them spilling out into a dress code violation. "I mean, don't get me wrong, we love working with you, but you've been here how long? Two years?"

"Three."

"Three years! Most people only stay like, a year, tops," Maureen said. "Haven't you noticed?"

"I've only been here since June and I'm already looking for something else," Vin told her.

Augusta began to get the creeping suspicion that she was the odd one out on an inside joke around the Old Jail. "You are?" she asked.

"Hell yeah. This is a great stepping-stone job, but no one can keep it up forever. Aren't you bored and exhausted from giving the same tour all day every day? I know I am." Vin scrubbed his hands through his curls, standing them on end. "I hate this uniform and I hate that Ron makes me 'tone down' my hair."

"I'm just doing it for the money while I take night classes in biology and chemistry, and then I'm going back to school for my forensic science degree," Maureen added. "God, if I'm still here in another two years I give you permission to put me out of my misery. I can't answer another question about the witches from a tourist."

Augusta bit her lip. It was easy to dismiss her own reasons for not wanting to stay, but it was much less so when it was spelled out in black and white for her by someone else.

"Here, pull up the application," Maureen demanded, scooting her chair closer. "I'll help you fill it out."

Augusta started to protest, but it was no use. Once Maureen was determined to do something, it was as good as done. Pulling out her laptop, Augusta started filling out the application, with Maureen occasionally telling her to change a word or to give herself more experience in a certain area. When Augusta began to draft the cover letter, Maureen drifted away, shifting her attention to Vin and giving Augusta a chance to compose it.

Augusta looked over her application package one last time and hit Submit. There. It was done. There was no going back now. A giddy sense of lightness bubbled up in Augusta's chest. She'd been brave, and now it was in the hands of the universe.

"Tilly had kittens. They are so cute it's nauseating. Look." Maureen thrust her phone in Augusta's face, snapping her out of her thoughts. "My sister's boyfriend is taking two of them, and Vin is taking the orange one with the white face."

"I'm going to name him Bruce," Vin said proudly.

Maureen rolled her eyes. "I'm *not* giving him to you if you name him that. You can't name a cat Bruce."

Shrugging, Vin resumed tipping his chair back to its precarious angle. "Then I refuse to bring you any more of my mom's pandan cake."

"You wouldn't," Maureen whispered, her face falling.

Vin smiled triumphantly. "Oh, but I would. Unless you let me name him."

"Ugh, you're the worst, but you know I'm obsessed with your mom, so fine." Maureen's gaze slid to Augusta. "Do you want one? I'd rather they all go to people I know, not randos off the internet or anything."

Augusta looked at the video of the mewling little babies one more time, before reluctantly handing back the phone. "I would love one, but my boyfriend is allergic. We can't have any pets in the apartment."

When Augusta looked up, she found Vin and Maureen staring at her like she'd sprouted an extra head.

"You have a *boyfriend*?" came the unified response.

Augusta opened her mouth. "I—"

"You've literally *never* mentioned you had a boyfriend," Vin said accusingly.

"I haven't?" Augusta was only half-aware that she had never mentioned Chris. It wasn't that she was hiding him, or didn't want people to know that she was in a relationship, he just felt like a separate part of her life from work. Besides, Chris was just...*there*. They never really did anything worth sharing.

Maureen held her gaze a beat too long, and Augusta shifted in her seat. "I definitely think I would have remembered if you said you were seeing someone."

A stocky white man wearing a ranger's uniform and a severe expression appeared in the break room doorway, saving Augusta from having to explain herself any further. "There's a two o'clock tour in the front and no one there to check them in." He let his gaze run disapprovingly over the three of them, Maureen's phone still playing the video of the kittens. "We're too busy for this kind of thing," he said. "Vin, you need to fix your hair before you even think of going on tour, so Maureen or Augusta, you're up."

Poor Vin's scowl could have eviscerated him, but Ron seemed oblivious as he perused the plate of muffins. "I'll do it," Augusta hurried to offer. Taking the tour would be a distraction from constantly refreshing her email to see if Harlowe House had replied, and she didn't need Maureen's knowing gaze sliding to her every few minutes. One more quick glance at her phone told her that Harlowe House hadn't responded yet, so, pasting on a smile, she greeted the dozen or so tourists waiting in the front entrance. She rattled off the script as she ushered them out of the early autumn heat wave and into the equally stifling hall. She probably could have done it in her sleep at this point, and any meaning the words had once held had long ago faded.

The Old Jail was one of many museums in Salem, a restored building that offered tours, had a gift shop and lots of photo ops for tourists to take pictures of themselves behind bars. Unlike some of the other tourist attractions in the city, the Old Jail wasn't related to the history of the witch trials in any way, didn't have creepy wax figures and, mercifully, didn't require its staff to give tours in costume. But, true to its original function, it was a barren, lifeless building. History was supposed to be alive, a way for people in the present to connect in meaningful ways from the past and learn from it. But that didn't feel like the case at the Old Jail.

A woman in a Myrtle Beach T-shirt and a fanny pack interrupted Augusta as she led them past the old cells. "Is this where they kept the witches before they burned them?"

"They didn't burn witches," Augusta told her with a smile, drawing on all the patience she could muster. "They hanged them. And this prison wasn't built until 1842—a hundred and fifty years after the witch trials."

The woman looked disappointed, and whispered something to her companion next to her. They moved on to the warden's office, and she resisted the temptation to sneak another peek at her phone. If she really did get the job, the best part would be never having to field questions about witches from belligerent tourists ever again.

2

Margaret

When cockle shells turn silver bells
Then will my love come back to me
When roses bloom in winter's gloom
Then will my love return to me.

—"The Water is Wide," Traditional Folk Song

DO YOU KNOW what it is to be lonely? Truly alone, even amidst a crowd? Even in a family? Perhaps if my mother had been a witch like me with powers of her own, she would have taken me under her wing and guided me on my singular path. But she did not, and I was left to discover what made me different on my own, stumbling and groping along.

I was not a stupid child; I knew that it was not normal for a girl to be able to call on spirits or send birds to do her bidding. Water should not shimmer with messages from beyond the veil. But it did mean that I was apart, different from other children my own age. How could I play at silly games, knowing that the trees speak a different language and will sing in the wind? How could I care about tea parties and town functions when the moon beckoned me to learn the secrets of the sea?

My childhood was uneventful, at least, if not quite normal. Witches are born, yes, but they are also made. Their powers are forged while communing with nature, their sight honed by waking dreams at night. I suppose I always carried my powers within me, but it was not until I was old enough to see the world for what it was that I truly came into my own.

One day—I could not have been much older than eight or so—I was watching the boats come in from the harbor when a fisherman returned with a dolphin that had gotten caught in his net and died. Sun glistened off its pearly skin, its black eyes little more than indifferent slits as it was carried down the dock. There was always a crowd of curious children and idle drunkards on the pier, and at the sight of the dolphin, there was a ripple of excitement. A tall woman with dark brown skin and a purple turban wound round her hair caught my eye from across the crowd, held it for a moment as if she could discern my thoughts, and then turned her attention back to the dolphin.

But it was not the spectacle that drew me in; I wanted to know to where had the spirit of that great animal flown. Why could it not swim and play anymore? If the flesh was too far gone, could another vessel still support an ember of life? I had heard of men, who, in years past, had tried to bring back the dead. They were known as the Resurrection Men, and they had stolen bodies right out of the cemeteries and brought them to laboratories where they had tried to reanimate them. I may have only been a little girl, but even I understood where they had gone wrong. A body, once dead and decaying, could not support life. A soul, on the other hand, needed only an abode in which to take root and flourish.

I pondered this truth many times over the coming years, but my interest in magic was not limited to just this question. Life and death, omnipresent and vast as they are, are best understood through the tiny details, the intricacies of the natural world. If one of my brothers suffered a scrape or bruise, I was fascinated by the pinpricks of blood that emerged from the skin. If I came upon a bird with an injured wing, I was quick to examine the fine, crooked bones. When I awoke one morning to sticky thighs and sheets stained with rusty blood, I was not frightened, only curious and awestruck that my body was capable of such a miracle. Where my mother taught me that a woman's body was something to be tamed and laced into submission, I celebrated the generous sea swells of my thighs and breasts, reveled in the crimson blood that flowed from me every month, as steady as the phases of the moon.

Every sunrise, every drop of rain was a paradigm of magic, proof of a miraculous world. I was particularly drawn to the herb garden that our housemaid Molly kept, and I would often pinch off budding rosemary and thyme, rubbing the fragrant stems between my fingers. "Mind you don't eat that," Molly told me one morning as I was helping her gather elderberries for tea. "It will give you a bellyache and sweats if it isn't prepared properly." I studied the innocuous plant, its tiny red berries so simple, yet so mysterious. How was it possible that the same plant that made such a comforting tea could also be deadly? I badgered Molly to tell me all she knew of plants and herbs, and when her patience and knowledge was exhausted, I turned to botanical encyclopedias procured for me by my brother George. But beyond the Latin names and taxonomic tables, a deep intuition guided my explorations. The plants sung to me in a language I had never heard, yet somehow understood. They told me secrets, things that no book would ever dare have printed in black and white: how to cure heartaches, and how to cause them. How to measure one's monthly courses against the waxing and waning of the moon. How to get with child, and how to stop one already in your belly from growing. My curiosity had no limits, and soon I was wading ever farther out into the vast ocean of forbidden knowledge.

My unusual abilities might have gone unnoticed had I not chanced across a man and a woman one day when I was deep in the woods collecting wild strawberries. I watched from behind a tree as the man pressed himself against the woman, despite her pleas. He was big and burly, and easily overpowered her. My blood grew hot as I watched. Why did men get to take whatever they wanted, just because they were bigger, stronger? Why did the poor woman's feelings not matter at all? I burned with rage. Would I be submitted to the same injustices when I was a grown woman? Was I destined for a life of subservience and violence?

Although I did not know what I was going to do, I could not sit idly by. Stepping out from behind the tree, I slowly walked toward the man, my hand outstretched, my fingers trembling. I was almost upon them when the man turned and caught sight of me. He sneered over his shoulder. "Run along, missy, unless you want a turn next."

But I did not turn and run. Calming myself, I focused all my anger, my disgust, until my fingers tingled with energy. My powers had only strengthened over the years, and I had been waiting for such a time as this to use them. Words came bubbling out of me, water from some long-untapped well.

With a cry, the man went reeling backward as if yanked by some invisible rope, landing hard on his backside. We stared at each other, us three, as clouds scudded across the sky, the wind tugging at the leaves above us. The air had gone very quiet, even the birds pausing in their song.

The man was the first to react, running and nearly tripping on a root as he shot one last look of horror back at me over his shoulder.

When the last of his crashing footsteps in the brush had faded, I addressed the wide-eyed woman. "If you find yourself with child, come see me and I will help you."

I'm not sure if she was more frightened of her ordeal, or of what she had just witnessed. She regarded me with terror, disbelief. I offered her a smile, but she did not return it, or even thank me. Instead, she took off running in the opposite direction.

Soon, word spread that the Harlowe girl possessed uncanny powers and the ability to offer remedies that the town's male physician would not, and women began making their way to my cabin in the woods. I did not ask for money in return for my services. I had money aplenty from my parents, and wanted for nothing. Instead, I collected secrets and gossip, stories from my customers. I knew which women found pleasure outside of their marital beds, and which men were impotent. I knew who had debts, and who hoarded their wealth. I knew that Delia Fisk's husband beat her, and that she still loved him and only wanted his affection. When she came to me asking for a love potion, I made sure to slip something in it so that he would suffer from digestive pains. It was not for myself that I wanted these secrets, but because I wanted a record of the events that transpired in the lives of those around me. In the eyes of society, Delia Fisk's husband was an upstanding, generous man who gave money to the local foundling home; who would know that behind closed doors he was a monster? He suffered no consequences, no punishment for his ill treatment of the woman who loved him. It was a rare thing for a man to be brought to justice for abuse of his wife, as men tend to band together, to protect one another. I collected these secrets and wrote them down so that somewhere in this universe, there would exist a sliver of justice for these women.

3

Augusta

THE HIGHWAY WHIZZED by through the Uber window. Augusta's palms were sticky, and the car's air-conditioning was only pushing tepid air through the vent. If she landed this job then she was going to have to figure out transportation; she couldn't take an Uber every day to work.

The operative word there was *if*. Full-time, benefited museum jobs in the area were few and far between, and highly competitive. She redid her ponytail for the hundredth time, and then tried to distract herself with her phone the rest of the ride.

The car stopped in front of a rolling lawn on the main street. Augusta stepped out into the muggy day as beach bag–toting tourists in flip-flops and sun hats strolled past her, enjoying the early autumn heat wave. She'd been to Tynemouth a handful of times before, mostly as a child during day trips in the summer. The coastal town was known for its fishing and whaling history, and was a popular tourist destination with its seaside hotels and up-and-coming restaurant scene. Shielding her eyes from the glare of the sun, she squinted up the lawn to the stately Georgian house.

Harlowe House was postcard-perfect, from its garden of luscious blue hydrangea and vivid daylilies to its peach clapboard sides with white shutters. Steep steps led up the lawn and Augusta took them slowly, willing her makeup not to run from sweat. Her short, sandy curls were already frizzing out to extreme levels, and her sale-rack J.Crew blouse was sticking to her back. If her nerves didn't do her in, this heat would.

Even with the bustle of tourists and shops nearby, the house belonged to a different time, a different world. It once must have stood among other houses just like it, but now—with the exception of some of the brick storefronts—it was the lone survivor of its era.

"Augusta?"

Augusta jumped at the voice as the front door opened.

"Sorry, I didn't mean to scare you. The bell is broken and I saw you coming up the steps. I'm Jill Wei, we spoke on the phone."

With a sleek black bob that defied the humidity, Jill was petite and put-together in crisp capris and a flowing top. Augusta shook her hand. "Nice to meet you."

"Oh, wow, I love your earrings," Jill said, returning her handshake. "You must be baking, though. Come on in. The air is terrible today—I'm so over this heat wave."

Augusta liked Jill immediately. Some of the tension lifted from her shoulders as she stepped into the cool interior, the familiar museum scent of old wood and citrus cleaner welcoming her inside.

"Monday and Tuesday are our administrative days, so there aren't any tours today," Jill said, as she led Augusta through a gracious hall tastefully appointed with a mahogany credenza and Oriental carpets. A grand staircase with ornately carved balusters and a brightly polished banister dominated the entryway.

The wallpaper was an understated chinoiserie in warm taupes and grays, illuminated by soft light filtering in from a window at the top of the stairs. Despite the lavish scale of the hall, the overall effect was warm and welcoming. After the dark cells and low ceilings of the Old City Jail, Harlowe House felt like a breath of fresh air. Jill caught Augusta taking in the period details and smiled. "If we have time afterward, I can give you a quick tour. I have a meeting in Boston at two, though, so it might be tight. Have you been here before?"

"No," Augusta admitted. "I've always meant to but never had the chance."

Jill didn't seem too concerned about it. "Well, I'll just give you the quick version for now. We have an endowment from the Harlowe family's living descendants. There are three properties—Harlowe House, a shipping office and residence in Boston that now houses our archives, and an unfurnished summerhouse that we rent out for weddings and functions. The bulk of the collection is here at Harlowe House, and in addition to our regular tours, we do lots of community outreach and public programming."

They passed through a sitting room and into a modern back hall, then up a set of carpeted steps. "There were Harlowes living in this house from as early as the 1780s, we think," Jill said over her shoulder, "but it was really the fourth generation in the second half of the nineteenth century that made their mark on the fishing and whaling industries."

"I've seen the name Harlowe on a lot of buildings in the area," Augusta said. "I didn't realize that this was the same family."

"They had a *lot* of money," Jill said. "That tends to get your name on stuff."

The floorboards creaked as Jill ushered her into an office at the end of the hall. It looked like it had once been a bedroom before being converted to an administrative area; crown molding edged the ceiling, and the walls were painted a soothing hue of goldenrod. Jill gestured to a chair across from the desk.

"I'm going to go grab our administrator, who'll be joining us for the interview. Make yourself comfortable, I'll be right back."

Augusta took the opportunity to catch her breath and send a quick text to Chris to let him know that she'd made it to Harlowe House. When she heard footsteps approaching, she slipped her phone back into her purse. But seconds passed and no one came in. Her neck prickled as if someone was watching her.

"Hello?" she said. Silence.

She must have imagined it. The feeling died as quickly as it had come on, and soon Augusta heard Jill's voice coming through the door. "Augusta, this is Sharon, she's our administrator."

Sharon was a little older than Jill, her peppered-silver hair framing a warm and kind light-skinned face. She gave Augusta a bright smile. "Should we get started?"

Augusta nodded, crossing her ankles under her chair so that her bouncing knees wouldn't be visible.

"It looks like you've had a lot of experience with visitor services and public outreach," Sharon said as she glanced through a printed copy of Augusta's CV. "That's great. Can I ask why you're interested now in switching gears to working behind the scenes?"

"My background is actually in collections," Augusta said. "My degree is in American material culture studies, and I concentrated in ceramics. The Old City Jail has been a great experience," she said, only gilding the truth a little. "Working there has taught me a lot about what goes into running a historic building, but I'd really like to get back to collections. I miss working with art and objects." It would be heaven to never have to work with the public again, to just be able to lose herself in a collection of beautiful things.

Jill shared a grin with Sharon. "You've come to the right place. Elijah Harlowe imported tons of porcelain in the 1820s, so we're up to our ears in ceramics. A lot of it was improperly cataloged back in the '80s, so that's a big project that we'd love to see tackled. I don't suppose you'd mind crawling around storage and seeing just what we have in there? Maybe even putting together an exhibit?"

"Honestly, that sounds like perfection," Augusta said. She relaxed a little. She could do this. The rest of the meeting flew by, more like a back-and-forth conversation than a formal interview. With every answer, Augusta grew more confident and excited. She'd be responsible for the health of the collection, monitoring objects and writing up condition reports. She'd have a hand in helping curate special exhibits. She'd have coworkers that shared her passion. Before, the job had seemed like a fantasy; now she knew that she belonged here.

The hot air hit her like a wall as soon as she stepped outside. Instead of calling a car right away, Augusta took a walk down Tynemouth's quaint thoroughfare. Even in the heat, the air held the hint of cool ocean spray, and the constant cries of gulls reminded her that she was only a few blocks from the water. On impulse, she followed the signs to the beach, where she slipped off her sensible ballet flats and waded into the shallow surf. Closing her eyes, she let the cold water flow and recede over her feet, a gentle and comforting rhythm. When was the last time she'd been in the ocean? The sounds of children playing and dogs barking faded into the background, and for a glorious, sun-warmed moment, it was as if the world stood still for her. A chill ran across her skin despite the heat, and from somewhere deep inside her, a voice hummed in time with the steady roll of the ocean. *Home*, it said. *Come home.*

Opening her eyes, she blinked against the glare of the sun on the water. She'd had moments of intuition before, but this was different. The voice had come from inside of her, but it wasn't her voice. Eager to get back to the world of air-conditioning and Wi-Fi she waded back to shore, brushed off her feet and promptly forgot all about it.

4

Margaret

'Tis a sigh that is wafted across the troubled wave,
'Tis a wail that is heard upon the shore
'Tis a dirge that is murmured around the lowly grave
Oh! Hard times come again no more.

—"Hard Times Come Again No More," Traditional Folk Song

THIS HOUSE IS my prison, but it is also my lens, a looking glass that allows me to view the physical plane. While I might not be able to observe what transpires outside these walls, I do wonder if passersby ever stay their step, their neck prickling as if being watched and look up to the windows, only to find themselves staring at nothing.

She hears me, though. She comes as if called, and perhaps she has been called in a sense, for this place will always carry my voice in the shafts of sunlight, and my desires creaking in the wood beneath her feet. How thrilling to know that after all these years I'm still capable of casting a stone in water and experiencing a ripple. With her glasses and prim clothes, she is unassuming, mousy. If I did not know who she is and what she carries, I would not look twice at her. But something sings when she enters, a harmony to the melody that hums throughout the house.

She is hungry, though I can sense she doesn't know for what. And I have so much to give, if only she will accept it.

For how can you hear my story and not believe that I am worthy of remembrance?

On a sharp, sunny day, with a crisp wind carrying salt and woodsmoke at my back, I ventured down to the beach in search of blood cockles.

Save for the loitering gulls and quick-footed sandpipers, usually I had the vast, rocky beach to myself. But that morning a tall, black-cloaked figure was bending over by the water's edge, a dark slash against the pale sand. Unaccustomed to sharing the beach with anyone other than the occasional fisherman, I squared my shoulders and walked purposefully to where the figure was busy gathering something from the ground.

Despite my silent footsteps in the sand, the figure slowly unfolded and stood up at my approach, the hood of her cloak falling away to reveal a dark-skinned woman. She was dignified and beautiful, with a long, slender neck and brown doe eyes that seemed to see right into my soul. She might have been as young as thirty, or as old as fifty.

My breath caught in recognition. "I've seen you before. At the docks, when the dolphin was brought in," I told her.

She raised her brows, clearly unimpressed with my introduction. "And I'm sure you've seen me many other places about town. I'm hardly a recluse."

Her frank speech momentarily addled me; I was not used to my own directness being received with anything less than acquiescence. "What are you doing here?" I asked her.

"You're not the only one who knows when the blood cockles come in." Stooping back down, she ran her small, rusty rake into the sand, stopping to pry out the shy creatures when the metal clinked against their shells.

I watched as she continued her work, both affronted and a

little amused that I was not so singular in my eccentricities as I had thought.

"What is your name?"

"Phebe Hall," she answered, without stopping in her work.

"I'm Margaret—"

"Margaret Harlowe," she finished for me. "Yes, I know who you are." At my incredulous silence, she graced me with a knowing smile. "Everyone knows of Clarence Harlowe Senior's pretty daughter and her wild ways."

I was more than a little pleased to have my reputation precede me. After that, I could not stay away from Phebe Hall. She never turned me away, and was generous with her knowledge of herbs and the life that flourished in the tidal pools. Here was someone else who understood the tiny miracles of the world and cared not if she was seen with sandy hems or in the company of the strangest girl in town.

Soft-footed and reverent, we would convene in the woods on nights when the moon was full. Everything that I knew about womanhood I learned from her, from how to carry myself, to how to keep myself from falling with child. If only I had heeded her warnings about young men and the lies they tell. But of course, I was young and thought myself invincible.

Before Jack Pryce came into my life, days were for heeled leather boots, tight-laced stays and a head bowed over work. It had always been thus. At nineteen years old I was the baby of the family, and with my three older brothers all grown and with vocations of their own, it was left to me to help my parents manage the house and entertain their business guests. But the nights were mine, and mine alone. Sometimes I would walk along the rocky beach just for the thrill of feeling the sand between my toes, and other times I would meet Phebe to harvest. But more often than not it was the forest into which I would lose myself. You might envision the coast as all rock and water and salt, but

Tynemouth was alive with wild woods and lush gardens, too. In the old days, there had been a settlement where the woods ramble, but in my time, all that was left were overgrown foundations and a pack of stray dogs.

The townspeople might have thought that I danced with the devil in the woods, that I held congress with demons. But there is no devil, and any demons with which I held congress were only those of my own making. The truth, of course, is always so much more mundane. It was there that I ran my practice out of an abandoned cabin, away from the prying eyes of servants and parents. It was there that I could find the herbs that I needed for my tinctures and drafts. I went because in the woods there are no expectations, no social mores. Now I wish I had not gone, for it was there that I first met Jack Pryce.

I had seen Jack in town before; it was impossible to miss the tall, lanky, young man who worked in his parents' dry goods shop where I often did our shopping. We had never spoken beyond the required pleasantries, so when we came face-to-face in the pale moonlight, it was like meeting a familiar stranger.

Cool air touched my neck, the briny scent of the sea mingling with the fresh pines as I gathered nettles. Something rustled in the underbrush and I froze, thinking it perhaps a fox or coyote. Although the pioneer settlement was long since abandoned, there was still the occasional recluse that haunted this area and I did not relish running afoul of one. With only my thin slippers on my feet, I soundlessly moved over the fallen leaves, and took shelter behind a tree.

From my vantage I could see a group of young men tramping through the leaves and brush. They made no effort to be quiet, no effort to respect the sacred sanctuary of the woods. These were not the business and tradesmen with whom my brothers associated. These were the rough-and-tumble sons of sailors and fishermen, young men who took their pleasures in the dark pubs that lined the backstreets of town.

"Did you see that girl in the Black Horse?" one boy asked his companions. "Could see from her ankles clear up to her thighs!"

Another boy scoffed. "I was more interested in what was on her chest, or better yet, what wasn't on her chest," said a voice cracking with puberty.

This earned him a few snickers.

"I bet the half of you haven't even touched a breast, let alone lain with a girl."

"You and Tom think you're awfully worldly just because you're seventeen," said the cracked voice.

If I had thought that young men were anything other than crass in private, then my assumptions were quickly put to rest. I could have easily slipped away, yet I was fascinated by this glimpse of unguarded interaction. So often, whenever I went into town, people turned away, or grew stiff and standoffish. I was so engrossed that I grew careless, snapping a branch as I moved to get a closer look.

"What was that?"

"Did you hear something?"

"I've heard these woods are haunted."

"Tch, you're all fainthearts."

I stayed my step, but it was too late. The moon betrayed me as a thick cloud slid away, bathing my hiding spot in light.

In that moment, I knew what the deer feels when circled by a pack of desperate, hungry wolves. They would never have dared in town, but here there was only the rule of the wild, and I was the quarry, they the predators.

"It's the Harlowe girl!"

"Say, little witch, what are you doing out here all by yourself?"

They had started advancing on me, and I, fool that I was, found myself backed up against one of the old stone foundations with nowhere to run. Could I dispel them with magic? It was possible, but there were at least four of them, and in my panic all my spells seemed to fly from my mind. Their eyes glinted with cruelty in the moonlight, their hungry expressions unmistakable. They might only have been children, but there is nothing so frightening as the energy that builds between boys as they spur each other on.

One launched a pinecone at my head, the others laughing as I ducked. I could just smell the cheap liquor on their breath as they moved toward me, when a deep voice rang out.

"Leave her alone."

Just like that, the boys fell back. "We were only having a bit of fun," one said.

"It's just the Harlowe girl."

The owner of the voice stepped into view. Tall, whip-thin and vibrating with a dangerous energy. I knew him at once as Jack Pryce.

"Why don't you all run home to your mothers now."

I expected the boys to protest, to insist that they were not children but men, but not one made a peep against Jack Pryce.

"Sorry, Jack."

"If you say so, Jack."

Cross-armed, he watched them scamper away through the leaves. I should have run also, but I was too transfixed by the moonlight in his dark hair, the dramatic shadows of his face.

"Are you all right?" he asked when they were gone.

I nodded. In truth, I had rolled my ankle and my heart was thumping furiously, but I knew how lucky I was to escape with nothing more than that.

"You're the Harlowe girl," he said. "I've seen you in town."

I nodded again. Usually when I was in the woods at night, I was at my most powerful, the moon above me, the wind in my hair, the damp earth coming up through the soles of my feet. But tonight, I was barely able to so much as form words.

"They say you're a witch." It was not a question.

Finally finding my tongue, I squared my shoulders and held his gaze. "Do you think I am?"

He considered me, his dark eyes glinting. Then he shook his head. "No. I think you're rather queer, but not a witch. Witches don't live in fine houses with a sporting coupe in the stables, or have successful brothers who work in shipping offices."

I might have laughed; if only he knew. But it didn't matter, because he didn't treat me as a curiosity; he looked me in the eye when he spoke, he acted as if having a conversation in the woods at night with the town witch was the most normal thing in the world.

"I don't know what to think about you," he said thoughtfully.

"You've only just met me. Perhaps you need more time in which to form an opinion," I countered.

"Now that I know you frequent the woods at night, I suppose I'll be walking this way more often."

I didn't realize until he gave me a long, slow smile how much I had ached for that connection with another person. I had thought that the trees and the brown rabbits and the moon were companions enough for me, but now I knew otherwise. I wanted a man to look at me with something other than leering curiosity. I wanted to know what a lover's touch felt like. I wanted a baby of my own, a little one to love. There are many things a witch can conjure, but a baby is beyond even the purview of magic. A baby requires a man.

Perhaps it was not love, not at first, that drew me to Jack Pryce. Though soon enough I would learn that love was not the tranquil stream I had thought, but a violent torrent of a river, one that could pull me under completely.

5

Margaret

It's a rosebud in June and the violets in full bloom,
And the small birds are singing love songs on each spray.

—"Rosebud in June," Traditional Folk Song

AFTER THAT FIRST chance meeting with Jack, I returned
to the woods every night for a week, hoping to see him again.
Of course, I could not admit that that's why I went, even to myself. Instead, I pretended that I needed a certain herb that could
only be found by the old ruins. With the moss soft beneath my
feet and the moon guiding my way, I stole outside every night.
Every night, I waited in vain.

On the eighth night, there was a rustling in the underbrush. I
held my breath, hoping that it was Jack, but fearing it was those
boys again. Make no mistake, I had taken precautions, like the
protection charm of cow's bone which hung under my bodice,
but I was not eager to come face-to-face with their hungry eyes
again, their hateful expressions.

But it was not the boys nor was it Jack who came limping
out from behind a tree, but a pitiful brown mutt with matted

fur. He stood awkwardly on his paw, and looked at me with big, imploring eyes.

"You poor thing." I bent to inspect his paw closer and found that he had suffered a deep cut in the pad. As meekly as a lamb, he allowed me to pick him up and carry him home, where I made a salve for him and bandaged him up. From that night on, he never left my side. Shadow, I called him.

Shadow proved a most faithful companion, and soon I ceased my night walks looking for Jack. My days were the same: helping with housework, sitting through painfully boring business dinners with my parents and roaming the coast with Shadow. Occasionally a woman from the town would find her way to my cabin in the middle of the night, and I would give her the herbs or charms she needed.

"Margaret," my mother said one day, bustling down the stairs, "we are out of cream of tartar for the sponge cake, and Molly is busy and can't go to the store. Your brothers are coming for dinner tonight, so it cannot wait." She ran a critical eye over my mud-speckled hem and the boots I had been wearing as I harvested seaweed on the beach that morning. "Make yourself tidy, then take this to Pryce's."

She pressed a banknote into my hand, and the next thing I knew I was whistling for Shadow, and preparing to make a trip into town.

It was not as if I was a leper, but there was no denying that I had my fair share of whispers about me as I passed by. The same women who came to me in the night to buy herbs and beg my help turned their noses up at me during the day. But I paid no mind; I kept my own counsel and liked it that way. That was, until I had met Jack.

Now, as I took my time strolling down Main Street, I found myself checking my reflection in shop windows to see if my curls were in order. I smiled at the bright-eyed girl that stared back at me. I had a sweetheart! Me! There were few opportunities for a young woman in Tynemouth, but having an admirer gave me wings, set me free from the confines of my mundane life.

Before I stepped into the grocer's, I beat the dust from my hem and pinched color into my cheeks. I instructed Shadow to stay put, though he would do what he pleased. Then I went inside.

I made an effort to look poised and collected, though I was apprehensive as my gaze landed on Jack standing at the counter. With sleeves rolled to the elbows, and a crisp navy vest over his linen shirt, he looked relaxed and unbothered by the heat. Unlike most of the men in town, he was clean-shaven, and I liked that about him, liked that I could see every inch of his comely face. He was busy with a customer, so I took my time browsing, keeping a corner of my eye trained on the front of the shop. It seemed like an eternity before the woman finally paid for her purchases and Jack bid her a good day. Then we were alone in the shop.

"Well," he said, coming out from behind the counter, "if it isn't the witch. I can't remember the last time I saw you in town."

"I only come to town when there is something that catches my fancy."

He raised a brow. "Oh? Something here catches your fancy, then?"

I let his question hang, giving an inconsequential shrug. I was not above a little pettiness; he had made me wait in the woods for him, and now it was my turn to make him wait, to wonder. But what if I had misread him? What if he did not want me after all? I would not hold out my heart, raw and bloody, only to have him dash it on the floor.

"My mother wants cream of tartar," I said.

"So she sent her daughter, and not the maid?"

"You flatter yourself if you think this errand has anything to do with you, and not the sponge cake that must be baked for my father's dinner tonight."

He placed a hand on his heart. "My lady knows how to land a blow," he said with mock hurt.

"*Your* lady does not like to be kept waiting," I said, trying for a light tone that did not betray my hurt.

His eyes registered surprise, then warmed with delight. "Why, little witch, you don't mean to tell me that you've been waiting in the woods for me the past fortnight?"

I scowled, though I was inwardly pleased. So, he had remembered. "Of course not. The cream of tartar, if you please."

He wordlessly obliged, going to measure out the white powder and sifting it into a little paper packet. When it was paid for and I had slipped it into my bag, I gave him a curt thanks. Throughout our exchange he had been lighthearted and flirtatious. But now, as I turned to leave, he stayed me by the sleeve. I looked down at his large, strong hand on the fawn linen of my dress. When I raised my gaze to meet his, I was startled to see desire smoldering there. "I want to see you again," he said under his breath. "I haven't been able to stop thinking about you."

My body warmed and my heartbeat quickened. I had no doubt in my mind that he spoke the truth, but I was still sour that I had waited like a fool for him in the woods. If I had thought that the trees and moon gave me power, it was nothing compared to the headiness with which being the object of this man's desire imbued me.

Jack's breath smelled of peppermint, and his touch filled me with electricity. It would have been the easiest thing in the world to tilt my face up, to brush my lips against his.

Though every tingling fiber in my body begged me to lean into his touch, even I knew that it was too soon. I carefully took my arm back, and though my heart was pounding and my body aching with desire, walked proud and tall out the door.

6

Augusta

"YOU'RE GOING TO work in Tynemouth?"

Chris was sitting at the breakfast table, absorbed in a book, when Augusta broke the good news. She hadn't wanted to tell him she'd applied until she knew for sure whether she'd gotten the job or not. It had only been three days since her interview when the call from Jill came, letting her know that the position was hers.

This was big. This was confidence-boosting, life-affirming big. The job at the Old Jail had been a step in the right direction after years of working soul-crushing retail jobs, but it hadn't been anything like this. At Harlowe House she would be responsible for projects, making decisions and working hands-on with collections. No more giving tours to bored tourists and cleaning gum off the walls. It had all fallen into place so perfectly that she could still hardly believe it. That's why her heart fell at Chris's apathetic reaction.

She was leaning against the counter, a mug of rapidly cooling coffee in her hand. "Yeah, why?"

He gave a shrug. "I dunno. It's just kind of far away, isn't it? How are you going to get there?"

He did have a point. Augusta had always been able to walk to work. There was no way she could afford a car, but she was unwilling to let her dream job slip through her fingers. "I'm sure we can figure something out. It's going to be good money, like, really good money."

This caught Chris's attention. "Oh, yeah?"

"Like almost double what I'm making now, and I won't have to work Sundays."

Leaning back and putting his book down, Chris finally looked at her. "That's great. Maybe we can go on a vacation next year or something. Put some money toward fixing up the back deck."

"Maybe." She took a sip of her coffee. She wasn't sure why it rubbed her the wrong way, but she didn't love that Chris was already planning out how they were going to spend her new salary. Most of it would be going to pay off her student loans, and she wanted to start putting some into savings, too. "This is a really big deal. If it works out here, I could actually be a curator of a house museum someday."

"Look at you, Miss Fancy Curator. Great job." Chris gave her one of his rare, big smiles, and she remembered why she was with him, how good it felt to make him smile.

A heavy autumn rain had subdued the bustling streets of Tynemouth, turning the wet air gray and heavy. Puddles formed in the uneven stone steps as Augusta texted Jill that she was outside and waited for her to come down and open the door.

Jill greeted Augusta with a big smile. She was just as impeccably put-together as the first time Augusta had met her, with her pin-straight bob, cherry red lipstick and chic linen shift. "Your first day! Come on in and let's get you set up!"

Carefully shaking out her umbrella and wiping her shoes, Augusta stepped inside. The house was cool and quiet, the gray skies and amplified sound of rain on windows making it cozy.

"If you want to drop off your stuff in the kitchen, I thought we might start with a tour of the house?"

Augusta hung up her raincoat to dry, stuck her yogurt in the fridge and then glanced around. Besides the hum of the kitchen appliances and a phone ringing somewhere upstairs from the offices, it was silent. Even the traffic was muted from the rain.

"Is it always so quiet on Mondays?" she asked.

"It's quiet compared to the days when we're open to the public, but usually Sharon is around. We also have a few other staff members that split their time between Harlowe House and the archives in Boston, so it can get busy if we have a lot of projects going on. Sharon is out today, so it's just you and me. On Wednesday, you'll meet all the tour guides."

After Augusta took a peek at her office—her own office!— Jill started the tour. "We're really trying to do more to tell the stories of everyone who lived in Tynemouth in the nineteenth and twentieth centuries, not just the upper class, white population. Immigrants were coming from Boston and the population here was incredibly diverse."

Jill flicked on a light and led her into a surprisingly modern space, complete with gleaming hardwood floors and pristine white walls. "This would have been the ballroom back in the 1800s, but now we have rotating exhibits in this space featuring local artists. Last summer we even had a bluegrass band perform. Our director of community outreach works out of our Boston office, but you'll see him sometime. He's responsible for putting these events together, and occasionally he'll ask for objects from our collection to highlight in the exhibits, usually to draw a parallel between the history of the area and the current art scene." She gestured to a display featuring a collection of embroidery hoops. "Like this one—we did a spotlight on local fiber artists, and used some of the baskets and embroideries from our collection. Do you think you'd be interested in helping pull objects for exhibits like that in the future?"

"Definitely. That's amazing." Augusta leaned over to read the placard on one of the hoops before they moved on.

"Great!" Jill motioned for Augusta to follow her as they left the ballroom. "Just through here," she said, as they passed through a narrow hall. "Not as modern as the staff kitchen, but I'm kind of jealous of the tiles in here."

It was easy to see why. Gleaming white tiles with bright, purple ink depicting every manner of country scene lined the back splash and countertops. It was a visual feast, like something right out of a French home-and-garden magazine. "We'll just scoot through the butler's pantry," Jill said, leading the way.

After the light and airy kitchen, Augusta wasn't prepared for the dark room they entered next. "Watch your step here," Jill instructed. "We don't usually take tours in here unless they specifically ask or it's a VIP, like a descendant. The step is uneven and the lighting isn't great."

Jill pulled a string and a single bulb buzzed to life in the middle of the room. "What was this room used for?" Augusta asked.

"We're pretty sure it was the original kitchen when the house was first built in the seventeenth century, but by the time the Harlowe brothers were living here it had long since gone out of use. It was probably used as extra storage or a pantry." Jill sheepishly gestured to some bins in the corner. "We, uh, might stash some stuff in here, too, on occasion."

There really wasn't much to see in the room. The rough-hewn walls were covered in chipped white paint, and the floor was packed dirt coated in some kind of concrete, like the bottom of an empty swimming pool. At the far end, what had once been a fireplace large enough to stand in was now just a gaping recess.

"How are you with spiders?" Jill asked. "Because we have a lot of them in here."

Augusta shrugged. "They don't bother me." She had done some pest management at the Old Jail which involved setting out sticky traps and tracking and recording all the insects in them. It had forced her to get over any squeamishness in a hurry.

"Well, I'm not a fan," Jill said with a shudder. "Let's head upstairs."

Augusta was just turning to follow her when a wave of dizziness overcame her. She shot her hand out against the wall to steady herself before she stumbled. Cold from the wall seeped into her skin and rooted in her bones. Closing her eyes, she cursed herself for not eating a better breakfast.

When she opened her eyes again, she was still in the same dark room, but sensing something above her, she looked up. Bunches of dried plants and flowers hung upside down from the ceiling beams, quivering in the still air. She could smell their dry sweetness, could make out every brittle leaf and petal. The formerly empty fireplace now glowed with use. From somewhere beyond her sight came the sound of a woman's voice, humming.

What the hell was happening? Some museums employed holographs or 3D projections to replicate historic settings, but Jill had been quite clear that this wasn't an exhibit space, and Augusta was pretty sure that she would have mentioned if Harlowe House had that kind of technology.

The roots of her hair lifted, and she was excruciatingly aware of every inch of her skin prickling in response to the closeness of the humming. Slowly, she turned her head, certain that she would see the source of the sound. There was someone there—someone who wasn't Jill. She could sense their presence, smell the sweet, floral scent of their perfume and the salty tang of perspiration under it. But then, just as suddenly as the room had changed, it was all gone again, leaving her in the musty darkness. The dried herbs and flowers that just moments ago had hung above her had vanished, and the humming had stopped.

She shot an alarmed look at Jill to see if she had noticed the dramatic change, but Jill was already ducking back through the low door and moving on to the next room.

Augusta looked back over her shoulder again; everything was back in its place, from the plastic bins to the electric light. Shaking her head, she hurried to catch up with Jill. She really should have eaten breakfast that morning, more than just a glass of orange juice and a slice of unbuttered bread. She had a job, responsibilities, and she had to make sure she was taking care of herself. But even as she forced herself to follow Jill, she had a sinking feeling that the hallucination hadn't had anything to do with calories, or the lack of them.

"So." Jill plopped a stack of books and binders onto the table. "This is totally not required, but it's probably a good idea to read through some of these and get a sense of the history of Harlowe House. You'll pick up a lot as you work, but this will provide a good baseline."

Jill had insisted on picking up lunch from the sandwich place down the street, and they were sitting in the small staff kitchen eating while Augusta flipped through binders. The rain had tapered off, leaving heavy humidity and an overcast sky in its wake. Since her strange episode that morning, Augusta hadn't felt any more light-headedness or had any disturbing hallucinations, but she still forced herself to bite into her sandwich, chewing slowly.

"This is really the only thing I would ask you to read," Jill said, tapping the cover of a slender folder. "It lays out the family tree and who was who. It will be helpful to get a grasp of what generation owned what things in the house."

Augusta flipped it open, tracing her finger down the sprawling tree, starting in the 1600s and going all the way to the present day. "So there still are living descendants?"

Rolling her eyes, Jill licked some mustard off her finger and put her sandwich down. "Yes, and you didn't hear it from me, but they are the *worst*. They show up unannounced all the time, looking to take friends on 'behind the scene tours' and expect us to drop everything. They have a picnic at the house once a year, but the public isn't invited. I guess since we don't have royalty in America some people like to imagine that they're above everyone else because of their bloodline."

Augusta nodded absently as she studied the chart. It was an impressive tree, with so much information corresponding to each name, and she felt a pang of jealousy that anyone could claim ancestry going back so far. She was an only child without much extended family and had grown up knowing little about her own family history.

Her finger stopped on a name, and a jolt of recognition passed through her, even though she was sure she'd never seen it before. Unlike the others in its generation, this one didn't have any information—no birth date, no death date, nothing. "Who was this?" she asked.

Jill leaned over to look. "Margaret Harlowe," she said. "She was the only sister of the three Harlowe brothers. We don't know a lot about her, or even if she really existed at all, since she doesn't show up in any censuses." Jill shrugged. "Unfortunately, that's kind of the case with a lot of women in the historical records— they got married and took new names, moved away, or they just slipped through the cracks. We do have a portrait in the dining room that we think is her, but we aren't even sure about that."

Augusta moved on, and Jill told her about each of the brothers and what they contributed to the narrative of the house. "Once you get your sea legs, we should chat about a possible exhibit you'd like to research and help curate."

The binder nearly slipped from her hand. "Are you serious?"

Jill laughed. "Yeah, I'm serious! You didn't think you'd just be sitting around and working on spreadsheets, did you?"

"Well, no. I guess I just didn't expect to take on such a big project right away."

Jill's expression softened. "Augusta, we're really excited to have you here. Your references had nothing but great things to say about you, and you bring a lot of knowledge and valuable experience to Harlowe House."

Augusta ducked her head, glowing. She'd never felt particularly valued at a job before, and this was the job of her dreams.

They were interrupted by a knock on the doorframe. Jill looked up and broke into a smile. "Hey, Reggie."

"Hey there." The man in the doorway had light brown skin and a dazzling white smile. With a T-shirt tucked into faded jeans and silver streaking his dark hair, he looked like the quintessential dad from a Hallmark movie. He returned Jill's smile before his glance landed on Augusta. "A new face! I don't think we've met," he said, sticking out his hand.

"This is Augusta, our new collections manager extraordinaire." Jill turned to Augusta. "Reggie is our properties manager. He splits his time between the properties, so you'll see him on days when we're closed to the public, working on projects."

"Or on days when there are doughnuts," Reggie said, looking around hopefully.

"It's your turn to buy the doughnuts," Jill reminded him. "What's up? I thought you were in Boston today?"

"Something keeps setting off the silent alarm in the basement," he said. "I don't know if it's a faulty wire or mice, but I keep getting alerts from the security company. Guess I'm going to go crawl around with the spiders and have a look." He patted the flashlight on his belt and gave Augusta a wink. "The excitement never ends around here."

After he left, Jill and Augusta finished up their lunches. "You said something about a possible portrait of Margaret Harlowe?" she asked Jill. For some reason, the lonesome female name on that branch of the family tree had piqued her interest.

"You want to go see her?"

Augusta nodded. She was more than a little curious about this woman who may or may not have existed.

Jill led her to the dining room. A large, polished oak table dominated the space, blue-and-white porcelain laid out on it as if just waiting for a family to come and sit down for a meal. Portraits dotted the green-papered walls, the gilt frames winking in the soft lamplight. Jill drew Augusta's attention to a small portrait at the far end of the room. "That's her. Or at least, we think that might be her, judging from the style of her dress. We have pictures of Jemima Harlowe from the time, and she would have been much older than the sitter here."

Augusta studied the young woman. She possessed a Mona Lisa–like quality, assessing the viewer with a cool, measured stare. Her dark curls were loosely pulled back, cascading down her shoulders. The tight-fitting sleeves and high-necked collar as well as the hairstyle certainly pointed to the portrait having been painted in the late 1870s or 1880s.

"Are there any photographs of the family?" Augusta asked. By the 1880s, photography would have been quite accessible, and she would have been surprised if a well-to-do family such as the Harlowes hadn't had any photos taken.

"We do have some daguerreotypes and cabinet cards in the collection, but most of them are of the brothers. I think there are a couple of the exterior of the house, too. We can pull them out later if you're interested."

A thought struck Augusta. "Are there any of the interior? Like of the old kitchen?"

Jill frowned. "I don't think so. Why?"

Just then Reggie stuck his head in again. "Sorry to interrupt. The sensor stopped, though I can't figure out what was causing it to go off in the first place."

"Must be the ghost," Jill said.

"That's about the only explanation I can think of," he said, without looking up from typing on his phone.

"We have a resident ghost," Jill explained. "He likes to hide important papers on us, turn off the lights, stuff like that. A few years ago, we even had a paranormal investigator from a TV show come in. They aired the episode and it was great publicity for the museum."

"What did they find?" Augusta asked.

"That it's an old house," Reggie said with a grunt. "Cold spots, creaky floorboards and dust orbs."

"Reggie doesn't believe in ghosts," Jill said. "He's no fun."

Augusta glanced at her phone and was surprised to find that it was already four thirty. She would have to leave right away if she wanted to catch the last bus before eight that night. But Jill and Reggie were bantering good-naturedly, and it was so peaceful and cozy inside. There was still so much more she wanted to explore in the house before she went home for the day, too. Sliding her phone back into her pocket, she decided she would figure out a way home later.

It was after five thirty when Augusta emerged into the crisp, overcast evening. Taking out her phone, she shot Chris a text asking if he wanted to meet her in downtown Tynemouth for a celebratory dinner. If he met her there, she wouldn't have to call a car or wait for the eight o'clock bus.

She walked around the outside of the house in the gathering dusk, snapping a few pictures for Instagram. No reply from Chris. He was probably at the gym, or engrossed in a video game with Doug.

She was just about to go in search of a café so she could hunker down until eight, when Jill and Reggie caught her coming out the back door.

Jill looked surprised. "Hey, do you have a ride home?"

Augusta didn't want to admit that her boyfriend wasn't answering her texts, or that she was planning on sitting by herself for three hours. "Yeah, I'm fine. Just going to call an Uber or something if my boyfriend doesn't get me first."

"Well, we're going to go grab a beer. You're more than welcome to come. Reggie lives near Salem—he can drive you home after."

"Or I can drive you home now," Reggie quickly offered. "No need to come out if you don't want to."

Augusta fidgeted with her phone case. She'd envisioned celebrating with Chris, but he hadn't answered, and she didn't really feel like going home yet. Checking her messages one last time, she made up her mind. "Yeah, okay. I'd love to."

It was almost eleven o'clock by the time Reggie dropped Augusta off. As she made her way up the carpeted stairs to their apartment, a knot tightened in her chest. She'd forgotten to check her phone until she was in the car and saw she had a text from Chris asking where she was. When she let herself into the apartment, Doug was nowhere to be seen, and the door to her and Chris's bedroom was closed.

The light was off but she could make out the faint outline of Chris in the bed. Quietly as she could, she slipped off her shoes and changed into her pajamas.

The rustle of blankets. "Where were you?"

"I went out for drinks with people from Harlowe House. I texted you," she added.

"Who?"

"Just some of the people who work there. Jill is the curator who I told you about, and Reggie is the building manager. They're both married," she added, knowing what his next question would be and hoping to avoid a confrontation.

Chris didn't say anything, just turned back over in bed. She stared at his unmoving form for what felt like an eternity before finally getting ready for bed and resigning herself to a night of the silent treatment. As she climbed into bed beside him, she felt a pang of grief for the days when he'd hugged and tickled her and then fallen into bed with her, glad for her company. How long ago those days seemed now. Had she and Chris changed, or had time simply eroded whatever chemistry they had once shared? Either way, it was lonely to lie so close next to someone, yet feel so very far away.

7

Margaret

The gardener standing by,
He bid me take great care;
For that under the blossom and under the leaves
Is a thorn that will wound and tear.

—"The Seeds of Love," Traditional Folk Song

MY MOTHER RECEIVED the cream of tartar with a *humph*, but did not ask me what had taken so long. "Clarence and Lizzie will be here soon," she said.

It was a rare thing for all three of my brothers to be in Tynemouth on dry land at the same time, but whenever it happened my mother was rapturous, insisting on throwing elaborate dinners for them. Her sons were her pride and joy. They did not embarrass her, did not give her cause for worry.

Nearly ten years older than I, Clarence was little more than a stranger who appeared at the house with his wife on occasion and talked business with Father. Clarence worked at the shipping office and did not actually go to sea himself. He had a head for numbers and the reserved demeanor of a scholar. Next oldest was George, and then Henry. George had salt water in his blood and was at sea more often than on land, and though I seldom saw him anymore, he had always been my favorite. The house was a duller place without him.

I often wondered why I was such an anomaly in my family. Mother did not show the slightest inclination toward the world outside the gossip pages, let alone the art of magic. And Father, while he was always kind and generous, had not an ounce of imagination. Aside from George, my brothers were dull and would rather sit inside an office hunched over a dusty ledger than look out the window at the world around them. Sometimes it felt as if I had been born from the morning dew, simply materializing from the air fully formed.

I wanted to divest myself of the wretched corset, but Mother had the eyes of an eagle, and I knew that she would insist upon my looking "presentable" for my brothers. There was always something wrong with me, always something worthy of her criticism. Sighing, I changed out of my lawn linen dress and into a stiff visiting gown of plum taffeta and made my way to the kitchen. I wanted rosemary and borage for a sachet to put under my pillow. Even though there was no mistaking the way Jack Pryce looked at me, there could be no harm in making a love spell to encourage his affections.

Molly greeted me warily from where she was mixing a bowl of eggs, watching as I passed through the kitchen. She tolerated my presence in her domain because her position demanded it, but her dislike didn't escape me. There was an unused pantry— once a kitchen from the early days of the house—which I used as my stillroom. It was my sanctuary, the one place where I might breathe freely. As soon as I opened the door, the warm, familiar scent of sage and lavender embraced me. The old kitchen had not been used for decades, but one window remained uncovered, and it let in a slice of soft, buttery sunlight.

When I was not able to go out into the woods or to the ocean, I would retreat into my stillroom. It was here with my herbs and dried flowers that I could bring time to a halt. Later I would look back at those days with fondness, longing. Dust motes hung suspended in the shaft of sunlight, and the sounds of the house were far away and muffled. I plucked and ground and mixed my little potions and tinctures, tipping them into bottles and labeling them.

When I had made my love charm, I wiped my sage-dusted fingers on my skirt, and emerged back into the hall just as my brothers began to arrive. Clarence and his wife, Lizzie, were first, Lizzie's stomach bulging with child. Her keen eyes seemed to calculate the price of every stick of furniture as she swept through the hall, the exaggerated bustle of her dress nearly knocking the credenza over as she passed.

"Margaret," Clarence said, giving me a formal kiss on the cheek.

"Hello, Clarence. Hello, Lizzie. You look well." But Clarence had already turned to Father, and Lizzie was complaining to Mother about the ache in her back and how she couldn't get the sugared almonds she'd been craving lately.

Henry and George arrived together. George, his usual good-natured self, gave Mother a big, loud kiss before turning to me and swinging me in his arms. "Maggie, but you've grown since I saw you last."

I hadn't, but it was a tradition of ours that he would comment on my height every time he returned from sea. He was also the only person who was allowed to call me Maggie. "That's what happens when you disappear for months at a time."

George had dark hair which he wore neatly parted and greased, and he'd recently grown a mustache. I had always thought him terribly dashing, and though George was seemingly oblivious to it, many other girls in town had shared the same opinion as me. "The sea is a fickle mistress," he said, tossing me a wink. "And look what your favorite brother has brought you." He dropped a strand of smooth, pinkish-red beads onto my palm. "Coral," he said. "From the Indies."

"George," I breathed. "It's beautiful." I fastened it around my neck, the blushing beads bright and lustrous against the dark taffeta of my dress.

George brushed my cheek with a kiss. "Your beauty puts them to shame, but I'm glad you like them." Then, as if just noticing that Clarence and Lizzie were there, he said, "Hullo there, Clare. Liz."

Clarence pressed his lips tight, and Lizzie gave him a lukewarm greeting, their rigid sense of convention no doubt ruffled by George's flamboyance.

Behind him, Henry stepped out and glanced at me from behind his dark fringe of hair. "Hello, Margaret," he said, his tone almost as formal as Clarence's. Though Henry worked as a clerk for a lawyer in Boston, he was restless and not suited to the life of an office man. Neither was he suited to the sea, though. "I suppose I should have brought you a gift, but I am not so courteous as George. Did you enjoy the book of poems I sent you last month?"

In truth, I had forgotten about the book, and had yet to open it. But before I could tell him as much, Mother was ushering us into the good sitting room, ordering me to let Molly know to bring us lemonade.

When I returned, everyone had made themselves comfortable. "Well, I have some news," George said, leaning forward in his seat. "I've asked Ida Foster to marry me."

Mother clapped her hands, and there was a murmur of surprise and approval from everyone.

"Oh, but, George, that's wonderful!" I exclaimed, and he gave me a shy smile. Though I was not acquainted with the young lady, I had heard George speak fondly of her for months in his letters, and I'd had my suspicions that he'd set his cap at her.

Father nodded thoughtfully. "Well done, George," he said, as if George had made a particularly savvy investment.

"She won't mind that you're away so often?" Clarence asked.

"Ida is a fine girl and understands the life. Besides, I daresay she'll relish a little quiet time without me around."

"Well, I think it's marvelous," Mother said. "You must pass

on our regards to her parents, and of course we will host a celebratory luncheon for you both."

"What about you, Henry?" my father asked. "When will we see you settled?"

Henry mumbled something and took a slow sip from his lemonade.

"Aren't there any pretty girls in Boston that catch your eye?" Clarence asked with a mocking raise of his brow. Henry had never expressed any interest in girls, and it was a great source of ribbing for my other brothers.

Henry glowered at him, but did not say anything.

"Come now, that's enough," Mother said, reaching out to pat Henry's hand. For reasons beyond my comprehension, Henry had always been Mother's favorite, her pet.

There were more well-wishes, and Father led a toast. Molly brought in a tray of little sandwiches, and everyone seemed to overlook the dark cloud that was hanging over Henry.

After Father took out the cigars, and Mother and Lizzie were busy discussing colors for the nursery, I went outside to bring Shadow some scraps. My parents didn't tolerate him inside, but sometimes I would sneak him into my bedroom at night so that he might sleep in my bed with me.

The warm air felt heavenly on my face, and I wished that I was not so encased in taffeta and stiff lace so that I might feel more of it on my skin. Birds sang from the flowering apple trees, and clusters of blue irises swayed in the breeze. It was too nice a day for stuffy conversation and to be sitting inside sipping from crystal cups.

Shadow rose from where he had been lounging under the apple tree and greeted me with a wagging tail, eagerly snapping up the ham. When he was done, he flopped over and I obliged him by rubbing his belly. "Good boy, sweet boy," I murmured. "Don't let the rabbits get too fat," I told him. "They've already eaten all my parsley." Shadow gave me a withering look; he was the best of companions and loyal to a fault, but guard dog he was not.

Rising, I found Henry leaned up against the wall, sulking and smoking a cheroot. I joined him. "Why aren't you inside with everyone else?" I asked. "Aren't you happy for George?"

Henry scoffed. "Oh, yes," he said, throwing his cheroot down and angrily stubbing it out with his heel. "How can I not be happy for George? The golden child."

"Don't be sour," I said. "It's not becoming on you."

Henry's dark eyes flashed. "Don't pretend *you* are happy, Margaret."

"Of course I'm happy. Just as I would be happy if you were to announce an engagement."

For all that Henry was my brother, sometimes I wondered that we were related at all. He had always been a broody child; he had a watchfulness about him, as if he was above the rest of us mere mortals. I thought of the boys in the woods, their hungry eyes. There had always been a gleam of something dark in Henry, something dangerous and slumbering. Was he like them?

"Don't lie," he told me. "You've always been a free spirit, with your nocturnal jaunts to the woods and the beach. You aren't like the others, and neither am I."

"I don't know what you're talking about."

"Oh, yes you do. You and I are different from the rest of them. We could never bind ourselves to someone who doesn't understand us. The Ida Fosters of the world are all well and good for George and Clarence, but not for the likes of us."

I rolled my eyes. The only thing different about Henry was that he fancied himself a poet, a tortured soul. "You're wrong," I told him, before I could stop myself. "I've found a man who knows what I am and loves me for it."

I don't know what perversion compelled me to say it. Did Jack love me? We'd only had a handful of exchanges, but the memory of his hand on my arm that morning, the urgency in his voice when he'd told me he needed to see me again, was still vivid in my mind.

Henry's gaze sharpened. "What? What man?"

The sun slid behind a cloud and in an instant the warm spring air had gone chilly. I knew that I had misstepped, that Henry was the last person I should confide in. "No one," I said quickly.

He reached for me, putting his hands on my shoulders. "Maggie," he said, his voice going soft. "You can tell me anything. I'm your brother, aren't I?"

I shrugged out of his grasp. "Don't call me Maggie."

"Of course," he said bitterly. "Only your precious George is allowed such a familiarity. Are you worried you won't hold pride of place in his heart now that he will have a wife?"

"I'm going back inside," I said. "Perhaps it is time for you to go home, as well."

He didn't say anything, but I could feel his eyes on my back, burning into me as I whistled to Shadow and walked back to the house.

The sound of footsteps in the yard roused me from my light sleep that night. Creeping to the window, I could see a woman, her lantern light slicing through the rainy night below, and I knew at once that I had a customer. I let out a curse under my breath. What was she doing here, at the house? I met all my patients in the old cabin in the woods, and even the uninitiated knew enough not to come to my door in town.

I was not quick enough to dress and intercept her before Molly knocked on my door. "You have a visitor," she said coldly.

Ignoring her disapproving glare, I picked up a lamp and made my way downstairs to the kitchen, where the woman was standing in the doorway, looking like a drowned rabbit. She carried in her arms a bundle of blankets, and despite her wet hair and frenzied look, I recognized her as Jenny Hough, a good, respectable woman who wouldn't have so much as glanced in my direction in the day. "Come along inside," I told her. "I won't bite you."

After a moment's hesitation, Mrs. Hough came the rest of the way in the kitchen, and I closed the door, shutting Molly out. Molly must have had her suspicions, but I knew that she would not tattle on me, for fear of what I might do to her in retribution. Good Catholic girl that she was, she knew to keep her distance from me. Did my parents know, too? Well, yes and no. Certainly they knew that I spent a good deal of time out of doors, and that I occasionally entertained women from town during odd hours, though they probably thought I fancied myself an herbalist or something innocent enough. They did not—could not—know of the dark powers I possessed.

My patient sat on a stool, arms crossed and shivering. Placing a cup of steaming tea before her, I did what I always did first: I asked her what ailed her, and then I listened.

It was always my hope that whatever ailments came through my doorway might be treated with herbs, or perhaps a little charm—something designed more to give the person peace of mind than to actually work magic. But sometimes they required something more, something darker and more powerful.

Mrs. Jenny Hough cupped the mug of tea, the steam wreathing her face as she recounted her troubles. Her little girl, it seemed, was insensible with fever, and the physicians had told her that it was hopeless.

When she was finished, she looked up at me with wide, frightened eyes. "Can you help me?" she whispered.

Of course I could help her, but she was not going to like what my help would entail. They never did. "Where is the child now?" I asked her, warily eyeing the bundle in her arms.

Her gaze dropped to the bundle, and I bit back a curse as my suspicions were confirmed. But there was nothing for it, so I bade her remove the blankets.

"Lay the child down on the table," I instructed her. She only hesitated for a moment, and then was arranging the limp body of the little girl on our kitchen table. Running my hands over the cold flesh, I assessed her condition. She was achingly fragile, her eyes moving feverishly under her paper-thin lids, her small hands curled into fists at her sides. What an exquisite burden it must be to love something so small, so delicate.

My fingers found a pulse, though it was faint and erratic. Mrs. Hough watched me, her knuckles white as she clutched the edge of the table. Gently laying the girl's arm down and tucking the blanket around her, I stood back. "She is very far gone," I told her mother. "Though you are not without recourse."

"Anything," she said, "I will do anything." Reaching into her cloak, she produced a thick roll of banknotes.

But I shook my head. "It is not a question of money. If you want your daughter to live you must find a new body for her. Her spirit lives, but her body is dying."

Mrs. Hough stared at me. "You cannot be serious."

"I am quite serious. You will need a body that yet lives, preferably of the same age and sex. Otherwise, do not waste your time dragging your poor daughter to witch's houses in the middle of the night. Make her comfortable and prepare your goodbyes."

"You propose that I kill another girl so that mine might live? I—I could never! They warned me about you, but I couldn't have imagined that you would be so craven...so—so unnatural!" Gathering up her daughter, she fumbled for the door as if she could not get away from me fast enough.

"You came to me asking the impossible, and I told you what would be required to achieve it," I hissed at her, aware that Molly was probably still listening on the other side of the door. "Did you think that it would be easy? Did you think that I would only have to snap my fingers and restore her to you?"

Mrs. Hough gave me one last fearful look over her shoulder before plunging back out into the rain.

After she had left, I returned to my bed, tired and restless. It gave me no pleasure to deliver such a grim verdict to a desperate mother. It gave me no pleasure to know that the girl would most certainly die. But there are prices to be paid for such magic, and balances to be kept.

8

Augusta

CHRIS'S HANDS WERE heavy on Augusta's shoulders, and everything was dark. "Where are we going?" she asked him for the hundredth time.

Behind her, Chris guided her down the apartment building steps and outside. When she'd come home that evening, he'd instructed her to put on a blindfold and prepare to be surprised. It was so out of character for him that she had been immediately suspicious. Was he playing some sort of joke on her? Or had Doug gone on one of his redecorating rampages and Chris was afraid to let her see? But now, as he helped her navigate the stairs, she could practically feel him vibrating with excitement.

"You'll see," he said. A few more steps in the darkness and they came to a stop. "Okay...open them!"

Augusta fumbled to remove the blindfold, and then blinked against the late evening light. They were standing in front of the apartment, facing the street. All that she saw were the usual things: parked cars, kids kicking a soccer ball in the park across the street, tomorrow's trash sitting in garbage bags on the curb. "What exactly am I looking at?"

Grinning, Chris pointed. "Right there."

She followed his finger. Parked right in front of her was a forest green station wagon. "I don't get it."

"It's a car. For you."

"You…you got me a *car*?" Chris didn't get her things. Or rather, he didn't make grand gestures. Early on in their relationship he'd gotten her flowers a couple of times, and occasionally they exchanged presents for the holidays, though never anything too pricey. She couldn't wrap her head around it. He'd gotten her a car. Granted, it was a little dinged up and looked to be at least ten years old, but it was a car. No more early morning bus trips to work, no more being dependent on other people to get around. Tears stung her eyes.

"Do you like it?" Chris asked, apprehension in his voice. "I know it's not brand-new or anything fancy, but now you won't have to take the bus to work anymore. It's all paid off, you just have to get insurance and keep the tank full."

She nodded, unable to speak. All those times she'd questioned if she and Chris were meant to be together faded away. He wasn't good at telling her how he felt, but he was showing her now, and that was all that mattered.

The next day, Augusta woke up feeling light, optimistic. Abundant sunshine poured through the windows, and a crisp blue sky promised a picture-perfect autumn day.

"We should go somewhere today—I want to try out my new car," she told Chris over breakfast. "I was thinking we could go apple picking or visit that new pumpkin patch in Danvers. There's that little breakfast place right down the street."

Chris barely glanced up from his phone. "I think Doug and

Gemma were planning on going for a hike. There's a cool abandoned settlement right outside of Tynemouth with tons of trails. Might be fun? Besides," he said, finally looking up and patting his nonexistent belly, "we could use the exercise."

Augusta deflated. She didn't have the greatest relationship with Gemma, and her relationship with hiking and the great outdoors even less so. Gemma had gone to school with Doug and worked with Chris, so every time they all got together, she, Chris and Doug all talked about stuff that Augusta had no knowledge of, or interest in. But if she didn't go it would mean Chris would just go without her, and she would be the odd one out later when they all came back.

So that's how she found herself behind the wheel of her new car, headed to Tynemouth on a Saturday, Chris in the passenger seat, and Gemma and Doug in the back.

They pulled into a gravel parking lot and parked among a handful of other cars. Dog walkers congregated and chatted at the trailhead, and a couple carried a kayak under their arms as they walked toward a sign for a portage. Stepping out of the car, Gemma stretched, her crop top riding up and showing off a generous breadth of creamy skin. Tall, dark-haired, with the statuesque body of a model, she was Augusta's polar opposite. Jealousy wasn't an attractive quality, Chris had told her on more than one occasion, but it was hard not to be jealous, especially when Gemma and Chris spent so much time together at work.

Doug was tucking his pant legs into his socks, even though Chris had assured him it was too late in the year for ticks. Augusta surveyed the area. The landscape looked mercifully flat, just the usual rocky New England terrain. Chris, sensing Augusta's relief, patted her on the shoulder. "It's a really easy hike— you shouldn't have any problems."

Biting back a scowl, she retied her tennis shoes and adjusted her thin socks. The group set out, Doug and Gemma laughing and chatting as they led the way, and Chris hanging back with Augusta.

The brilliant autumn forest welcomed them with gently swaying branches and an abundance of chatty birds and quarrelsome squirrels. Aside from the occasional stone foundation, overgrown and decaying back into the earth, no one would have ever known that it must have once been a bustling little settlement. Faded wooden plaques marked the trail loop's miles and provided some sporadic information about the ruins. Despite the lack of hills and the cool, pleasant weather, about half an hour in, sweat started to slick her back, her leg muscles burning. Why exactly did people think hiking was anything other than an exercise in self-inflicted torture? Nature was meant to be enjoyed from a picnic blanket or well-lit patio with lots of cold drinks and easy access to indoor plumbing.

Chris had gradually caught up with Doug and, ahead of her, the sound of the group's movement and laughter carried through branches. Bringing up the rear at least meant that she could ignore how small she felt when everyone else talked about video games or computer stuff she didn't fully understand.

She'd just lost sight of Gemma's bright pink leggings when the coffee she'd had on the drive hit her. God, if there was one thing worse than walking in nature, it was having to pee in nature. There had been a highly suspect port-a-potty back in the parking lot, but she wasn't *that* desperate. Better to risk a few moments of exposure than whatever lurked in an unmaintained port-a-potty. She called for the group to wait up, but the wind carried her words away, and she didn't feel like running over the uneven trail just to catch up and announce that she had to pee. With one more glance at where she'd last seen the group, she plunged off the trail in search of a private spot. With any luck, she'd be able to catch up to everyone else afterward.

Bladder finally, blessedly empty, Augusta took stock of the thick woods where she found herself. Above her, the orange canopy danced and flickered in a sudden rush of wind. Lifting her ponytail, Augusta let the cool air skim across her neck, grateful for the few moments of rest from the hike. It was only when she was ready to get going again that she realized she had no idea which direction she was supposed to be facing. Her sense of modesty had led her so deep into the underbrush that she had completely lost her bearings. By now she'd been separated from the group for at least five minutes. Had Chris even realized that she wasn't with them anymore? She checked her phone, but she had no messages, and no reception.

Despite the abundant daylight and the sound of a dog barking not too far away, her body tightened with panic. What if she'd somehow stepped onto the wrong trail and couldn't find her way back? What if she was still lost by nightfall? What if she wandered onto someone's private property and was shot for trespassing? This was why sane people didn't go into the woods for fun. She and Chris should have been at the apple orchard, enjoying a cup of fresh cider and taking photos of the scenery from the comfort of a picnic bench.

The sun slid behind a clutch of clouds and a chill raced across her skin. If not for the distant hum of traffic, she might have been the only person in the world. Except that she had a very real sense that she was not alone in this dense pocket of woods. Her neck prickled. It wasn't that she felt like she was being watched, it was as if *she* were the one intruding. A thousand spirits seemed to crowd the air, pressing around her, making it known that she was on hallowed ground. What was it about this place, about Tynemouth in general, that seemed to speak to her?

One more gust of wind was all it took to send her blindly scrambling, hoping that she ended up on the right path. Every sinister tree and jutting rock looked the same, and her head spun as she tried to regain her bearings. Eventually the trees thinned, and sunlight began to peek through the clouds. A jumbled pile of rocks told her that she was at least back near the ruins, and, not wanting to risk getting turned around any further, plopped herself down to wait, her heart still beating fast. Chris and the others would realize soon that she wasn't lagging behind—if they hadn't already—and come looking for her. In the meantime, at least she could rest, give her pulse a chance to slow. Closing her eyes, she let the sounds and sensations of the natural world weave and swirl around her. The foreboding atmosphere had faded, a sense of serenity washing over her. Birdsong crisscrossed above her like far-flung telephone wires. Layers of scent—earthy dead leaves and sun-warmed stones—rose like baking bread.

The sound of approaching footsteps and voices pulled her from her reverie, and a shadow passed over her closed eyes. When she opened them, she found Chris, Gemma and Doug standing over her, all wearing equal expressions of concern. How long had she been sleeping? What had come over her that suddenly the woods felt so unthreatening that she could actually fall *asleep*?

"Look at Mother Nature over here," Chris said, helping her to her feet. "We were wondering where you were."

Clearly, they hadn't wondered enough to actually come looking for her. "I had to go to the bathroom and I got turned around," she told him as she brushed dead leaves and dirt off her pants. "Didn't you notice I wasn't with you guys anymore?"

Gemma flicked her long ponytail back, surveying her with detached scorn. "You're like, two minutes away from the parking lot," she said, pointing to where Augusta could just make out the tops of a couple of cars.

Gemma's attitude would have usually left Augusta mumbling with burning cheeks, but after the surreal experience of getting lost, panicking and then slipping into a meditative state, wasting her energy on Gemma felt like less of a priority. She'd started the day ambivalent about having to spend time in nature, but as she slid into the driver's seat and started the car, she was inexplicably sorry for having to leave behind the woods, and the secretive wind that blew through it.

★ ★ ★

*Do not think that because I have no corporeal form that I am com-
pletely divorced from the goings-on of the present day. If you have ever
hastened home ahead of an approaching storm, then you know that the
energy hanging in the air is as real as the lightning that follows.*

*Tethered to my home as I am, I can only see that which transpires in-
side the house. Yet all the same I know that she has been to the woods,
trod over the rocky ground where once my secret cabin stood. Do not ask
me how I know; it is the same way that birds know to fly south, the
same way that a fox can pick up a scent on the wind. How I envy her
freedom to come and go, to sit among the craggy rocks and lichen-painted
trees. All the same, I am glad she feels called, because I have more to
show her. So much more.*

The next week Augusta disarmed the alarm system and let
herself into the back door of Harlowe House. After nearly a
month, she was feeling more at home at her new job, and even
though she didn't need to get up at the crack of dawn anymore
to take the bus, she still came in early. She liked the mornings
when she had the house to herself before the rest of the staff arrived. It was quiet, and she was able to listen to her music while
she worked.

After dropping her stuff in the kitchen, she sat down at her
desk and got out the binder of the Harlowes' collection. The
community outreach guy from the Boston office was coming
by later that day, and Jill said that he'd be looking for some objects to showcase in their summer exhibit.

Augusta flipped through the collection catalog and sipped her
tea, the sounds of the old house filling the silence around her.

But there was one sound that was out of place. She lifted her
head, trying to isolate it. Over the hum of the air purifier and
the muffled car traffic outside, she could hear someone walking
downstairs. It couldn't be Jill or Reggie because the door sensor hadn't gone off, and it definitely wasn't the guy from Boston

because Jill had said he didn't have the code and would need to be let in. The tour guides didn't have codes either, and anyway, the house was closed to tours today. If someone had broken in the alarm should have gone off, shouldn't it? She reached for her phone, the hairs on her neck standing up.

Her instinct was to sit as still as possible and not make a sound, but she was responsible for this house now. She wasn't quite sure what she would do if she came face-to-face with an ax murderer, but she had to do *something*. As quietly as she could—which wasn't easy given the old, creaky floorboards—she stood up and made her way to the office door. Pausing, she listened again for the footsteps.

Nothing.

If there was someone else in the house, perhaps they'd heard her and stopped moving. Reggie's words about the creaks and sounds an old house made came to mind, but this didn't sound like the natural settling of an old structure. This was the sound of very deliberate movement.

She was just about to call Jill when the door sensor went off and she heard Jill herself come in, talking on her phone and dropping her bag in the kitchen. Letting out a giant sigh of relief, Augusta grabbed her mug and went down to meet her.

When Jill saw her, she waved and motioned to indicate that she would be off the phone in a minute. After she'd hung up, she gave Augusta an apologetic smile. "Hey, sorry about that. Our water boiler broke last night and I'm trying to get a repair guy scheduled." She paused, studying Augusta's face. "Are you okay? You look a little green."

"Oh, yeah." Augusta was about to tell her about the footsteps, but something stopped her. Had she really heard anything? Jill had said they had a resident ghost, but Augusta didn't really believe that was anything more than a cute way of explaining the phenomena common in old houses. More likely it just had been the house settling, or even another episode like her first day when she'd had that hallucination. "Just had a late night," she said, with a forced shrug.

Jill didn't look convinced, but before she could say anything, Reggie popped his head in. "Doughnuts?" He flipped open a box, revealing a tempting array of doughnuts, crullers and sticky buns.

Jill took a chocolate one. "Oh, God, why do you do this to me, Reg?"

He grinned, then offered the box to Augusta. She forced herself to shake her head, even though they looked mouthwatering. "No, thanks. I'm not hungry."

"More for me," he said with a wink, grabbing two. "If you ladies need anything, I'll be out back."

Augusta returned to her desk, forcing herself to ignore the rumble of her stomach. Jill was across the hall, the reassuring sound of her classical music floating from her half-closed door. A text from Chris lit up Augusta's phone, asking what she wanted for dinner that night. Things had been good between her and Chris the last couple of weeks since the car, yet she still felt restless, anxious. It was probably just from the new job, getting used to her new schedule. At least, that's what she told herself. She was afraid that if she examined her feelings too deeply, she might find that there was truly something wrong in her relationship, and if that was the case, she wasn't sure what she would do.

Flipping open the collection catalog of jewelry, Augusta quickly lost herself in the glossy pictures of precious stones, gold stickpins and all sorts of treasures. Jill had told her that the theme for the upcoming exhibit was "personal adornment by the sea," and Augusta had already identified five objects from the collection that would perfectly complement the pieces that local artists would be displaying.

She was so absorbed in her work that she didn't hear Jill's music stop or the light knock until Jill was in the doorway.

"Hey, Augusta," she said. "Sorry to interrupt. Is this a good time?"

"Oh, yeah. Totally." Shoving a bookmark in the catalog, Augusta looked up and realized there was someone with Jill.

"This is Leo," Jill said, gesturing to the fair-skinned thirty-something guy next to her. "He does all our community outreach and public programming."

Augusta had never really understood the meaning behind the phrase "boy next door" before, but seeing the young, clean-cut man with the chestnut hair and easy smile, suddenly she got it. If this guy had lived next door to her growing up, Augusta would have never moved out of her parents' place.

Augusta smiled and stood to shake his hand, trying not to focus on how absurdly cute he was. "Hey, nice to meet you."

"Nice to meet you, too," he said, his handshake firm, his smile warm and genuine. "I know Jill is excited to have you here."

Augusta was about to respond when Jill's phone rang. "It's the repair guy calling back," Jill said, glancing at the screen. "I have to take this, but you guys can get started without me. Hello?"

She left the two of them, and suddenly Augusta felt awkward in the small office alone with a stranger. But Leo didn't seem to notice. "Should we go down to the ballroom where we can spread out?"

"Let me just grab my notebook," she said, grateful for the chance to compose herself. As she followed Leo, she instantly felt like a creep for noticing the way the rolled sleeves of his black button-down showed off lean, muscular arms. She also couldn't help but feel preemptively guilty about being alone with a good-looking guy, like somehow Chris would find out and grill her on every aspect of their interaction. That was silly, though, she reminded herself. She was an adult and she was doing her job. That was all. She had seen attractive people before; this wasn't some new phenomenon. *Professional, Augusta. You're a professional. And you're not single.*

The ballroom was in between exhibits at the moment, and Jill and Sharon had been busy pinning up photos, trying out paint swatches and all the other things that went into the planning of an exhibit. It looked like Leo had been helping before he'd come up to meet Augusta, and his laptop was open on the floor, books and binders piled up next to it.

"Hold on," he said, jumping up and pulling out a folding chair from the corner.

"Thanks." Augusta perched on the chair while Leo grabbed a stool and pulled it up close enough that she could smell the clean scent of his bodywash.

He looked at her with that disarmingly genuine smile again. "So, how are you liking it at Harlowe so far?"

"I love it," she said, shifting slightly in her seat, aware of how close they were even in the large room. "Everyone has been so welcoming, and the house is amazing."

"Isn't it? The Boston office is nice, but I love the days when I get to come to Harlowe. It's like stepping back in time."

Leo was one of those charismatic people who probably made every woman in the world feel like she was the *only* woman in the world when she spoke. His frank gaze never left her face, his head tilted in consideration. Why was Augusta so tongue-tied? She was an adult, a *professional* adult, but she suddenly felt as if she were an awkward teen again, blushing from the attention of one of the popular guys. "I'm glad to be here," she said weakly.

"So, what do you have for me?"

"Right," she said, snapping out of it. "Jill told me that they're exploring 'personal adornment.' I wanted to get a good cross section of what people at Harlowe House would have worn, but also other people in the town who weren't upper class." She opened her folder and pulled out the catalog listings for the objects she'd chosen and handed them to Leo.

He leafed through them, nodding occasionally. Then he looked up and flashed her a brilliant, lopsided smile. "These are great, really great. I like that you've gone outside of just the obvious stuff like jewelry and accessories."

She didn't realize she had been holding her breath until she exhaled. She knew that they wouldn't necessarily incorporate all her choices, but she was proud of the work and thought she had put into it.

The more her excitement about the exhibit grew, the more relaxed she became. "Jill has mentioned that an Irish maid worked here in the 1870s or 1880s—do you think we could find something of hers? It would be cool if we could have some immigrants represented, too."

Leo nodded, typing something into his laptop without looking up. "Yeah, definitely. I'm not sure if they have anything that belonged to her—that's more Jill or Sharon's wheelhouse, but I like the immigration angle. Definitely worth asking about."

Augusta scribbled some notes down herself, her mind whirring with ideas. Leo was likewise absorbed in typing, so she took advantage of the moment and let herself finally really study him. His face might have been all softly squared angles and gentle demeanor, but there was a hardness, a guardedness that manifested at the corners of his gray eyes. Was there more to the boy next door than just his good looks and easy manner? Well, even if there was, it certainly wasn't Augusta's place to investigate it further.

After a few moments of quietly working, Leo suddenly sat back and raked his hands through his hair. "No, no, no," he muttered, frantically hammering the keys on his laptop. "Oh, fuck me," he cursed under his breath.

Augusta swallowed. "Sorry?"

"Shit, sorry," he said, briefly glancing at her before mashing the keys again. "This computer is the bane of my existence. It just crashed on me and I think I lost all my notes."

"Can I see it?" Augusta asked before she could stop herself.

He looked dubious, but he stood up and handed her the laptop. "Be my guest."

Augusta forced it to reboot and got it to start up in safe mode. "Can you type in your password?"

He leaned over her shoulder, so close that his sleeve brushed her arm, sending heat racing through her. She looked away while he typed.

When he was done, she quickly scanned his recent documents. "Your files aren't lost," she said, breathing a sigh of relief as if they had been hers. "You just have to go into recovery and save them as new files."

He was looking at her as if she was Prometheus bringing fire to humanity. "You're a lifesaver, thank you."

It was a simple fix and she was surprised he didn't know how to do it, but was pleased with herself all the same. If nothing else, living with Chris and his brother had taught her more than she ever needed to know about computers.

"It's really nothing, I can show you what to do if it happens again." In an effort to stop the blush she could feel blooming on her cheeks, she changed the subject. "So how long have you been working at Harlowe?"

"Let's see, about four years now. I started in education, but then they merged that with public outreach so I've been in this role for the last two years. What about you? Where are you coming from?"

She told him about her last job, and how draining it was to give the same tour day after day. He nodded encouragingly when she told him about her goal of someday becoming head curator of a historic house museum. Leo was easy to talk to, and before she knew it, the light was fading outside the windows.

They started packing up. She saw a text from Jill, explaining that she wouldn't be back in for the rest of the day and could Augusta forward her the notes Leo and Augusta had taken.

"So, hey," Leo said, sliding his laptop into his shoulder bag,

"I don't know what your lunch hours look like, but what would you think about going out to grab a coffee sometime later in the week? We could chat more about your exhibit and I can give you all the dirt on Harlowe that Jill and Sharon won't tell you."

Augusta froze. Was he asking her out? Should she tell him that she had a boyfriend? No, of course he wasn't asking her out. He wanted to get some coffee with her during work hours and talk about work stuff. But then, what would she tell Chris? She hated lying to him by omission, but she also knew that he wouldn't like her going out with a guy, even if it was just for work.

"I didn't mean to make you uncomfortable," he said quickly, at her hesitation.

"No, no," she hurried to reassure him. "Coffee sounds good."

"Great," he said, smiling and holding her gaze. "Looking forward to it."

After she'd helped him pack up and locked the door behind him, she couldn't help but feel she should have mentioned Chris. If it was no big deal, then why did she feel like she was hiding something?

9

Margaret

A ship there is and she sails the sea
She's loaded deep as deep can be
But not so deep as the love I'm in
I know not if I sink or swim.

—"The Water is Wide," Traditional Folk Song

THERE WAS ONLY one other soul in Tynemouth who knew and understood my craft, and it was to her that I set off on a fine summer's morning, with a basket full of herbs and tinctures. Phebe lived on the edge of town in a little cottage and made her livelihood through the mending of fishing nets. Townspeople often left her offerings of food and dry goods, as it was said she could charm the storm out of the sea. Of course, she no more had the power to do that than I, but I think she liked the reputation. I went there at least once a month to trade her herbs in exchange for her company and stories.

Periwinkles and sand dollars hung on twine from the little porch, tinkling like music in the wind. My boots crunched the oyster shells that lined her front path, releasing white puffs of dust. Phebe greeted me with a grunt, barely looking up from her work. Her warm brown skin glistened with perspiration as she drew her handkerchief across her forehead. "Put that basket down and help me with these nets," she instructed as soon as I'd opened the rickety gate. "Rain is coming, and these will tangle something fierce if they get left out."

Though there was not a cloud in the sky, I did as I was told, and followed her inside. We worked together in silence, fishnets spread around us. Her hands were quick, working deftly to mend the tangle of netting. Her little mahogany shuttle flashed in and out of the ropes ten times for each clumsy pass of mine. When we were done, she wiped her hands off on her patchwork apron and looked over our handiwork before turning to me. "You bring me anything?"

I handed her the herb bundles and she inspected them. Nodding her approval, she gestured for me to make some tea while she sat down in the only upholstered chair in the small room. "Oh, my back is aching today," she said. "Always does when it's going to rain."

When the tea had finished steeping, I poured it out and handed her a chipped cup. Outside, rain was starting to patter, just as she had predicted. "There's a dance being held at the assembly hall next week to celebrate the docking of a Norwegian ship. Should be a fine time, especially if Mr. Brody decides to take up his fiddle." She paused before asking, "You going?"

"Of course I'm not going," I said, surprised that she would even ask.

She shrugged, as if it made no difference to her, but there was a telltale tug to her lips. "I just thought you might be interested. There should be some fine young men there. Tall, fair-haired. Like the Vikings of olden days."

I stared at her. Never once in the ten years I'd known her had Phebe spoken of dances or the opposite sex in anything other than tones of scorn. "What makes you think I have any interest in young men?"

"I hear things," she said without looking up. "Things about a *certain* young man meeting a *certain* young lady in the woods at night and making love to her."

Nothing happened in Tynemouth without Phebe knowing about it. But still, to hear that Jack and I were being spoken of in town was like a dousing of cold water.

"He's a smart-looking boy," Phebe added lightly.

I concentrated on my tea, not rising to her bait.

"Broken a lot of hearts, left a lot of girls wishing maybe they hadn't been so quick to fall for his pretty words."

This was a bridge too far. I put down my tea and looked squarely into my friend's deep brown eyes. "Phebe, is there something you want to say to me?"

There had always been an unspoken agreement between Phebe and me, that whatever odd things we might engage in, we never questioned the other about them.

She answered me with another question. "How old are you now, Margaret?"

"Nineteen," I answered, suspicious of the sudden change of subject.

She nodded. "You look like your mama at that age."

I paused, my cup raised halfway to my lips. "You know my mother?" I couldn't think of a less likely friendship, never mind that my mother had repeatedly told me that I was not to associate with Phebe Hall.

"Oh, I knew her," Phebe said. "I made her a promise that I would tell you about her when you were grown."

I frowned. "Tell me what?"

I'd never known Phebe to be at a loss for words, but she sat back now and studied me with sharp eyes. "You mean they still haven't told you?" she finally said.

"Who hasn't told me what?" I asked, growing exasperated.

She sucked her teeth. "Child, if they haven't told you by now then it isn't my place to say anything. But you had better ask your mama where you came from. It's not right that they let you go on all this time not knowing."

"What do you mean, 'where I came from'?"

But she only shook her head. "Ask your mama," she said again.

Though I burned with curiosity, I knew better than to press Phebe. Perhaps she was mistaking my mother for someone else. But she was sharp as a tack, and I had never known her mind to wander. We drank our tea in silence, each nursing our own private thoughts. "Bring me some of that gingerroot next time and I'll make you a cake like you've never seen," she promised me when we were done. "And you go talk to your mama," she said. "You need to know the truth of things."

When I returned home that evening, Clarence and Lizzie had been there for supper, and there hadn't been an opportunity to speak to my mother about Phebe's cryptic advice. I spared it no further thought, for I had other matters on my mind. Matters that had dark hair and sensuous lips. Matters that had me aching with desire, counting the minutes until sundown.

Jack and I had seen each other but a handful of times since our meeting in the store, but each time his gaze would cut across the street to find me, sending thrills racing down my spine and pooling between my legs. And I would walk by, as if he were no more than a perfect stranger, unworthy of my attention. It was a game, and I savored every delicious minute of it. I wanted a child, yes, but I also wanted a conquest.

After my parents retired to bed, I slipped out into the cool, clear night with a basket on my arm. Roseroot collected by the light of the full moon is particularly powerful, and I wanted some for a charm. But that was not the only reason for my errand. A salty breeze swept around me, carrying with it the sound of footsteps. I smiled; he was coming.

I had barely turned around when his hands were on my waist, his mouth on my neck. "I need you," he said between hot breaths. He backed me up against a tree, and I dropped my basket, fragrant herbs spilling on the ground. "I can't see you on the street again and not know what your lips taste like, or the shape of your legs beneath your skirts. You torture me, and I only want you the more for it."

This time there was no pretense of waiting or propriety. I didn't have the patience to be coy any longer; I ached for his touch, for his body against mine. "Tell me," I demanded. "Tell me what you want from me."

"I want your heart, little witch," he gasped into my hair as I undid his trousers. "I want your soul, and I very much want your body."

"They are yours," I told him, though I did not add that if I was his, then he was equally mine.

For as much as I wanted a child, I admit that as he took me against that tree, I had little thought in my mind about conceiving. All I wanted at that moment was to feel him inside of me, to know what it was to reach the peak of pleasure and come crashing down in the arms of my lover, and if I got a baby from it, so much the better.

Afterward, we lay tangled together on the forest floor, leaves blowing over us as he idly twined his fingers through my hair. I was not so naive as to think that Jack would honor any of the words he had spoken in the heat of passion; thanks to my three brothers, I knew something of the ways of men. So I was surprised when he rolled toward me and lifted himself on one elbow, and asked, "When can I see you again?"

10

Augusta

AUGUSTA WAS IN a prickly mood. That morning she and Chris had gotten into a fight over something stupid (he kept putting his dishes in the sink even though the dishwasher was empty and RIGHT THERE), and she'd thought they had made up, but when she went to kiss him goodbye, he'd pulled away. Now the day had an anxious cast, and everything seemed off.

After refreshing her mug of coffee for the third time, she sat back down at her desk, squared her shoulders and resolved to get some brainstorming for her exhibit done. If Chris wanted to keep ignoring her texts then she wasn't going to let it ruin her day.

Curating her own exhibit was a thrilling prospect, but she didn't have the faintest idea what it should be about. Jill had mentioned the ceramic collection as a possible starting point, but Augusta found that, for once, she didn't want to get lost in a dusty collection. Harlowe House was so dynamic, and she wanted to do something that would bring in otherwise unheard voices, something that would make the story of the house come to life. As she reached across her desk to turn on her computer, the binder of Harlowe family history caught her eye. It was open to the family tree.

The name *Margaret Harlowe* again stood out. It was a shame that, in a family of brothers, there was no information on the only woman of that generation. If the portrait of the woman with the knowing eyes in the dining room was indeed of Margaret, then she had clearly been a vibrant, urbane young woman. How could such a beautiful portrait exist with nothing known about the sitter? In an instant, Augusta knew what—or rather, *who*—she wanted her exhibit to be about. She broached the idea to Jill at lunch that day.

"I mean, we would love to know more about Margaret," Jill said, as she put her plate of leftovers in the microwave. "Hell, we would love to know *anything* about her. I think the exhibit is a great idea, but unfortunately, I'm just not sure there's enough there to make it work. Our archivist has scoured everything looking for something about Margaret and found nothing more than a couple of clues, and even they don't conclusively link back to her."

Augusta's heart sank. There was something about the mysterious name on the tree that had captured her imagination completely. How could she walk through this house and care for the collection not knowing if this woman had walked the same hallways, touched the same things? She stirred her yogurt, lost in thought. "How about something broader, then, like women in nineteenth-century Tynemouth in general?" Maybe while she was researching, she would unearth something about Margaret.

"See if you can narrow it down a bit further. Leo might have some input, too, if you want to shoot him an email. I think he's done some work with our archivist before as part of an outreach program for women in the arts."

Augusta and Leo had planned to get coffee the next day, so she would ask him then. Augusta said she would keep thinking about it, but she knew that regardless of what the exhibit subject ended up being, she was going to be hunting for mentions of Margaret.

After lunch, Augusta trudged back up to her office. Hauling out the stack of books Jill had left her, she began idly flipping through one, hoping for inspiration to strike. How many other women were written out of the history of Tynemouth, of this house? Women whose names didn't even appear on a family tree or a census? Margaret Harlowe at least had some record of her existence, even if it was nothing more than speculation. There were probably domestic servants, enslaved people even, and others who were lost to time completely. It was a melancholy thought; would Augusta leave behind some sort of legacy, or would she someday be forgotten, as well?

Jill stuck her head in the office. "Hey, I'm going to go grab a coffee and a muffin—do you want anything?"

Augusta had only had a cup of yogurt for lunch, and hunger gnawed at her insides. "No, thanks," she said automatically.

Jill hesitated, looking like she wanted to say something else, but then nodded and left.

Tuesdays at Harlowe House were quiet because they were closed to the public, and aside from Jill and sometimes Sharon and Reggie, Augusta had the house to herself. She hadn't had any more hallucinations since her first day, when she'd been overtired and hungry, full of nerves. Still, she couldn't help but get goose bumps occasionally when she was alone with the sounds of the house. She'd worked in old properties before and she'd never been scared or bought into the ghost stories that inevitably sprang up around them. But as she flipped through the books alone in her office, there was a very eerie, very real sense of the air pressing in around her and lifting the hairs on her neck. She went completely still. She wasn't alone.

Footsteps, coming from downstairs. Slowly, she pushed back her chair and stood up, careful not to make any noise. It could just be Jill back already. She had to remind herself that just the other morning she'd thought she'd heard someone, and it had turned out to be nothing at all.

But as soon as she stepped foot into the hallway, the air turned cold, and the edges of her vision blurred. Just like her first day, her surroundings grew unfamiliar, the electric wall sconces fading away and replaced with oil lamps. The floral printed wallpaper morphed and swirled until it was a dark geometric pattern. Her stomach dropped. *Oh, no. Please not again.*

When she was younger, she'd had a book of ghost stories and unexplained phenomenon. It was mostly hokey stuff that was obviously fake, but a few of the stories had stayed with her over the years. One in particular stood out in her mind now. In it, two women had been visiting an old estate in England in the 1980s, and had experienced some sort of shared paranormal vision. Both of them reported seeing people dressed in Victorian garb, and, thinking that they had stumbled upon some sort of reenactment, they tried approaching and speaking to someone, only to find that the person could neither see nor hear them. Afterward, they had described everything they had seen in detail, including a Victorian-style greenhouse that had been absent from the modern building. A historian had been able to confirm that the house had indeed once had an attached greenhouse. Could something like that be happening to her? And what did it mean? The story had been an unexplained phenomenon, with skeptics claiming that the women were only looking for attention. Yet why would they make it up? And if it had happened to them, were there other people around the world who had similar experiences?

She wanted nothing more than to turn around and flee back to her office. Or better yet, run outside into the broad daylight and throw her arms around the first pedestrian she came across and reassure herself that the modern world was still there. But some invisible force drew her forward.

Although her heart was pounding loud and fast in her ears, she had the impression of a different kind of silence in the house. Gone was the hum of appliances, the muffled sounds of traffic from far beyond the walls. The air was fresher, a sharp floral scent that was at once foreign and familiar lingering around her.

She didn't know where she was going, but she found herself heading for the stairs. They, at least, were much the same. They creaked under the same spots as always, and a series of framed miniatures hung over the banister. Through the window downstairs, she could see linens hanging to dry in the yard, undulating gently in the breeze. From somewhere just beyond her vision she could hear the murmuring of two men in conversation. They were speaking English—she was sure of it—but no matter how hard she strained her ear, she could not make out their words.

It was all so strange, like moving through someone else's dream, yet somehow familiar. There was an ache in her chest that felt very much like homesickness. No, not homesickness exactly. Loss. It felt like the sharp sting of loss after her father had died. Not the days immediately afterward when the world was upside-down and throbbing with fresh pain, but later, when she'd gone back to school and the sympathy cards had stopped coming. It was that numb, persistent ache that she had carried with her even as she got on with her daily life. As frightening and unsettling as the hallucination was, it was the loneliness that made her want to huddle into herself and cry.

The heaviness pressed harder in her chest as she made her way to the kitchen. The differences were the most stark here. There was no microwave, no refrigerator, no brightly lit countertops. Instead there was a large wooden table in the center of the room, and the wall was lined with white dishes displayed in an oversize hutch. A simmering pot of something savory sat on the iron range, the aroma of herbs filling the air. As she continued moving dreamlike to the door, her body met with something solid, something flesh and blood. She jumped back, her heart rate spiking.

Disembodied arms shot out and steadied her. "Whoa, whoa, whoa…are you okay?"

In an instant, the wooden table and simmering pots vanished, the scent of herbs gone. She was back in the bright staff kitchen looking up into the concerned face of Leo. "Oh, Jesus Christ." A whoosh of relief rushed through her as she steadied herself against his solid forearms. "Did you see that?"

Leo looked around, frowning. "See what?"

"The kitchen—it was all different. There were sheets outside in the wind and pots on the stove except the stove was iron and…" But just by looking at his face she knew that he hadn't seen anything, that it had only been her. It all had been in her head, again. "I thought…" She trailed off, not sure what she had thought, what she had experienced. The ache in her chest lingered, but everything else was back to normal; outside she could hear a car horn and the distant drilling of a jackhammer. "I thought I heard someone down here," she said, unconvincingly. "I came down to look."

He studied her, and she tried not to focus on how warm he felt, how safe. He was a balm to the crushing loneliness, and she wanted to press herself into him. Self-conscious, she took a step back.

"Nope, just me," he said with a wry smile. "Is Jill around?"

Augusta shook her head. "She just went out to get some coffee. How did you get in?"

"Reggie gave me the code the other day. Are you sure you're all right? You look pretty shaken up."

"Yeah, I'm fine," she lied, her head still spinning. On top of the lingering fright, she was mortified that Leo had stumbled upon her in such a state.

"Are we still on for tomorrow?"

"Tomorrow. Right." She felt as if she was in the hazy aftermath of a dream. The lights were too bright, the buzz of the electricity too loud. "I'm going to go back up to my office. Just give me a shout if you need anything." She didn't wait for him to answer as she quickly retreated, pounding up the stairs to the safety of her office. Below, she could hear him moving about the kitchen and then heading to the ballroom to work.

Taking a long drink from her water bottle, she took a few deep breaths and forced herself to concentrate on her research. It was nearly impossible to clear her mind of the hallucination, though. She played it over and over in her head like a movie on repeat. It had been so *real*, from the way the light slanted in from the windows to the smell of food cooking. It wasn't just that she had seen the house as it must have looked one hundred and fifty years ago—she had really been moving through the space as if she was part of it. How could she explain that away? Maybe she had some sort of undiagnosed psychosis that had never manifested until now. Jesus, what if she had a brain tumor? The idea that there was something wrong with her mind was a frightening one, but at least it was one rooted in science, in reality. The alternative was something she didn't even know how to begin to approach.

Her eyes glazed over as she sightlessly scanned the pages in front of her. She frowned. The book on the desk wasn't one she remembered pulling from the shelf, and it was open to a page she definitely did not remember reading. Glancing at the cover, it appeared to be a collection of stories taken from an oral history of Tynemouth in the 1970s. It was open to an interview with an old woman who had been in her eighties, and was probably long since dead. The woman reminisced about her childhood in Tynemouth, and the people and places that had made lasting impressions on her.

Harlowe House was rumored to be haunted, and us children had a game of daring each other to run up to the porch and knock at the door before running away again. This was before the house was a museum of course, but after it had been abandoned. The name of the ghost was Margaret Harlowe, and it was said that she would appear on the night of the full moon, walking the grounds of the property, looking for her body. You see, after she disappeared, her body was never found.

Augusta sucked in her breath, her hallucination momentarily forgotten. Margaret Harlowe had disappeared, and the story implied that she had died. This wasn't proof that she had existed— after all, it was an old woman remembering an urban legend—but it *did* show that at the very least the name Margaret Harlowe had been around for decades before the museum came along. She flipped forward a few pages, scanning the lines of text, but the story moved on from Harlowe House to other local haunts for the town children. Leaning back in her chair, Augusta stared down at the book, lost in thought as her water bottle perspired in her hands. What on earth had happened to Margaret Harlowe?

My efforts have not gone unnoticed. Every time she muses on my name, every time she discovers a little piece of me, I grow stronger. Fragments of myself fly back from the ether, a skeleton regenerating flesh, a spring bulb dying in winter only to grow back again the next year.

I existed, I still exist, and I shall exist again.

When Augusta left work that evening and waved goodbye to Jill, she looked up to find Chris parked outside.

"Hey!" She should have been excited to see him, grateful that he'd taken the time and effort to come visit her, but all she felt was a little disappointed not to have the car ride home to herself to regroup from her strange day. Forcing herself to smile, she gave Chris a side hug and peck on the cheek. "What's up?"

"I was in the area. Do you want to get dinner?"

She left her car at Harlowe, and as they drove to a nearby tavern together, Augusta told him about her day, careful to omit the hallucinations. She wouldn't tell Chris about those—he wouldn't believe her, and she didn't want to give him the opportunity to doubt her. He nodded along, putting in a word here and there. This was why they were together, she reminded herself. They were compatible, comfortable. Who cared if it wasn't exciting anymore? Why did it matter? But since starting at Harlowe House, a spark had been lit in her, and deep down she knew she could never go back to the way things had been.

11

Margaret

Black is the color of my true love's hair
His face so soft and wondrous fair
The purest eyes
And the strongest hands
I love the ground on where he stands.

—"Black is the Color of My True Love's Hair,"
Traditional Folk Song

IT WAS OCTOBER when my courses ceased. My breasts grew tender, and I often found myself sick at the sight of food. For all my wishing and dreaming of a baby, I was terrified of the physical changes that seemed to happen overnight. Would I still be beautiful? Would Jack still find me desirable? Would I even recognize my reflection in the mirror come this time next year? Though my body was no longer my own, I liked having a secret. Who was this stranger who was growing inside of me? Would they love me as fiercely as I already loved them? Would they be my ally, my companion, my dearest little friend?

I had not yet told Jack about the child, as I knew that the early months were fraught with danger, and that I could lose it at any time. Jack and I had spoken at length about what our future might look like. We would lie on the sun-warmed rocks and watch the tide seep in as we built our castles in the air. And though I was content with these snatched moments of happiness, I wished that he was not so hesitant to be seen with me in town, for he still did not want his parents to know of our attachment. They would need time to come round to the idea of his marrying me, he explained. Never mind that my family was wealthy and well respected; it was understood that I was different, that I was not fit for marriage.

On a crisp day when the late afternoon sun slanted through the reddening trees, I laced on my boots and slipped out the back door. I had hardly reached the gate when I heard footsteps in the fallen leaves approaching me at a leisurely pace from behind. Shadow growled, his hackles standing on end.

"Hullo, sister."

I stopped, groaning inwardly. "Hello, Henry," I said, unlatching the gate without turning.

"Where are you off to this fine afternoon?"

"Just going for a walk."

Henry hurried to catch up to me, slipping through the gate before it could shut. "All alone? Where is this beau of yours that supposedly worships the very ground that you walk on?"

I didn't particularly care if Henry believed me about Jack or not, but I certainly didn't want him interrupting our precious time together. "Just walking today, no beau," I said.

"Excellent. Then I don't suppose you would mind your doting brother escorting you?"

He didn't bother waiting for an answer before he fell into step beside me, his sleeve brushing my arm. Shadow trailed us, sulking. He did not care for Henry.

Henry chatted with me about the weather, George's engagement and how he wished he didn't have to return to Boston to work. The sun was dipping ever lower, and soon it would be dusk and I would miss my rendezvous with Jack. Henry was going on and on about how boring his work was and how he was destined for greater things, when I spun and faced him. "I have to go. I promised Mrs. Crenshaw that I would bring her seaweed for a poultice."

Henry frowned. "It's almost dark."

"The tide is going out, and I'll miss it."

I could see the indecision warring on his face. I knew that, on one hand, he would not want to get his clothes dirty scrambling down the rocks, but on the other hand, that he was unwilling to let me go.

"I'll be fine," I said, giving him my warmest, most sisterly smile. "Tell Mother I'll be late, and not to wait for dinner on my account. I'll make myself a plate later."

When at last Henry's reluctant footsteps had faded back down the path, I hurried toward the rocks where I had promised to meet Jack.

When I saw him waiting with his hands in his pockets, I nearly lost my breath at how beautiful he looked with the wind in his dark hair. The weather had turned cool, and though I shivered beneath my shawl, Jack was only in his shirtsleeves and vest. He must have felt my eyes on him, for he turned and gave me his crooked smile. "There's my wildflower."

I fell into his arms, hungry for his touch and the heat of his lean body against mine. I knew I should tell him about the child, but a part of me was frightened that it would change everything between us. It was such a perfect moment, with the crashing waves behind us, his arms wrapped around me and his chin tucked over my head. Our hearts beat in unison, the wind binding us tightly together.

"There's something I must tell you," I made myself say.

He pulled away slightly, tilting my chin up to him. "What?"

He was looking down at me with such heat in his clear blue eyes, such longing. Had there ever been a woman so adored, so loved? "Nothing," I said, managing a small smile. "It is nothing."

I led him away from the rocks and into the woods where he

took me with no less passion than he had the first time or the hundred times since then. Afterward, we lay on a bed of damp autumn leaves, my shawl wrapping us together in a cocoon. Above us, a canopy of black branches fanned out against the dark lavender sky. I was in such a daze of contentment that I hardly realized he had said something.

"Maggie," he said, twining a finger through my hair, "there's something I have to ask you."

I caught my breath. Here, at last, was my proposal.

But it was not a proposal, nor even the pretty words to which I'd grown so accustomed. "The stories about you...that is..." He cleared his throat, looking suddenly uncomfortable. "How much is true?"

I didn't need to ask him what he was talking about. I tamped down my disappointment. I suppose it had only been a matter of time before he would ask. "You want to know if your 'little witch' is indeed practicing some dark art, is that it?" He didn't say anything, but I could see the confirmation in his eyes. I sighed, sitting up. "Very well. Give me your hand."

Reluctantly, he sat up and gave it to me. It was a beautiful hand, large and strong, fingers elegantly tapered at the tips. Taking my time, I drew my finger down the meandering lines of his palms, my featherlight touch eliciting a sharp intake of breath from him.

"Your love line is very deep," I told him. "You love intensely and with your whole being. But it is not long." I raised my gaze to meet his, and found that he was staring at me with an unreadable expression. "I hope that means you will not be unfaithful to me," I teased.

Abruptly, he took his hand back. "I don't like this, Maggie," he said. "It's all nonsense anyway, isn't it? You can't truly see all of that, can you?"

"It's as true as any preacher's sermon," I told him.

Jack went very still, as if just struck by an unpleasant thought.

"You can't...that is, you can't see into the minds of others, can you?"

I nudged him in the side, amused by his discomfort. "Why, do you have dark secrets you'd rather keep hidden from me?"

"Of course not," he said gruffly.

If only I did possess such a power, I might have saved myself considerable heartache. "Here, look at this." If he didn't want to see the truth, I could at least show him a pretty trick. Taking up a dead aster, I held it between my thumb and finger and murmured the words I knew so well. Jack's eyes went wide as the withered leaves uncurled back to life, pink color returning to the petals.

I had never shown my magic to anyone before, and my heart was beating fast, my palms sweating. I had not thought that I would care, but I suddenly realized how very important it was to me that Jack understood what I was. Who I was.

"Maggie," he said, his voice husky and almost breathless. "I don't know if I should be afraid, but I can't seem to be anything other than amazed. My remarkable girl."

We watched the aster complete its transformation in silence, until the last petal had opened and I let the sea breeze carry it away.

"I want to speak to your father," Jack finally said.

I must not have heard him correctly. We had built many castles in the air that started out in just such a way, and I assumed that was what he was doing now. Propping myself up on my elbow, I arched my brow at him. "Why, whatever for, Mr. Pryce?"

"Don't, Maggie," he said. "I'm in earnest."

And indeed he was. I could see it in his eyes, the way he looked as if his next breath relied on my answer. My heart raced, my thoughts in a jumble. I wanted my child. I wanted love. I wanted to be my own mistress and escape the stagnation of my parents' house. The first two only required a man, but the third required a husband. A husband would give me certain freedoms, yes, but I would be no less beholden to him than I was to my parents now. I studied Jack out of the corner of my eye. Would he expect me to work in his family's store? Or would he keep me home to raise his children? Would he tolerate my wild ways and let me go where I would? Or would he grow bored with me after he had captured his prize? The chill that we had kept at bay with our lovemaking returned.

"And what of your parents?" I asked him. "Do they approve?"

His pursed lips and the way he evaded my eyes was all the answer I needed. "I am a grown man," he said, almost as if he was reassuring himself and not me. "If they do not approve, then what can they do to stop me?"

A great deal, it turned out. Nearly a week later when I saw him next, Jack admitted that his parents had threatened to withhold his inheritance from him if he were to marry me, small though it must have been.

"What need have we for money?" I drew my finger down the length of his torso, teasing at his waistband. "I shall charge for my midwife services, and you are strong and clever. Why, my brother George would give you a position at the shipping office if I were to ask, I am sure of it."

But Jack didn't say anything. A cloud seemed to have settled over us, a wall of thorns springing up around our castle in the air.

The knock at the door the following week was sharp and angry. Mother and I had been mending in the parlor, though my mind was far away, spinning through my memories of Jack and the night we'd spent together. Mother shot me a questioning look, but I just shook my head. I was as surprised as she was to be getting a call so early in the morning, and on a Saturday, no less. Could it really be that Jack had already spoken to his parents again and was now here to ask for my father's blessing?

Or perhaps he had decided to forfeit his inheritance altogether and had come to abscond with me.

My heart raced as I stood behind my mother as she opened the door. It was not Jack, but three men in work coats and rough trousers, their skin raw and chapped from the sea. After my initial disappointment wore off, it took me a moment to recognize one of the men as Jenny Hough's husband, Bernard. My stomach tightened; I knew why they were at our door. I only wondered that it had taken them so long.

I had always been able to keep my worlds separate, the wild witch that worked magic in the nights, and the dutiful daughter of my parents in the daytime. So I could only watch, frozen, as those two worlds met in a spectacular collision.

"Gentlemen, can I help you?" Mother looked perplexed, but she was as polite as always.

"That's her!" shouted Bernard, pointing at me over my mother's shoulder. "That's the unnatural woman what told my wife she could bring back our little Suzy. Said that we had to kill another child and bring her the body if we ever wanted to see our girl again."

The other men howled their agreement. Perhaps the only thing more unnerving than a group of wild boys in the woods was a group of angry men on your doorstep.

"I said no such thing!" I exclaimed.

By this time my father had overheard the commotion and come to the door. "What is this?" he demanded.

"They say that Margaret..." My mother trailed off, looking at me as if I were a stranger in her house. "They say that she told them to kill a child."

My father shot me an alarmed look, color blooming behind his mustache. But I just held my chin up, unfazed. Let them hurl their insults and accusations, they could prove nothing.

"Bring her out! She must be made to answer for this. My wife hasn't stopped crying in weeks."

"She gave my wife a draught to keep from conceiving," another man shouted.

There was jostling, and I realized that the men meant to gain entrance, to do what I wasn't sure, but no doubt nothing good.

"Stand back!" I'd never heard my father raise his voice in such a manner. There was a vein throbbing in his neck and he was bright red. He'd stepped in front of my mother, his arms braced on either side of the doorframe. "If you have a grievance against my daughter, then do the civilized thing and hire a lawyer. I won't have angry hordes beating down my door with baseless accusations."

Their hateful looks could have eviscerated me, but the men must have known that they had no other recourse, so they left, cursing over their shoulders and spitting on our front walk.

When they had gone, Father shut the door, and I was left with my parents in the silent hall.

"What," my father said, mopping his red brow, "was that all about?"

"I'm sure I don't know," I said innocently. "They must have mistaken me for someone else." But I could tell from my parents' expressions that I would have to do better than that.

"I do not know from what kind of encounter their bizarre accusations sprung, and I'm certain I don't want to know. Your mother and I have been patient with you, looking the other way at some of your more…aberrant behavior. But I will not have people knocking down my door with craven accusations about my daughter. I have a business to run, a reputation as a good, honest family man to uphold."

Mother's gaze had not left me the entire time my father had spoken. "What did they mean," she asked quietly, "when they said that you told them to kill a child to save their own?"

I might have told her the truth, but she wouldn't have believed me anyway. I decided to meet her in the middle with a version of the truth instead. "His wife came to me asking for a cure for her sick child. There was nothing I could do, and in her grief she must have imagined such a scenario."

It was the first time I had admitted anything to do with my practice, and I was more fascinated by what my parents' reaction would be than anything else.

"There's to be no more of this…of this herbal or medicinal practice," Father said, pacing about the hall. "We have looked the other way while you pursued this hobby, but you want for nothing in this house, and I won't have my daughter engaging in a debasing trade. Perhaps it is time we began to think of marriage, or sending you somewhere for some polish."

For the first time since the knock at the door, a real sense of panic began to set in. Was he in earnest? I was nineteen years old and I could not go to some faraway boarding school—I was pregnant. And I could not—I *would* not—marry any man but Jack.

Though it prickled my pride, I bowed my head in what I hoped was sufficient obedience. "I will leave off in my herbal work and give you no cause for reproach," I murmured. "You have my word. It was only a fancy to pass time—I never thought it would cause any trouble."

The look my father gave me was unreadable, but eventually he nodded. "Very well. Perhaps you should go upstairs and spend some time thinking on how you might improve yourself and be an asset to this household. Your mother and I will discuss this further."

As I climbed the stairs, I could hear my mother's distressed whispers, and then my father angrily stalking back to his study. I did not believe that I had truly fooled my parents, and it was only a matter of time before the truth leaked out around the seams of my lies and omissions. I had seen the anger in those men's eyes; there was a reckoning coming.

12

Augusta

AUGUSTA WAS ON her hands and knees in one of the second-floor bedrooms, examining a bedpost, when the murmur of women's voices floated up from downstairs. Condition reports were one of Augusta's favorite parts of her job, and once a week she would slowly walk through the house, dusting the furniture and art, taking note of any damage that might have occurred during the previous week. The guests that came through the house were usually respectful and careful, but accidents still happened and occasionally someone would bump into a chair and scrape the floor or knock a painting with their shoulder in passing.

Pausing in her evaluation, she listened, trying to make out what she was hearing. There weren't currently any tours underway, and as far as she knew, Jill was in her office. She set aside her clipboard and slowly made her way out into the hall and down the stairs. The closer she drew to the dining room, the clearer the voices became. Taking a deep breath and completely expecting to be met with another ghostly hallucination of the past, she was relieved when she opened the door to see Jill and another woman, both very much in the present day. At her entrance, they both looked up at her, breaking off their conversation.

"Hey, I was just about to come up and get you," Jill told her. "This is Shayna. She does most of our painting conservation, and she's here to do a pickup."

"Nice to meet you," Shayna said, reaching to shake her hand. "Harlowe is one of my favorite stops—you guys always have something fun for me."

Augusta's hand was still shaking a little, but she joined them at the table, returning Shayna's handshake.

"I know you were interested in this portrait, so I thought you might like the chance to take a closer look since it's coming down for conservation," Jill said, gesturing to the portrait of Margaret Harlowe on the table.

Careful not to get too close, Augusta leaned over and studied the crackled veneer crisscrossing Margaret's pale visage.

She was vaguely aware of Jill and Shayna conversing, but their voices quickly faded to the background as she lost herself in the brushstrokes of the painting. Up close, a thousand little details leaped from the canvas that Augusta had never noticed before. The smallest dimple touched Margaret's cheek where her lips curved up knowingly at the edges. The sitter was a beautiful woman, but her allure transcended just the physical; there was a vibrance about her, something completely bewitching. Though more than a hundred years separated them, Augusta could have seen herself being friends with this young woman, perhaps even loving her.

"I never realized how beautiful she was," Augusta breathed.

"Wait till you see her all cleaned up," Shayna said, breaking the spell. "All this varnish was probably put on in the 1950s, and it's obscuring the original colors. She's going to look like a whole new woman when I'm done with her."

Augusta felt an unexpected tug as Shayna and Jill carefully covered the painting with a sheet and carried it out to Shayna's van. Without the enigmatic portrait, the dining room felt cold and empty, bereft of its soul. She could have stood there all day lost in a rapture, but a ping from her phone reminded her that she was supposed to meet Leo for lunch. With a last glance at the bare spot on the wall, Augusta forced herself to push the laughing green eyes from her mind and headed out.

Leo was already at the coffee shop when Augusta arrived. She hadn't realized how much she was looking forward to seeing him again until she spotted him on the sofa in the back of the shop. He had been looking at his phone when she came in, his face lighting up in a smile when he saw her.

If he remembered her strange behavior the day before, he didn't say anything. For her part, Augusta didn't want to think about the hallucinations anymore or what they might mean for her health. She was doing her best to eat breakfast before she came in, but deep down she knew that wasn't what was causing the strange sensations. When she'd asked Reggie if it was possible that the carbon monoxide detector might be malfunctioning, he had taken it seriously and checked it out. But of course, the meter and the detector had both been in working order, just as Augusta had suspected they would be. Whatever was causing the hallucinations was inside of her.

Leo hadn't ordered yet, so they went to the counter together. "What are you having?" he asked, pulling out his wallet.

"You don't have to pay for—"

But he just waved her off. "Harlowe is paying, don't worry about it. We're talking about work stuff, right?"

"Oh, right," she said. "Nitro cold brew with a splash of almond milk and an extra espresso shot, please."

"I've never tried that, but it sounds good. I'll have what she's having," he told the barista with a wink. "I've always wanted to say that."

"Are you sure? It's pretty strong."

"That's okay, I like trying new things." There was something in his tone that made her body flood with heat. They took their drinks back to the couch, where they sat next to each other, the cushions dipping so that their knees touched.

Leo took a sip of his coffee and nearly gagged. "You weren't kidding. That's...intense."

"Told you," she said, laughing. Some of the froth had stuck to his lip, and his eyes were watering.

"Wow." He swiped the froth from his mouth and placed the offending beverage back on the table. "So, how's everything going? Still liking it at Harlowe?"

"Definitely," she told him. "It's basically a dream come true." She didn't tell him about the hallucinations or that she was beginning to believe in ghosts. It was bad enough he'd caught her in the middle of one and she didn't want him to think that she was completely out of her mind.

"So, do you have any ideas for your exhibit? Anything I can do to help you get going with it?"

She told him about her exhibit idea, and how she wished there was more information on Margaret Harlowe. Seeing the painting up close had only fueled her interest in Margaret. She wanted to know everything about the woman who made her feel so deeply connected to the painting, the house.

He nodded. "She's definitely an intriguing topic. You should ask Jill if she could spare you for a day to come into Boston and check out the archives there."

"Jill made it sound like the archives wouldn't be worthwhile, that they've already looked for anything relating to Margaret."

Leo tilted his head in consideration. "Well, I think to some extent that's true. Our archivist has a fairly good grasp of what is and isn't in the collection, but a new set of eyes might turn something up. Besides," he said, "you should really see the archives and the Boston site at some point."

Before she could respond, he added, "Why don't we take a drive over there next week?"

The opportunity to research in the archives *and* spend an hour car ride with Leo was almost too good to be true. "I mean, if it's not too much trouble, I would—"

But Leo was already waving her off. "Are you kidding me? You'd be doing me a favor—that drive bores me to tears."

"Okay, then," she said, and found that she was grinning. "That sounds good."

Leo took another sip of the coffee and nearly gagged. "I'm sorry, but I don't think I can do this. I'm going to go get an iced coffee with two creams and two sugars, the way it was intended to be consumed."

"Quitter."

"Ouch," he replied, but he was smiling. "Be right back."

She watched him order and then stuff a dollar into the tip jar. He looked so urbane in his posture, so confident. In another life she could see herself falling hard for him, a life where she wasn't with Chris. A life where she wasn't painfully shy and unsure of herself. The barista was leaning her elbows on the counter, clearly flirting with Leo as the coffee brewed, but either he was oblivious, or uninterested. He must have been used to it.

"Much better," he said with an exaggerated sigh as he sat back down.

They sipped their drinks, and Augusta suddenly found herself tongue-tied again. She desperately wanted to have an easy conversation with him, but couldn't think of something to say. "So, do you think you'll stay at Harlowe for a while?" she finally asked him, hoping that her voice didn't betray the extent of her interest in his answer.

"Oh, yeah, I'm not going anywhere. The Harlowe Trust is

probably one of the better gigs out there in terms of funding, plus you can't beat the benefits. What about you?"

Augusta nodded. "I really like it here so far, and honestly I didn't think I'd be able to find a job like this for years yet."

"Glad you'll be sticking around for a while," he said. Was it her imagination or did his knee brush hers more deliberately when he said that?

She felt a smile tugging at her lips and she forced herself to bury her face in her cup. It was getting harder to convince herself that the looks he kept stealing in her direction didn't mean anything, but she couldn't bring herself to mention that she had a boyfriend. She didn't even know if he was single, for goodness' sake. Besides, she didn't really *know* Leo; he could just be a really friendly, nice guy. But something told her that there was more there, if only she were free to look.

13

Augusta

THEY TOOK THEIR time walking back to work, occasionally stopping so Leo could point out some of his favorite spots in town. Aside from the day of her interview, Augusta hadn't spent much time exploring Tynemouth, and she liked discovering it with Leo as her guide. He seemed to know a lot about the town for someone who only came up from Boston a couple of days a week.

"Are you from here?" she asked him. They had stopped on the promenade that ran alongside the beach to wait for the drawbridge to go back down. A parade of small fishing and pleasure boats were headed out into the harbor, and pedestrians had stopped to wave at them as they passed under the bridge. With the sun sparkling on the water and a salty, fresh breeze, it felt like an exotic vacation, not a workday lunch hour.

"No, but it reminds me of the little town in Maine where I grew up. What about you?"

"Salem," she told him. "I still live there."

"Oh, yeah? I bet it's nuts on Halloween."

She rolled her eyes. "All the locals get out of there before the Halloween madness descends on the city. If you go early, it's usually just families and people dressing up for fun, but sometimes it gets out of control. Last year a guy dressed as the Joker got really drunk and smashed a bunch of gravestones in the historic cemetery."

"Yikes. Well, the people-watching alone would be worth it, I bet. I'd like to see it one year." He grinned at her and she found herself grinning back.

The drawbridge had lowered, so they continued their leisurely walk. They were just about at Harlowe House when Augusta stopped dead in her tracks. Ahead of them, right in front of the house, Chris was leaning against his car. What was he doing here? She went from walking on air to feeling like a lead weight had been tied to her ankles. She automatically took a step away from Leo to put some more space between them.

Leo noticed, and followed her gaze. "Everything all right? Do you know him?"

She swallowed. "That's my boyfriend." Shouldn't she have been excited? Proud to show him off to her coworker? But all she felt was a vague sense of disappointment mingled with apprehension.

She thought she caught a flicker of surprise across Leo's face. "Well, I better get back to work," he said. "I'll catch you later."

Before she could say anything, Leo was heading inside. Maybe it was the coffee, but she felt jittery, unsettled as she walked over to meet Chris.

"Hey, fancy seeing you here," she said, trying for a light tone.

Chris didn't look at her; he was watching Leo disappear into the house. "Who was that guy?"

She shrugged. "Just a guy who works here. We were having a meeting."

"Must have been a pretty long meeting," he said. "I came to surprise you for lunch half an hour ago and your boss said you were out. You didn't answer your phone either."

There was that old guilt again. She'd been out having a great time with Leo, and Chris was trying to do something nice for her. "Oh," she said, trying to sound sorrier than she felt. "Sorry, I forgot to check my phone."

"I guess I wasted a trip," Chris said bitterly.

"Wait—" She reached out to stop him but he pulled away.

"I'll see you at home," he said, getting into the car and slamming the door.

Augusta stood there, watching him drive off, feeling guilty, yes, but also oddly relieved.

She avoided Leo for the rest of the day, which didn't turn out to be hard since she had a feeling he was avoiding her, too. Occasionally she heard him across the hall talking and laughing with Jill. Jamming her earbuds in, she tried to focus on her work.

There were condition reports to write and stuff in storage to inventory, but all Augusta wanted to do was get lost in documents and search for Margaret. She wondered if Leo would still take her to the archives next week. Of course he would. He was a good guy, and professional. He didn't care if she had a boyfriend or not, and he certainly wouldn't let it affect their work relationship. She was blowing this way out of proportion.

And that's when it hit her. She was staring at the Harlowe family tree again, the spidery lines dancing across the paper, the soft cadence of Leo's voice just audible from across the hall. She knew people fell out of love, knew that her parents had had rough patches over the years, but this was a sudden, clean flash. She wasn't happy. She hadn't been happy for a long time. She wanted to break up with Chris.

It wasn't that she thought that Leo really had any interest in her, or that she wanted a relationship with him, for that matter.

It was that she would never be able to explore that possibility because of some misplaced sense of loyalty to Chris. Maybe she really did love him, but what good did that do her if she was miserable all the time? Did she really owe him anything? Or did she owe herself the chance to be happy, whether that led to another relationship or not?

That evening as she climbed the steps to the apartment, she began to second-guess herself. Where would she live? How would she afford a place by herself? Most of the furniture belonged to Chris and Doug; she would need to buy all new things. She could move in with her mom, who lived on the other side of town, and who would be thrilled to have her. But Augusta didn't love the idea of moving back home; it felt like a big step backward. Maybe it would be easier to stay with Chris just a little longer. She ran through a mental list of her friends that she could possibly stay with, but came up empty. All her friendships had gradually deteriorated during her relationship with Chris, and any friends she had now were more Chris's than hers.

But there would always be some reason to stay. She'd already stayed this long, and the longer she stayed, the harder it would be to eventually break free.

Doug was nowhere to be seen when she let herself in, and Chris barely looked up long enough to glare at her from his video game. He was clearly still upset about that afternoon. Taking a deep breath, Augusta perched on the other side of the couch. She had to do it then, while she still had the nerve, or she wouldn't do it at all. "Can we talk?"

This time Chris didn't look up at all. "That sounds ominous," he said, a sarcastic edge to his voice.

He must have known what was coming. Maybe he even wanted the same thing and was just waiting for Augusta to be the one to pull the trigger. Was he happy with her? She couldn't imagine that he was. Their relationship hadn't been remotely passionate for a long, long time. They didn't have much in common except their history, and even that was fading further into the years. Augusta traced the geometric pattern of the couch cover with her finger, glad for once that Chris was distracted by a video game. "Yeah, I guess it is. It's just…well, I love you. I really do."

"But?"

"But um, I don't know. I don't think that's enough anymore. I think I need some time to find myself and figure some stuff out."

Chris didn't say anything, and his silence made her keep talking, tripping over her words in her haste to get them out. "I think we should take a break. I might go to stay at my mom's for a while."

She knew that she was taking the easy way out, trying to peel a Band-Aid off little by little when she should have just torn it off in one go. But it was either baby steps or nothing, and she couldn't do nothing anymore.

"It's your new job, isn't it?"

"What do you mean?"

Chris finally threw the game controller on the couch and looked at her. "You're hanging out with your new friends after work all the time. You're different now."

"I…um, I guess?" She did occasionally go out after work with Jill and Reggie, but it was a stretch to claim that she had a whole new social life.

"I was going to ask you to marry me, you know."

That stopped her cold. But then a burst of laughter threatened to erupt. "No, you weren't."

Chris looked injured. "Yeah, I was. I was saving up for a ring, and since you got that new job, I thought we could look for a house together."

The laughter died on her lips and her heart beat faster. How many times had she wished that Chris would propose? That he would make some sort of gesture that showed he was serious about their future together? And now that he had made it, why did it feel like such a hollow victory?

"I'm sorry," was all she could make herself say.

"Yeah, me, too."

She stood up, her body tight and achy from the tension. The longer she talked to Chris, the more opportunity she was giving him to change her mind, or to hurt her.

But then Chris was dropping to his knees, taking her hands in his. "Don't go. We can still get married, still get a house together. Doug is taking a job in California next year so it will be just you and me. Come on, it will be good. I know I'm not always the best at saying what I'm feeling, but I'll try harder. We'll start over." He was looking up at her, his hazel eyes bright and hopeful, more emotion on his face than she'd seen in years.

She swayed under his words, wanting so desperately to believe them. She *did* want to stay, but for the wrong reasons. She wanted to stay because it was convenient, safe. She wanted to stay because she hated conflict and wanted to make everyone happy. But if she didn't put her foot down now and take a stand, then she never would.

She shook her head. "I'm really sorry. I just… I'm sorry."

For the first time Chris seemed to really understand that this was it. They'd had their false starts and close calls before, but this time she was sticking to her guns. He abruptly dropped her hands and stood up, and Augusta was reminded how much bigger than her he was.

"You know, I really thought you were in it for the long haul." He shook his head. "You always play it safe with everything. But I guess this is the safe option for you. You'll probably start dating the first guy you find at work and move in with him." He gave a humorless snort of laughter.

"This isn't easy, and I'm not playing it safe now," she said, her voice small.

"Yeah, and that's why it's so fucking sad. You strung me along until you did the first brave thing in your life, and now you don't need me anymore. Jesus, I can't look at you right now. I'm going out."

"Chris," she started, but it was a half-hearted plea. There was so much pent-up anger in her, so many reasons why they didn't work as a couple that she could explain to him, but what would be the point? They weren't right for each other, and starting an argument wasn't going to solve anything. Maybe it was better if he left while she packed up her stuff. What on earth had compelled her to do this today? She had work tomorrow. How was she going to hold herself together?

The door slammed shut, and a few minutes later she heard his car start outside. She stood in the silent apartment, afraid that if she so much as moved a finger, she might shatter completely. It was the kind of moment that she would look back on years later, understanding it as a pivotal step in her life. But right now, it was real and raw and horrible, and she wanted nothing more than to disappear.

14

Margaret

Young men are plenty but sweethearts few
If my love leaves me, what shall I do?

—"The Queen of Hearts," Traditional Folk Song

"NOT HUNGRY TONIGHT, Margaret?"

I glared at Henry from across the table. He hadn't taken his gaze off me all dinner, and I didn't like the knowing glint in his eye. It had been nearly two weeks since my last meeting with Jack, and I still had not told him of my condition. My stomach had been in turmoil all day, and I was in turns ravenous and then sickened by the mere thought of eating. I had spent most of the meal pushing food around on my plate to make it appear that I had eaten some of the wretched-smelling meat.

My mother frowned at my plate. "Don't waste your mutton— it's good meat," she admonished. It didn't matter that we could afford it and then some; my mother was ever the frugal New Englander.

Since Jenny Hough's husband and his friends had come to our house, there had been a shift in the dynamics between my parents and me. My mother's ever-present mild annoyance with me had curdled into downright dislike, and my father avoided me altogether. I didn't know if they had told any of my brothers of what had transpired, but I rather thought they hadn't, for they would not want word to spread even further. Still, I dared not see any more women, for fear of more rumors spreading, more angry mobs at our doorstep.

Dinner dragged on, and I forced myself to nibble at a roll. When my mother's attention had shifted back to her conversation with Father, I excused myself.

I only barely made it to the basin in my room before I was sick. When I'd rinsed my mouth and put myself to rights, I stepped back into the hall and came face-to-face with Henry.

He must have been waiting for me, listening as I moved about the room, because he pulled me toward him by the arm as soon as I opened the door.

"Take your hand off me," I snapped.

But his grip on my arm only tightened. He was looking down at me as if he could see all my sins written plainly across my face. Did he know about Mrs. Hough and her accusations after all? Did he know about what I did at night, about the abilities I had kept so carefully hidden all these years?

His words surprised me. "I know about you and your secret lover," he hissed back. "So you might consider being a little kinder to me, lest I tell Father."

My blood ran cold. This was somehow worse. "How?" I asked before I could stop myself. But he didn't need to answer; I already knew. He had followed me after all, seen me with Jack. "What do you want?" I asked with a dry mouth. It wasn't that I was ashamed or scared to tell my parents about Jack, but I had no assurance from him yet. I wouldn't go to them until he had proposed, made some promise to me. The humiliation of rejection would be too much to bear. If they even suspected that I was carrying on an affair it would only cement their decision to send me away.

Now that he knew he had my attention, Henry drew back

slightly with a smile. "I want my sister back. I want the pretty girl with dark curls to laugh and talk with me again like when we were children. I want you to stop treating me as if I were an afterthought, an annoyance. I've only ever wanted what was best for you." He took my chin in his hand, gently tilting it up so I had no choice but to meet his gaze. "This lover will be the ruin of you."

I didn't like the way he was looking at me, a way a brother should never look at his sister. "You're mad," I said, pulling away. "Leave me alone."

He feinted toward me as if he would grab me again, and I automatically shielded my stomach.

I realized my mistake at once as Henry's eyes grew wide. Silence swelled around us, thick and suffocating. "There's a child," he said at last in a whisper. "You're carrying his child."

"So what if I am?" I said with a confidence I did not feel.

"Does he know? Does Jack Pryce know that you're carrying his child?"

I pressed my lips tight, but didn't say anything. The hallway was dark, the faint sound of Mother and Father finishing their dinner floated upstairs. Outside, the birds sang their last songs of the day.

"Margaret." Henry's eyes softened with pity. "My poor darling sister. I thought you too clever for this."

I had thought myself clever, too, and so above the young women who came to my cabin in the night begging for the evidence of their transgressions to be erased. How foolish I must have looked to Henry. I had thought only of my pleasure, and my ache for a baby to call my own, and not the practical consequences of my actions. How could I have thought that the very same baby that would be my heart's love would not also be my downfall? There was a reason why after weeks of Jack promising that he would sway his parents that he had hadn't been round to ask my father's permission. There was a reason why he had not come for me to elope. All the love potions and spells and prayers couldn't save me. Oh, how could I have let myself fall in love!

Before I knew what was happening, I found myself folded into Henry's arms, my tears staining the rough wool of his coat.

"Oh, my dear sister. My own dear love." His chin tucked over my head, just as Jack had held me. We did not move for a long, long time.

Perhaps if it had been George holding me in his arms in the dark hallway, I would have been able to unburden my hopes and fears to my favorite brother. But it was Henry, not George, so I held the deepest of my thoughts to myself.

He saw me tucked into bed, making certain that I had water and fresh linens. It felt good to be taken care of, to have my burdens eased just the smallest bit, even by Henry. For all that Jack worshipped me, he was not there when I needed him, did not seem to exist outside of our stolen nights in the woods. Henry was here, though, sitting beside my bed, dabbing at my clammy temples with a cloth until the worst of the nausea passed.

"Poor darling," he crooned.

In the dark, with his hand reassuringly in mine, it was easy to forget the reason for our confrontation in the hall. "Henry," I whispered, though there was no one that might overhear us, "may I ask you something?"

"Of course, anything."

Though I didn't know exactly what it was I was asking, I felt my way as I went. Phebe's words about my family tickled the back of my mind. "Is there something about our family—something about me—that I don't know?"

It wasn't my imagination; Henry went very still, and I could hear his slow swallow. "What do you mean?"

"I don't know what I mean exactly, but I think you do."

Abruptly, he dropped my hand and stood up. "You should sleep," he told me, brushing a kiss against my brow. "You're overwrought and need rest."

Before I had a chance to protest, he had shut the door, leaving me with my festering doubts.

15

Augusta

AUGUSTA'S CHILDHOOD HOME sat on a quiet side street in a diverse neighborhood of working- and middle-class families. It was only a fifteen-minute drive from her old place with Chris, but it felt like another world. At least four bathtub Marys welcomed her back with outstretched arms, and American flags and seasonal banners fluttered from porches. Pulling up in front of the two-family house with light blue vinyl siding and neatly swept patio, Augusta turned the ignition off and drummed her fingers on the steering wheel, her resolve faltering.

At least getting out of the apartment hadn't been too bad. Chris had never returned after their fight, and Doug had been holed up in his room and hadn't come out to say goodbye. There had been no awkward conversations, no chances to second-guess herself. It was better that way. A clean break, a fresh start.

Except that her fresh start included moving back to her childhood home with her mother and facing all the ghosts that still lingered there. After her dad had died, she'd been desperate for a change of scenery, but her mom had insisted on staying in their family home. The real estate developers would just love for her to move out, her mother would always say, but they would have to pry her dead body out of her reclining chair before she gave them the satisfaction of turning the house into luxury condos for yuppies.

As if on cue, her mother threw open the screen door. "There's my girl!" She was wearing house slippers, but padded out to the sidewalk to meet Augusta and pulled her into a tight embrace. Holding her at arm's length, her mother studied her. "Look at you! Have you lost weight?"

"Um. Maybe."

"I hope you're hungry because Ginny from next door brought over a Tupperware of sauce and I'm making meatballs." Her mother grabbed a suitcase and started carrying it inside.

"I'm vegetarian, Mom," Augusta said, hurrying to catch up.

"No wonder you're so thin. Well, I have some chicken breasts in the freezer. You'll eat chicken, won't you?"

Augusta followed her mother down the hall, half listening to her steady stream of chatter. The Podos house could have been a museum in its own right, a time capsule of family life from the 1980s to the 2020s. The hallway carpet was still faded and stained from the infamous Kool-Aid Spill of 2003. An unfinished needlepoint—on which her mother refused to admit defeat—was still propped up half-heartedly on the mantel. Maybe in two hundred years a harried tour guide would usher tourists through the living room, pointing out the robust collection of snow globes on the bookshelf and speculating about the people who had collected them.

"What about lemonade? Should I make some lemonade?" Her mother had already moved on from unloading the car to bustling around the kitchen. Her frenetic energy was always a lot for introverted Augusta. A pediatric nurse at one of the hospitals downtown, Pat Podos was tough as nails, and didn't suffer fools lightly. She always wore shirts with slogans or puns when she wasn't in her scrubs, and today's said I CAN'T KEEP CALM—I'M ITALIAN!!!

She caught Augusta looking at it and grinned. "Isn't that a riot? I got it at Savers."

Augusta frowned. She'd never heard that saying before. "Are we Italian?"

Her mother waved her off. "Don't they say everyone has a little Italian in them?"

She had no idea where her mother had heard that, but she nodded as if she agreed. After they set the table—her mother insisted on using the "good" china—they sat down to eat. Augusta had barely picked up her glass when her mother raised the dreaded topic.

"So what happened with Chris? Did he break up with you, or was it mutual?"

"I broke up with him," Augusta mumbled into her lemonade.

Her mother shook her head, gold hoop earrings jangling. "I always liked him—so good-looking and so polite," she said with a wistful sigh. "Why didn't it work out?"

"I don't know," Augusta said between gritted teeth. "It just didn't." How could she tell her own mother that her boyfriend was an asshole and had treated her like crap? Having to explain everything out loud only made it all the more mortifying that she had stayed so long.

"Okay, okay. Message received. I know when to leave well enough alone." But Augusta could tell it was killing her mother not to have all the details.

Augusta ate around the chicken on her plate, pushing her food around while her mother brought her up to speed on all the neighborhood gossip. When Pat paused long enough to take a breath, Augusta took the opportunity to broach something that had been on her mind. "So I thought while I was here, I might go through some of Dad's stuff."

The fork stilled in her mother's hand and there was a beat of silence. She pressed her lips. "If you want."

At some point over the years, her father had become a taboo subject between them. Augusta wasn't sure why exactly; her mother had seemed to get on with her life after his death, had even dated sporadically. Everyone grieved differently, but something told her it was more than just grief. Coupled with the fact that her mother had always been hesitant to talk about their relatives and family even before her father's death, Augusta was starting to see little red flags everywhere.

"I mean, yeah, I do want," Augusta said, a new sense of determination giving her courage. "I feel like we've just shoved Dad under the bed and agreed to not talk about him. I don't want to do that anymore."

Setting down her fork, her mother pinned her with a stare. "Augusta, you are a grown woman. If you want to go through your father's stuff, I'm not going to stop you."

Augusta didn't have a chance to respond before her mother abruptly pushed her chair back and stood up. "I'm doing a Paint and Sip party tonight with the girls at that new place by the mall," she announced, her dark expression gone. "Will you be all right here alone? Do you want me to run to the store first to get you any snacks?"

Still rattled from her own outburst, Augusta answered without looking up from her plate. "No, I'll be okay, Mom."

After her mother had left, Augusta changed into some sweats and headed to her old room. She had thought going through her dad's stuff would be a good distraction, but the pile of boxes was bigger than she remembered, and suddenly she felt exhausted from the emotional whirlwind of the day. She had envisioned sitting at the kitchen table with her mom, dumping everything out of the boxes and going through it all together. Doing it alone was not only daunting, but she wasn't sure she was emotionally prepared for what she might find. Well, the boxes would be there later. For now, all she could manage to do was push aside the pile of teddy bears and decorative pillows on the bed, slip under the covers, and close her eyes. Now that she was home, there would be time to talk to her mother, to really talk to her. And maybe, just maybe, she would find the family she had always been denied.

16

Augusta

AUGUSTA STILL DRESSED in her same capris and ballet flats every morning, still battled with her curly hair, still tracked all her food in her calorie counter app, yet she was a new person. She'd thought she'd cry a lot more than she had or be depressed in general. But once she'd broken up with Chris, she'd realized that she'd already said goodbye long ago. Her body was simply joining her mind and heart now.

Between the breakup and moving in with her mom, she had lost track of time and had almost forgotten that she was supposed to go to the archives with Leo today. She'd avoided him for the past week, though he'd mostly been in Boston anyway. When she heard his knock at the door and looked up, her breath caught in her throat. It seemed a cruel trick of the universe that he looked extra handsome that day in a dark blue button-down, his chestnut hair adorably tousled.

"Ready for a road trip?"

If she had been afraid that seeing him so soon after the breakup might complicate her feelings, she was right. How could she share the same room, let alone car, with someone who made her heart race just at the sight of him? And that was not what she needed right then. She needed time and space to find herself. But they had already arranged the trip and he didn't have any clue about her feelings or the storm that was raging in her heart. Besides, she was dying of curiosity about what might be in the archives concerning Margaret.

"Yep," she said, trying not to appear flustered. Gathering up her notes and water bottle, she followed him out to his car.

Outside, Leo clicked a key fob and a sporty black sedan beeped from the road. Cars were not something Augusta really ever gave much thought to—they were meant to get you from point A to point B as far as she was concerned—but for some reason she found herself intrigued by his. Maybe it was because it reminded her of him: sharp, understated and playfully sophisticated. "You can throw your stuff in the back," Leo said as he hastily brushed aside some papers from the passenger seat.

It was a strange, intimate thing to be sharing so small a space with Leo. Everywhere there were little glimpses of his personality, like the seasonal pool pass hanging from the rearview mirror, the gym bag and stack of library books in the back seat. He was polite and kind as ever, but there was a slightly more formal edge to his demeanor today, and Augusta wondered if it was because of their encounter with Chris the week before.

Leo plugged in an old-school adapter into the dashboard and began scrolling through his phone. "What kind of music do you like?"

The old Augusta would have carefully curated her answer before she spoke, trying to anticipate what kind of music someone like Leo would like and matching that. But she had wasted too much of her life already trying to mold herself to what she thought a man would want from her. "Florence and the Machine is my favorite, but I also love Stevie Nicks, Rihanna, Adele..." She'd been listening to a lot of powerful female vocalists since the breakup, and though she would never admit to it, belting out anthems in her car on the way to work made her feel empowered.

"I definitely have Fleetwood Mac," he said. As they pulled out, he hit Play and the sound of "The Chain" filled the car.

They stopped for coffee and doughnuts, and Augusta randomly chose a giant, chocolate-glazed monstrosity that she held in her lap, picking at it without really eating.

"Any plans for the weekend?" Leo asked as he brushed powdered sugar off his pant leg.

Her only plans consisted of dodging her mother's attempts at setting her up with a coworker's son, and maybe finally going through her dad's stuff. "Not really," she said, gazing out the window. Maybe she would finally pick up her sketching again, a hobby she'd let fall by the wayside over the past few years.

"Are you okay? You seem...distant."

Augusta forced a smile, which she was sure looked as fake as it felt. Leo was probably the last person in the world she should confide in, yet she was desperate to talk to someone. She had no close female friends anymore, and she was way too mortified to talk to her mother. "Yeah, I'm fine," she said. "It's just been a weird week."

She could feel Leo glancing at her before merging onto the highway. "Want to talk about it?"

Shrugging, she pretended to be absorbed in peeling a sticker off her water bottle. "My boyfriend and I broke up. It was a long time coming, but it's been rough all the same."

Again, the sensation of Leo's gaze flitting to her. "Oh, yeah?" His voice held an undeniable note of interest.

"Yeah," she confirmed.

"Sorry, that came out wrong. I'm really sorry to hear that."

"Thanks," she mumbled into her water.

"If you want to talk about it, I'm a good listener," he said, flashing that lethally disarming smile of his.

Augusta hesitated. Was he offering because he legitimately wanted to help? Or was he just hoping for a juicy story? But there was something about him that made her think he was in earnest, that he actually cared. "There's nothing really to tell. We weren't right for each other and things finally came to a head."

"So it was mutual?"

"Um." Since the breakup, Chris had sent her several texts. They'd ranged from pleading to angry, and eventually she began deleting all of them without reading. "He wasn't completely on board with the idea."

"Either way, that must have been hard, for both of you."

The highway whizzed past them, and Augusta chewed on her lip, replaying in her mind the absurdly horrifying moment when Chris had dropped to his knees and asked her to marry him. "He proposed to me," she blurted out before she could stop herself. "He said he'd been planning on asking me to marry him when I broke up with him."

She could feel Leo digest this, studying her from the corner of his eye while he drove. "That kind of sounds like coincidental timing. Had you guys talked about marriage?"

"I think he just said that to make me feel guilty. I don't think he really wanted to get married."

"Did he do that a lot? Try to make you feel guilty?"

Augusta shrugged. "I'm kind of a guilty-by-default person," she said. "I always thought the fights were all my fault. Anytime something was wrong, I blamed myself."

There was silence for a beat, and she wondered if she was getting too personal too fast. But then Leo spoke. "I know I don't know you that well, but you don't strike me as someone who has a lot to feel guilty about. You seem like someone who tries really hard and goes out of her way to make people feel comfortable. I'm sure some people take that as license to shift blame away from themselves, but that's on them, not you."

Augusta blinked. Damn, he *was* a good listener. And he was right—he didn't know her, but his kindness was enough to bring tears to her eyes. She sniffed them back. "I just can't believe I let myself be manipulated for so long," she said with a groan. "I was so stupid."

"Hey." Leo leaned over and let his hand hover over her knee as if he was going to pat her leg. He must have thought better of it because to her disappointment, he placed it back on the wheel. "You're not stupid, Augusta. He sounds like a manipulative bastard."

Her first instinct was to defend Chris, the way she had for years every time someone rightly pointed out a red flag about him, but she didn't owe him that anymore. "Yeah, he is," she agreed. It felt good to finally say it.

"Do you have somewhere safe to stay?"

It took her a moment to realize what he was asking, and she almost laughed. Chris might have been overprotective and obstinate about some things, but he wasn't violent. "I'm staying with my mom," she said. "Until I can find a place of my own."

"That's good."

She desperately wanted to ask if he was in a relationship himself, but there wasn't a good way to say it without betraying that she was interested. Which, to be fair, she supposed she was.

As if reading her mind, Leo said, "My girlfriend and I broke up two years ago."

"Oh, I'm sorry." Did that mean he was single now? Two years was a long time—had he not dated since then? "Was it on good terms?" she asked cautiously.

His expression clouded. "It was complicated," he said. "She passed away a few months after we broke up."

"Oh, Leo. I'm so sorry."

He gave a little shrug, and though it was a casual gesture,

Augusta knew from personal experience how much emotion it probably held. "Like I said, it was complicated."

They lapsed into silence. The car began picking up speed, and Augusta shifted uncomfortably in her seat. They were in the fast lane, the scenery whizzing past them. Reaching for the safety handle, Augusta took a peek at the speedometer and nearly did a double take. They were going almost 85 mph.

"Do you, um, always drive so fast?" she asked, her knuckles tightening around the handle.

"Hmm?" Leo glanced at her as if he'd forgotten she was there. "Oh, sorry. I like opening up on the highway and sometimes I get carried away." He slowed down and Augusta's heart rate likewise slowed back to normal.

The rest of the trip was spent listening to Stevie Nicks belt out the classics. Gradually, houses and neighborhoods replaced the trees, and then the suburbs transitioned to the dense city blocks of Boston. They pulled up behind a stately brick building in the heart of the city across from the Public Garden.

"You said you've never been to the Harlowe mansion before, right?" Leo asked as they pulled into the small side lot.

Augusta shook her head. "I never even knew it existed until I was hired."

He grinned. "Well, you're in for a treat. I'll give you a quick tour before getting you set up in the archives."

Augusta was itching to get her hands on those documents, but she couldn't turn down a private tour from Leo. They went in through the front where a ticket counter was set up in the front hall. "Hey, Monica," Leo said, waving to a young woman with long brown hair in a white button-down behind the desk. "Have you met Augusta yet? She's our new collections manager at Harlowe."

Augusta shook her hand, then stood by awkwardly while Leo and Monica caught up on some small talk. "We're going to zip through the house real fast before heading up to the archives— is that all right?" Leo asked.

"They're between tours right now, so just be quick and you'll be fine."

"Great." Leo motioned for Augusta to follow him out of the front vestibule and past the counter.

If she had thought that Harlowe House was elegant, the Boston mansion was a picture of Victorian refinement at its best. Leo led her through a formal dining room that made the dining room at Harlowe House look quaint by comparison. The table was set with crystal stemware that twinkled in the sunlight let in from the floor-length windows. "How often was the family here?" she asked him. It was nowhere near as homey and welcoming as the house in Tynemouth.

"The history of the family isn't my strong point, but I'm pretty sure Harlowe House was their main residence until the 1870s or so. I think after that one of the brothers lived here and the place in Tynemouth was more of a summer retreat."

The 1870s. So, right when Margaret was supposedly living. Would she have come here to visit her brother? Had she dined in this very room, surrounded by the elegant, powder blue molding and gilded mirrors?

They headed up a gracious marble staircase just as a tour was starting downstairs. Leo swiped his card at the door at the top. "I just have to grab my charger from my office," he told her over his shoulder as he led her down the hall.

Augusta stood in the doorway while he rifled through his desk drawers. There were a couple of framed photos on the desk facing away from her, and a neat row of Matchbox cars. File folders sat in piles, and there was a shelf of binders with labels like "Summer Programming 2016" and "Tynemouth Artist CO-OP Directory." A shriveled fern sat next to the only window. "So, this is the wellspring of public engagement, huh?"

He flashed her a grin before returning to his search. "Oh, yeah. All the magic happens here. Don't blame me for the plant, though—I think it was dead when I got it. Aha, there it is."

He waved the charger triumphantly and then led her down the hall to the archives.

Augusta had pictured a grand hall lined with books and old-fashioned green library lamps, but in reality, it was a modest room with two reading stations and a modern shelving system.

A middle-aged woman with light skin and a silver pixie cut sat behind the desk. "Hey, Lori, this is Augusta."

Augusta shook her hand. "I think we've emailed a couple of times."

"Of course! So nice to meet you in person. So, Leo says you're doing some research on the Harlowe women around the 1860s through the 1880s?"

Augusta had decided that she would have the best chance of finding information about Margaret if she kept the parameters of her research vague. She nodded. "That's right."

"I got out some reels for you to start with on the microfiche, mostly of transcribed journals and ledgers from that period. When you're done with those, I can pull out specific correspondences."

When Lori had gone back to her desk, Leo made sure that Augusta had everything she needed. "I'll be down the hall in my office. Just come and find me when you're ready. Or, actually..." He paused, glancing at his watch. "Why don't we grab some lunch across the street at one? You'll probably be about ready to give your eyes a break by then."

Augusta instinctively prepared herself to turn down the invitation, especially since it involved food. But why shouldn't they grab lunch? She didn't have to worry about Chris grilling her later about who she'd been with, and she knew she had to eat to something. There couldn't be any more fainting spells or hallucinations at work. "Lunch sounds perfect," she told him.

Jill had been right: there wasn't even so much as a mention of Margaret Harlowe. Dizzy from whirring through the microfiche, Augusta let her mind wander as she stared sightlessly out the window. Why wouldn't a wealthy, notable family want any trace of their daughter to survive? Had she committed some sort of unforgivable transgression? The Victorians were notoriously prudish when it came to scandals and love affairs, and Augusta had come across more than one case when a zealous descendant had decided to take things into their own hands and censor the historical record. But this was different. There wasn't even so much as a scratched-out name in a family Bible, or a veiled reference to a disappointing daughter.

She was going to have to get creative. Scrolling through the rest of the journals, she skipped to the ledger entries. Correspondence and diaries could tell a story, but numbers didn't lie. There had to be a record of expenses that showed that Margaret Harlowe had existed.

The portrait in the Harlowe dining room suggested that the sitter had been in her teens or early twenties in the 1870s, so Augusta raced through the reels from about twenty-five years earlier. If Margaret had been born sometime in the 1850s, then there should be *something* from that period that suggested a birth had occurred. Perhaps there had been an expense for a doctor to come and deliver the baby, or maybe her mother had needed a new wardrobe of maternity clothes. She checked her notes to see when the three brothers were born so she could rule them out, and then she began carefully scanning the cramped rows of numbers and shorthand.

It was mind-numbing work, so she almost missed the innocuous entry in the ledger. She paused the microfiche and then rolled it back another page. There. She squinted at the entry, double-checking that it really said what she thought it said.

She was hurriedly scribbling notes when her phone buzzed with a message from Leo asking if she was ready. Two hours had flown by, and she found that she almost wished she didn't have to pause her work to meet up with him.

But as soon as she stepped out of the archives onto the busy streets of Boston, she was glad for the break. It was like stepping out of the past and back into the present. They wove through groups of tourists and college students, the aroma of roasted nuts and fried dough hanging in the crisp air. As much as she loved the quaintness of Tynemouth, there was an energy to the city that made Augusta feel as if anything was possible. Coupled with her newfound singleness, walking across the Boston Public Garden with Leo beside her gave her a heady sense of freedom.

The Thai café Leo had recommended was mostly empty, so they slid into a big booth in the back. It was dimly lit and cozy, with soft instrumental music playing, and Augusta had to remind herself that this wasn't a date.

"So, did you find anything good? Any Margaret sightings?" Leo asked after the waiter had taken their orders.

"Well, not exactly," she admitted. "But—" She pulled out one of the photocopies that Lori had made for her and handed it to Leo "—I did find this. It's the Harlowe household ledger from 1858."

She tried to hide her excitement as she watched him scan the document. "What am I looking at exactly?"

"Right here," she said, leaning across the table and tapping at one of the entries. "It's an expense for five bolts of fabric. Then if you look down here—" she craned her neck, trying to find the other entry upside down "—there's a dressmaker's charge for 'girls' dresses, times five.'"

Leo looked up, and she could tell by his expression that he understood the significance. "There were three brothers, so why would Jemima and Clarence Harlowe be buying girls' dresses unless…"

"…unless they also had a daughter," Augusta finished for him.

"Wow." Leo leaned back, his appreciative gaze making her shiver. "That is some amazing detective work."

Their food came and Margaret was momentarily forgotten.

The noodles smelled amazing, but she'd picked at that giant doughnut in the car already, and she was probably way over her calories for the day. She'd have some of the bean sprouts on top, maybe a piece of the tofu, but that was it.

Leo was tucking into his curry. "God, this is so good. How's yours?"

"Good," she said, though she hadn't actually taken more than a nibble.

She could feel Leo watching her, wanting to say something. She was used to that from friends and family, always commenting on her eating habits, and it only heightened her self-consciousness around food. Why had she agreed to lunch?

He slid her plate closer to her. "Go ahead, I promise you it's good."

She hesitated. What was she going to do? Just sit there staring at her plate like she'd never seen food before? All she had to do was lift the fork to her mouth, yet it felt as if her hands were made of lead.

When she looked up from her plate, she found that he had resumed eating. No, not just eating, *inhaling* his food, noodles dripping out of his mouth. He smacked his lips loudly and grunted. It was like watching a three-year-old trying food for the first time. "This is *really* good."

Aghast, she flicked her glance around at the mostly empty restaurant. "What are you doing?"

"I'm eating," he said around his mouth full of food.

"That's how you eat?"

"Yeah—" he paused to swallow "—is that how *you* eat?"

"I—" She stopped as his meaning became clear. He was trying to put her at ease, trying to show her that she didn't have anything to feel self-conscious about. "No..." she said carefully.

Leo was suddenly absorbed in his phone, and she had the feeling he was doing it for her benefit. Taking a deep breath, she picked up her fork and took a bite. He had been right; the noodles *were* good. She would figure out the calories later, when it wouldn't spoil her precious time with Leo.

When they had finished and Augusta had gotten a container for her leftovers, Leo flagged down the waiter and asked for the check. She couldn't be sure, but the card he slipped into the billfold didn't look like the Harlowe credit card.

"So, what's next?" Leo asked, signing the check. "More Margaret hunting?"

"Yeah, I want to go back a few years earlier and see if I can find anything about her before the charges for the dress." Because something still wasn't right with the numbers. She had easily been able to find evidence that matched up with all three births of the brothers, but there had been nothing that even hinted at the birth of a fourth child. A daughter wouldn't have needed dresses until she was at least a couple of years old. So where was the proof of her birth? Where had Margaret Harlowe come from?

17

Margaret

The love that I have chosen I'll therewith be content
And the salt sea shall be frozen before that I repent.

—"The Lowlands of Holland," Traditional Folk Song

NO MATTER HOW much I wheedled and begged her to tell me of my origins, Phebe had remained resolute that it must be my parents who shared this secret with me. But I could not simply ask them, especially not now they were already so on edge around me. It was not just my pride, but my suspicion that if there was truly something amiss with me, that they would not give me a true answer. Henry might have thought that he had laid my doubts to rest, but he had only strengthened the idea that there was something no one was telling me.

There must have been someone who knew me as a child besides Phebe. But when I thought back to my early days, my memories were few and vague. I had been a solitary child, with only my older brothers for playmates. Had a midwife or physician attended my birth? Was there record of my baptism in the church?

Since I could not ask my parents, and Henry would not relent, I decided to find my own answers. On a gray, chilly autumn day, I donned my coat and boots, and paid a visit to old Dr. Hardy, our family physician.

Dr. Hardy practiced medicine in an office above his home on Main Street. A harried servant admitted me into the building, and I swept upstairs, ignoring his plea for me to wait in the parlor.

Ensconced in a velvet dressing gown, Dr. Hardy was hunched over his desk, engrossed in reading through a looking glass. "You must have an appointment," he said, without looking up from his papers. "I cannot see patients without one." Pausing from his reading, he spared me a glance. "If you are in some sort of trouble, then I regret to inform you that I do not perform such procedures."

Ignoring him, I seated myself on the wooden examination bench opposite his desk, arranging the folds of my skirt. "I am not in trouble," I said. Of course, this was not strictly true, but he did not need to know of my situation in *that* regard. "I have come to ask you some questions about your service to my family."

"You still need an appointment. I'm a busy man and I can't see every person who comes in off the street to—"

"But you will see me," I interrupted him. "Because I know what transpired between your wife's sister and yourself." I paused for dramatic effect. "Whips and chains," I said. "I really would not have imagined you possessed such proclivities by looking at you, Doctor."

The color drained from his face, his little gray mustache falling. "How—how did you—"

"Never mind how. Now," I said briskly, "I would like some answers to my questions. I believe that you have been my family's physician for at least twenty years, is that correct?"

"That is correct," he said stiffly.

"And you attended my mother through all of her pregnancies? Delivered all her children?"

134

At this, he shifted uncomfortably in his leather chair. "Delivered the three oldest, yes."

My body went very still, the tension in the room heightened, pressing in around me. I proceeded cautiously. "So you didn't attend my birth?"

"I just said that I did not."

"You attended the births of all of my brothers," I pressed. "Why did you not attend mine?"

"I cannot remember," he said testily, "but there are a hundred reasons I might not have. Your mother might have employed another physician. I might have been away or otherwise occupied. It's all beside the fact, though it is hardly appropriate for you to barge into my office with all these questions." Color was returning to his face. "Spread your rumors all you like, but it is your word against mine, and after your episode with Mrs. Hough, I assure you that it is mine that will be believed."

Oh, but he thought he was clever. I should have left well enough alone, but I have never been one to turn the other cheek. "So, you have heard about Mrs. Hough and what I told her, then? Perhaps you had even seen the girl for yourself before and deemed her case to be hopeless. Many women come to me after they see you, and I help them in ways that you will not."

I had his attention. Throwing down his spectacles, he leaned back in his chair with an impatient huff. "You fancy yourself a wise woman, but it is clear that you are simply an unnatural young woman who thrives on chaos and attention."

Brushing aside his accusations, I perched on the corner of his desk, as familiar as a house cat. "Some of the rumors are exaggerations, I will own that. But there is a seed of truth to even the most unruly vine of gossip. I would hate to have to demonstrate my power."

In truth, there was little that I could do to him. But I knew a few tricks, and that was all I needed. With a click of my fingers, I summoned a flame to life from the cold wick of his desk lamp. Another click, and I extinguished it again.

Dr. Hardy's eyes went wide and he shrank back into his chair. "Wh-what do you want?"

"I want the truth. Tell me what you know of my birth."

"And then you will leave?"

I held my hand to my breast in a pledge. "And then I will leave. You have my word."

He swallowed. "Your...your mother was confined and it was deemed unnecessary by your father for me to attend to her. I never saw your mother, either in her confinement nor immediately after your birth. Your father assured me that I was not needed, and that all had gone smoothly."

"But you saw my mother during her previous pregnancies?" I prodded.

"Yes, it was only yours. And it was strange, because..." He trailed off, his cheeks coloring as he darted me a worried look.

"What was strange?"

"She never appeared to be...that is, she never looked pregnant. I wasn't aware of her condition until I was informed that she'd entered her confinement in her last weeks."

My mind raced to complete the puzzle. The truth dangled just out of my reach, elusive and shimmering. "When did you first attend to me as a child?"

"I wasn't called until you were at least six months old." He cleared his throat, his gaze shifting away.

"Yes, Doctor?"

He fiddled with the looking glass on his desk, turning it over in his hands, unable to meet my eye. "I wondered if perhaps... perhaps you were the product of an affair, and I was kept away so as not to expose a family secret."

For the first time since storming into his office, my composure started to slip. I'd had my suspicions, but hearing them voiced drained me of all my fortitude.

"Miss Harlowe?" Dr. Hardy was looking at me with something between concern and fear. "That is all that I know, I swear it. Please, please leave now."

Using the edge of the desk for support, I stumbled toward the door. Gulls shrieked above me as I slowly made my way down Main Street, my thoughts churning. Why had my birth been a secret? I was the youngest of my siblings; it wasn't as if I had been born out of wedlock. And really, it had been the 1850s, it was not the Middle Ages when my mother might have faced corporeal punishment for a transgression. But for some reason, my parents had not wanted it known that my mother was pregnant.

The pungent smell of roast pork greeted me when I arrived home and let myself into the house. I'd forgotten that my mother was hosting a luncheon for George and his betrothed, Miss Ida Foster. She was a nice enough girl, a little mousy perhaps, but I was in no mood to entertain.

I silently slipped into my seat at the table, too distracted by my thoughts to apologize for my tardiness. My mother shot me an irritated look. I should have been glad to see George, but I was consumed with trying to make sense of what Dr. Hardy had told me. At least Clarence and Lizzie had not come as they had just welcomed their baby boy the previous week, and Lizzie was still recovering.

My parents had visited them the day before. "He's handsome as anything, and you can tell he's always thinking," my mother was saying proudly of her new grandson. "A Harlowe through and through."

"He's not thinking," Henry muttered. "He probably just has gas."

"Henry!" Mother protested.

"And he has his favorite uncle's gray eyes," George said merrily.

I could bear it no longer. "What about me?" I asked suddenly. Everyone turned expectantly in their seats at my outburst. I had to know, and now I at least had some information on my side, some ammunition in the battle to discover who I was.

"What about you, what?" Father asked.

Taking a deep breath, I folded my hands neatly on my lap before I spoke, the picture of a demure and obedient daughter. The daughter they had always wanted. The daughter they had never gotten. "Where did I come from? Am I a Harlowe through and through?"

"Of course you are. What a thing to ask," my mother said, vigorously sawing at her pork without meeting my eye. Despite my mother's assurance, I felt my heart turn heavy in my chest. There was indeed something that they were keeping from me about my origins. Was I truly the product of an affair? Why would my father not only tolerate my presence, but raise me as his own daughter? I studied my father, his olive complexion, his dark eyes. My mother was lighter in color, but her eyes were brown as well. I alone had green eyes and dark auburn hair. How had I never realized it before? How could I have missed it? They were neither of them my parents.

George opened his mouth to say something, but my father stopped him with a sharp look.

"Margaret—" he said, his posture stiff, his jaw tight.

"Who. Am. I," I demanded, cutting off my father's words.

Now my mother put down her napkin, her dark eyes flashing. "I refuse to play along with your antics."

"I know that I am not your natural child, so who am I? Why have you lied to me all these years?"

"Who told you that?" my mother asked, her voice dropping to a hoarse whisper.

"Aha!" I cried, my darkest suspicions confirmed. "So it is true!"

My mother and father shared a long look, and suddenly I felt as if I were a child again, small and unsure of my place in the world. My position in the family came into sharp focus, the way

I had always felt like an outsider, as if I didn't belong. The powers which I alone possessed.

I gazed at everyone in turn, studying their reactions. Father was tugging at his moustache, and Ida looked exceedingly uncomfortable. Who else knew beside my parents? Did my beloved George know? They had let me live a lie, pretending all these years to be my brothers. I hated them all in that moment.

The silence prickled. Molly came in with a tray of jellies, and my mother summarily ordered her out of the room again.

When the door had clicked shut behind her, and the only sound was the hiss of the oil lamps, my mother cleared her throat. "You are the illegitimate child of my sister." She paused. "You are our niece."

My head reeled as the room slanted and shifted. A small part of me had held out hope that perhaps there was no secret about my origins. "What sister?" I asked. The only aunts of which I knew were on my father's side, and they all had children of their own.

"I had a younger sister, Eliza," my mother said tightly. "She got herself into trouble and you were the result. We took you in shortly after you were born to protect her reputation."

Heaven forfend a Harlowe reputation be tarnished. "Where is she? Where is my mother?" I had never met her, had never even known she had existed until a few seconds ago, and yet all at once my heart beat fiercely with love for her. Every missing piece inside of me, every question without an answer suddenly became illuminated. I didn't belong in this family. I had never belonged.

My mother pressed her lips, dropping her gaze to her plate. "She suffered an infection from childbirth and died, not long after you came here."

And just as suddenly as my heart had come alive, it died again. My ears were ringing. Pushing my chair back, I stood up. I was vaguely aware of George rising and murmuring something to me as he tried to take my hand. I pulled away. I didn't want to be near any of them, even George. I wanted Jack, only Jack. He, at least, had never lied to me. He was more soothing than laudanum, more warming than whiskey. I wanted to lose myself in a burning haze of passion and never come out. But I had not seen him in weeks, and did not know if I would see him again.

I could hear the sharp murmur of my family's voices as I left and went to find Shadow outside. He must have sensed my pain, for he nosed my hand open, licking my palm. "I will not be like my mother," I whispered into his fur. "I will not suffer having my child taken away from me and raised by someone else."

After a sleepless night spent trying to imagine my mother's face, wondering what her voice had sounded like, I set out to visit Phebe. At last, I would be able to learn about my mother, to speak to someone who had known her. My foot hadn't so much as touched the oyster shell path when Phebe appeared at the gate, her arms crossed across her blue checked dress. "So they told you, huh," she said. "Come on in, then." She opened the gate and stepped aside so that Shadow and I might pass through.

I made us tea while she worked on her nets and hummed a song. Shadow lazed at her feet, occasionally snapping playfully at the twine passing over his head. My mind was a jumble, trying to make sense of the lie that was my life. There were so many questions that I wanted to ask, but every time I settled on one, a thousand more sprang up. Who was my mother? Had she been beautiful? She must have been to have fallen. Who would I have been if she had raised me? Who was my father? Would I ever know? Would I ever make sense in this world that didn't see or appreciate magic? Would I have made sense if I'd had a mother who nurtured and encouraged my wildness?

As if reading my mind, Phebe finally spoke. "She was pretty. Long dark hair like you, but she wore it up in a braided crown. Clever, except when it came to men." At this Phebe raised her eyes and gave me a meaningful look. "I didn't know her much outside of church, so I was surprised when she came to me in trouble. I guess she thought that I could fix her problem."

I winced at being referred to as a "problem," but I wanted to hear more, so I said nothing.

"I told her that I didn't do that kind of thing." Phebe abruptly stood up and disappeared into the back of the house, her long skirts swishing. When she returned, she was holding a book. "Your mama gave this to me for safekeeping. It was her wish that you should have it when you were of age. Well, you're of age now, I suppose."

I ran my fingers over the butter-soft leather of the cover. Inside, an elegant script covered the pages, interspersed with an occasional sketch. This had been my mother's; she'd written these words and left them for me. As I imbibed her personality through the slanted cursive and looping *P*s, I suddenly felt a little less alone. Here was an explanation of who I was, of that which I was capable. Here, at last, was a link to my past. I was not a ship adrift on lonely waters, but a boat in harbor, anchored, safe.

I could feel Phebe watching me, pressing her lips like she wanted to say something. "You be careful of what you read in there."

"Have you read it?"

"Of course not. It wasn't mine to read. But I knew your mama and I know the sort of magic she favored, the darkness in her that could flare up like a candle flame."

I thought of my mother, of Jack and the baby inside of me. It was too late for my mother, but perhaps I didn't have to make the same mistakes she had. "What about you? Have you ever used dark magic?"

Phebe gave me a long look, and I had the impression that I had offended her, though I didn't know how.

"I'll tell you the same thing I told her when she asked me. People make assumptions, they like to conjure up some romantic and silly notion about what they think I ought to be. Now, I don't mind being known as a wise woman, but I'm not a witch and I don't work dark magic. What's more, I'm not here to hold your hand as you figure out who you are. If the darkness calls to you, then you'll have to find your answers within the book."

Chastened, I closed the book and spoke of it no more. I wanted to know every single thing about my mother, from the color of her eyes, to how she carried herself, to the songs she used to sing. But I would have to make do with the book, and the hope that my aunt and uncle would share some crumbs with me about my mother, low though their opinion of her seemed to be. If she had followed a dark path, then so, too, would I.

After the tea was finished, I tucked the book into my pocket. Phebe hung on the gate as I said my goodbyes. "You be careful, Margaret Harlowe," she told me. "Don't let the promise of easy magic lead you further into the trouble you're already in."

18

Augusta

IN HER DREAM, Augusta was standing behind a young woman, watching her comb her long dark curls. The woman was wearing a tightly fitted bodice, and though her back was to Augusta, she somehow knew it was Margaret Harlowe. *Turn around*, she willed the woman in her dream. *Turn around and let me see your face.* But Margaret did not turn around, she continued combing her hair in long, deliberate strokes while quietly singing under her breath.

And then, as was the way with dreams, Augusta wasn't just watching Margaret, she *was* Margaret. She could feel the comb sliding through her hair, could smell the lily-of-the-valley perfume dotted on her neck.

Just as she was looking up to meet her reflection in the mirror, a car alarm went off outside and Augusta jolted awake. The delicate melody that Margaret had been singing still spun its way through her mind, though. *Let no man steal your thyme.* It was so familiar, yet she couldn't for the life of her think where she might have heard it before. With her eyes closed, she lingered on the edge of waking, desperately trying to keep the dream from fading away.

But it was gone. When she finally opened her eyes, it took her a moment to remember where she was. Some days she still woke up and expected to see the hanging plants and tapestry pinned to the wall of the room she and Chris had shared for years. Instead, now she was greeted by the slightly demonic grin of Mickey Mouse on her dresser, and a faded *Titanic* movie poster.

It was Saturday, which usually meant pancakes. Sure enough, when she'd sleepily shuffled into the kitchen, the smell of sizzling batter greeted her.

"Look who's awake," her mother said, expertly flipping a pancake. "I was about to go in and check that you were still breathing."

"Yeah, yeah," Augusta managed between yawns. Already the dream was little more than a hazy memory. "Is there any coffee?"

Her mother nodded toward the coffee maker on the counter and went back to her flipping.

Perching on one of the counter stools, Augusta blew on the piping hot coffee. "I found some boxes under the bed," she said, watching her mother's reaction.

Her mother didn't look up. "Oh?"

"It looked like there were papers and some photos in them." She paused. "I think they belonged to Dad."

Now her mother's hand stilled. "I think I put some of his things in there to store, now that you mention it."

Augusta knew that her mother didn't want to talk about it, but she pressed anyway. "I'd like to go through it all, maybe do some research on our family." Working in the archives looking for Margaret had made her hungrier for answers about her own origins.

Finally turning, her mother gave her the patented Pat-Podos-Is-Not-Doing-This-Today look. "I already told you, you don't need to ask my permission. Do whatever you want with it."

Augusta brushed her mother's cheek with a kiss. "Okay, Mom. We don't have to talk about it," she said. She grabbed a plate of pancakes to placate her, and then went back to her room.

Her parents had been separated when her dad had died, and his death had left a host of what-ifs in its wake: what if he had lived—would her parents have eventually gotten back together? What if they hadn't split up in the first place? Would his heart still suddenly have stopped beating while he was eating dinner alone in his apartment?

Apparently, her father hadn't updated his will in a while, because her mother had been listed as his beneficiary, and after he'd died, all his boxes and personal stuff came back to the house. Augusta doubted her mother had even so much as looked in them, and she was curious to see what there was.

Coffee in hand and music on, Augusta got comfortable on the floor of her old room and pulled out the boxes. Most of them looked like old work papers, invoices and receipts, and that kind of stuff. A thick envelope held snapshots from what must have been her parents' honeymoon in Hawaii. A younger version of her mom with big, curly hair stood in front of a waterfall with a broad smile on her face. There were a couple of them snorkeling, her dad looking goofy in his flippers and too-small swimming trunks. Underneath the honeymoon photos there was one of her dad at a Red Sox game, wearing a faded Boston sweatshirt and eating a giant hot dog. That had been his lucky sweatshirt, and he'd worn it for every single postseason game.

Putting aside the photos, she pulled out a big manila envelope full of what looked like legal documents including her father's discharge papers from the navy and her parents' marriage certificate. Then something else caught her eye. Augusta sat up straighter, ignoring the stabbing pins and needles from sitting in the same position for so long. A family tree.

Her father's side didn't have any surprises; his family had emigrated from Poland in the 1920s and had married into other Polish-American families. But her mother's side had always been a bit of a mystery. Since her parents had been older when they had her, her paternal grandparents had died before she was born and her maternal grandparents while she was in grade school. Her mother had been an only child, and her father had one sister with no children of her own. Family gatherings had always been small and subdued affairs.

She traced her finger up her mother's side of the tree. Her grandmother's maiden name sounded vaguely familiar, but she couldn't place why or where she might have seen it. The line went back almost to the mid-nineteenth century, when her mother's ancestors had made the journey from Italy to Ellis Island. But there was an American line, too, full of names and offshoots that Augusta had never known even existed, like Hale and Montrose, Barrett and Bishop. She wanted to copy them all down and put them in some sort of spreadsheet, maybe even get an account on a genealogical website to investigate further. It was an overwhelming prospect at the moment, so she carefully folded the family tree back up and put it in a folder for later.

There wasn't much else of interest in the boxes, but as she was putting all the papers and photos back in, something slid out from between them.

It was a tortoiseshell comb, glossy and delicate, and clearly very, very old. There was something familiar about it, as if she'd seen it before, maybe as a child, and she wondered if her mother had once used it. On a whim, she lifted it and ran it through her hair. It snagged on her curls almost immediately, but that wasn't what made her breath catch. She'd felt this comb before, felt the weight of it in her hands, felt the teeth slide through her hair. It was the comb that Margaret—that *she*—had been using in her dream.

★ ★ ★

Monday couldn't come fast enough. As soon as she stepped foot inside Harlowe House, Augusta said some cursory hellos to Jill, Sharon and Reggie, and ran upstairs to her office. She hadn't been able to forget the dream or the tortoiseshell comb. There had to be something about Margaret, somewhere. What was the link between her and the comb? Could it really be a coincidence that she'd had a dream about Margaret using a comb, only to find the *exact* same one later that day?

Reaching for the book of Tynemouth oral histories, Augusta flipped through it for the umpteenth time, rereading the scant lines about Margaret as if she hadn't already memorized them. Maybe there were some other mentions of her in the book, however oblique. Hopefully, Augusta began at the beginning, hungrily reading every interview. Eventually her need for information about Margaret faded to the background as she lost herself in the stories of other people who had lived long ago.

As she read, an idea took root in her mind. There were a lot of other interesting interviews with women in the book that would be good for her exhibit, but they were all older, from at least the 1970s. It would be great to get new interviews done, bring in a fresher perspective of Tynemouth from the women who lived there. The only problem was, Augusta had no idea who lived in Tynemouth or where to start. She decided to solicit some advice at lunch that day.

"You should interview my aunt," Reggie told her. He was leaning against the counter, eating leftovers out of a Tupperware container. "She's lived here since she came from Portugal in the '60s and has some wild stories about going out on the fishing boats with her father and brothers."

"Oh, you know who else?" Jill chimed in. "Who was that artist that did the driftwood sculptures for our winter exhibit? She was fantastic, and I remember her having tons of stories about Tynemouth from when she was a child. Claudia Linton. She lives right in town."

Augusta returned to her desk buzzing with excitement. Her afternoon consisted of phone calls and emails, setting up interviews, and putting the word out on the local community website that Harlowe House was looking for women to be interviewed for an upcoming exhibit.

The sculptor who Jill had suggested answered her phone right away, and Augusta had barely had a chance to get organized before she found herself at a cottage tucked on a little side street. Clouds had moved in from the ocean, a light rain starting to fall on the large driftwood sculptures in the yard. Ringing the doorbell, Augusta stood back, drumming her fingers on her thigh. As she waited, she found that she was suddenly nervous. She had no experience conducting interviews, and this was all happening faster than she had expected.

But she didn't have a chance for second guesses, because the door opened revealing an older woman with warm brown skin and a broad, friendly smile.

"You must be the girl from Harlowe House," she said, extending a hand that jingled with bangles. "Come on in."

"Thanks for agreeing to speak with me, and so quickly," Augusta said, returning her handshake.

Claudia waved her inside. "Are you kidding? I love Harlowe House. They've always been good to me and the local artist community. It's the least I can do." She invited Augusta to get comfortable on the couch, then turned off the music that had been playing on a record player. "Can I get you some tea or coffee? I think I have some pop, too."

"No, thank you." Augusta wanted to get started as soon as possible and hopefully put her nerves to rest.

"I've never done something like this before," Claudia said, sitting on a chair and carefully arranging her wool poncho. "Are you going to record it?"

"I do have a recorder, if you're comfortable with that," Augusta told her. "I'll take notes, too, but Harlowe House would love to also have the oral record. It's totally up to you, though."

Claudia nodded. "Yeah, okay. That's fine. Just to warn you, though—I've been told I have the gift of gab, so you might get more than you need."

Breathing an inward sigh of relief that her interviewee was making this so easy, Augusta set up her phone to record. "When you're ready, just tell me your full name and age."

Claudia sent her a sharp look. "You can have my name, but I don't even tell my children my age."

Claudia was a dream to interview. She mostly talked about her childhood in Tynemouth, and she was a natural storyteller, peppering her anecdotes with vivid details. "I know I'm going to sound like an old lady, but everything really was cheaper back in the day. I could get fried clams at Tony's for fifty cents and see a movie with the change."

Augusta dutifully took notes, asking the occasional question to guide her along.

"How long has your family been in the area?"

Pursing her lips, Claudia appeared to do some mental calculation. "Oh, a long time. My mother's family was always here as far as I know, and my father's family emigrated from Trinidad in the 1950s."

"Do you have any stories passed down from your relatives about Tynemouth? Like, really old ones?" Maybe if she was lucky, Claudia would be able to corroborate some of the other stories in the oral history book, like the one about Margaret Harlowe's ghost.

"How much time do you have?" Claudia laughed. "If I'd known you were interested in old stuff, I would have pulled out some of my family keepsakes. Let me see what I can put my hands on." She got up and started rummaging around in a desk in the corner. When she returned, she handed Augusta a faded shoebox held closed with a rubber band.

"Those are family mementos from over the years. Stuff I don't really know what to do with, but is too important to throw out."

Augusta opened the box. Just like her father's, it was filled with snapshots and old papers, little mementos. Carefully rummaging through everything, her hand found a palm-sized wooden object the shape of an arrow. It was impossibly smooth and beautiful. "What's this?"

Claudia leaned over to look. "I think it's called a shuttle. It would have been used for mending fishing nets back in the day. Kind of like a big sewing needle."

"Was someone in your family a fisherman?"

"Oh, probably. But this didn't belong to any of them. This belonged to a great-aunt in the 1800s. According to my grandmother, she had a little business mending nets for the fishermen."

Augusta ran her fingers over the satin-smooth grain of the wood. "That's amazing. I never thought about women being in the fishing industry back then, but of course they must have been."

Claudia nodded. "From what I remember my grandmother telling me, this auntie was a real character."

"How so?"

"I don't know if it was because there weren't many other Black folks around or what, but she had a reputation for being a bit of an outsider, maybe even a witch."

Augusta looked up at this. "Really?"

"Mmm-hmm. I heard all kinds of stories, but you have to take them with a grain of salt because they've been passed down over generations and probably embellished a bit over the years. Apparently, sea captains would pay her to calm the seas for them before they set sail, and they said that she could weave spells into the nets to double or even triple their catch."

"Okay, that's awesome," Augusta said as she continued turning the shuttle over in her hands. "Do you know anything else about her? I'd love to include her in our exhibit."

Claudia tapped her finger against her chin in thought. "There was some kind of drama around her and how she left Tynemouth. I remember my grandmother making a big deal of it, saying that Phebe got mixed up with a rich white girl who got her into trouble. My grandmother was pretty angry on her behalf. If there was ever a woman to hold a grudge, it was Grandma Lou, so I tend to believe that she knew what she was talking about. Anyway, she said this girl got mixed up in some sort of occult business, and Phebe ended up taking the fall for her. Forced Aunt Phebe right out of town."

The hairs on Augusta's neck stood up. She wasn't sure how she knew, but she was certain that Claudia was talking about Margaret. She hadn't even been thinking about Margaret, but there she was all the same, a shadowy figure living on through the story of this woman. Flicking her tongue over her suddenly dry lips, she asked, "Do you know what the girl's name was?"

Claudia shrugged. "I have no idea. Whatever happened, no one thought it was important enough to write it down. Phebe ended up moving out of the area, and my grandmother mentioned her being buried somewhere in Boston."

Claudia had moved on and was telling her a story about a beached whale back in the '90s, but Augusta couldn't seem to focus. All she could think about was Margaret and what had transpired between her and Phebe. She could practically envision the dark-haired Margaret, beautiful and tempestuous. How many other people had fallen under her spell, had found themselves in trouble when her passion had turned stormy? For the first time since starting her hunt for Margaret, she began to wonder if her beautiful muse from the painting had had a darker side, as well.

19

Margaret

I lean'd my back against some young oak
Thinking it a sturdy tree
But first it bent and then it broke
So did my love prove false to me.

—"The Water is Wide," Traditional Folk Song

WHY WAS I so nervous? I had always known what I wanted, and I cared little for the opinions of others. Yet as I left Phebe's cottage with Shadow at my heels, my palms were damp, my breath short and fast. Perhaps some part of me knew what was to come.

The day was fine and fair with crisp blue skies, the kind of day for which sailors pray. I had decided that whether Jack claimed the baby as his and married me or not, that I would keep and raise the child. Henry was convinced that Jack would abandon me. "Fear not," Henry had said, "I won't let anything happen to you. Come to Boston and I'll see that you and the babe are cared for." Oh, what a child I had felt like then, as my older brother had laid out my options and taken control of the situation. I wanted to prove Henry wrong, but deep down I feared he was right.

Taking a deep breath outside the shop, I pushed open the

door, only to find that a young Black man was working behind the counter, not Jack. I mumbled my excuse when he asked if I needed help, and then stumbled back outside. I had assumed that Jack would be at the store, even though I knew little of what he did during the days when I did not see him. I could not go to his house—or rather—I *would* not go to his house. I had too much self-respect to throw myself upon his step and beg admittance.

I was standing in the street, pondering which way to go, when I saw him. He was dressed sharply in plaid trousers and a frock coat, and it struck me that I rarely saw him in such a way; usually in our encounters his arms were bare, his collar open and hair tousled. No sooner had I taken in these details than my gaze slid to the young woman hanging on his arm. She was saying something, and he was leaning down to hear her, a faint smile on his lips. Lucy Clerkenwell was everything that I was not: petite, blonde, demure and modest. She was the picture of a seaside rose with her blushing cheeks and her pretty frock of blue silk with lace peeking out of the collar.

Perhaps he was just escorting her home from the shop or something else equally innocent, but there was something in the way she was looking up at him with naked adoration that told me it was anything but. The bottom of my stomach felt like it was falling, falling, falling.

A cart reeking of fish rumbled by, and someone shouted at me to mind myself before I was run over. My shock lasted only a moment, and then was replaced by seething anger.

I knew the rumors about him and Lucy—how could I not? I kept abreast of everything in Tynemouth—but it was one thing to hear about it in passing, and quite another to see her hand possessively wrapped around the crook of his arm.

Jack only looked momentarily surprised when he saw me marching toward him, murder in my eyes. Lucy clung tighter to his arm.

Jack made the mistake of speaking first. Clearing his throat, he gave me a short nod. "Hello, Miss Harlowe."

Oh, but I could have smacked him. "'Miss Harlowe' in the street, is it? Do you only reserve pet names such as 'wildflower' and 'my little witch' for such occasions when your trousers are down and my back up against a tree?"

Lucy recoiled, her big blue eyes going round as saucers. I took some satisfaction in making her pouty lips go tight, the roses in her cheeks fade in color. "Maggie, I—" Jack started.

I spit at his feet. "Don't you call me that, Jack Pryce. Don't you dare."

People in the road had stopped to watch the spectacle unfold, but I couldn't spare them an ounce of care. Let them stare, let them think the witch girl mad. The man to whom I'd entrusted my heart and my future was parading down Main Street with another woman and I couldn't muster an ounce of shame or modesty.

He pulled his arm out of Lucy's grasp and I reveled in the displeasure in her pretty blue eyes. "Please, Maggie, not here. I can explain everything." His voice was low and urgent, and I hated that he looked so beautiful with the sun in his dark hair.

I would not give him the satisfaction of explaining himself. Turning on my heel, I stalked back home to the woods. Loitering oyster shuckers in their rough caps and coveralls stared at me, their fingers crooked and malodorous from years of prying open shells. Sooty buildings, crusted in salt and disappointment, rose up on either side of me, threatening to grind me down into the mud and fish guts that polluted the road. It was a small town full of small people and smaller dreams. I might have settled for any number of the men here, but I wanted only Jack. Though my heart was fit to shatter, I would have given anything to hear the sound of Jack following after me, to have him catch me by the arms and demand that I forgive him and give him another chance. But there were no footsteps, no grand declarations. He was not coming after me. He had made his choice, and I was left to suffer the consequences.

20

Augusta

AUGUSTA TOOK HER time walking back to Harlowe House after her interview with Claudia, the sharp salt air bringing her muddled thoughts into focus. If only there was some way to find material evidence of Margaret and what had transpired between her and Phebe. It would be like finding a needle in a haystack, and that was if there even *was* any evidence. There was one place where she hadn't looked, so as soon as she got back to her office, she grabbed a clipboard and headed out back. She waved to Reggie, who was across the lawn weed-whacking, and let herself into the carriage house.

Ghosts or no, there was no getting around the fact that the Harlowe carriage house storage was creepy. It was stuffy and quiet, the sounds from outside muffled, the stillness amplified, and even with the lights on it seemed shrouded in shadows. Yet it was one of the best places on the property to work, just Augusta and the objects with no distractions.

This was where all the objects that had never properly been inventoried or accessioned had ended up. Jill was eager for her to get everything inventoried so they could start moving things to their climate-controlled storage in Boston and convert the carriage house into a space for community functions and exhibits.

She set herself up with a chair, propped up her phone on a shelf to play some music and then picked up where she had left off in cataloging. As much as she wanted to jump around and dig for something that could have been Margaret's, she forced herself to go in order. Most of the objects were from when the house had been bought in the 1960s and furnished with reproduction antiques, but there was also a good amount of stuff that had been left in the house when it was abandoned. A big cardboard box filled with mildewed *National Geographic* magazines and rusted tools was next on the shelf, so Augusta dutifully recorded everything, snapped a picture for her condition reports and moved the box to her pile to bring back to the house.

When she reached for the next item on the shelf, her hand stilled. Amongst the cardboard boxes and rusted tools there sat a gleaming mahogany lap desk, seemingly untouched by dust or age. It was the sort that would have sat on the user's lap, the slanted top providing an inviting surface for writing.

Carefully, Augusta opened the lid with her gloved hand, releasing a puff of warm, woodsy air. Her heart skipped a beat when she saw the faint inscription of a name. Gently lifting it closer, she was disappointed to see that it wasn't Margaret Harlowe, but Ida Foster. She frowned. The name was familiar, but she couldn't immediately place it. Inside the writing desk was a time capsule of accoutrements for a young woman's correspondence in the nineteenth century. Each item, from the inkwell to the pens to the faded stamps, would need to be individually cataloged and assessed for conservation. Just as Augusta was closing the lid to put it back, her fingers found a ridge underneath the lid. A false panel.

She hesitated. It could be risky to open it if the wood wasn't stable, but just like in her hallucinations, she felt herself moving as if from beyond her control, and before she could stop herself, she was sliding the wood to the side.

Tucked flat inside the hidden compartment was a slim bundle of letters bound with the faded remnants of a pink ribbon.

She really should put the letters back in the drawer, make a note, and then let Jill know what she had found; opening them would be unprofessional at best. But instead, she found herself carefully leafing through them.

A quick scan through the first couple of letters revealed that Ida Foster had been George Harlowe's wife. Augusta remembered now that George and Ida had inherited Harlowe House after Clarence Harlowe Senior's death, and had lived there with their four children well into the 1910s.

For all Augusta knew, these could be duplicates, with copies already in the archives. But something told her that she was the first person to see these letters in over a century.

Scanning the looping cursive lines, she gathered that Ida had been corresponding with George Harlowe following their engagement, but before their marriage. They weren't steamy love letters by any means; they were disappointingly mundane. Ida talked about her trousseau and plans to have some new gloves made. There was some gossip from a day trip she'd taken up the coast with girls from her church group. It wasn't exciting, but this kind of information would be invaluable to the historical interpretation of the house and the family. Augusta was just resolving to put them back and let Jill know when a line caught her eye.

I understand if you wish the wedding to be postponed. Of course, it is not what we had hoped, but my parents will understand. It is a great tragedy, and I cannot imagine how this must be weigh-

ing on your heart. You will forgive my indelicacy in asking, but do the authorities suspect foul play?

Augusta sucked in her breath. Foul play? She flipped through to the next letter and scanned past the initial pleasantries.

You yourself often spoke of her queer ways and independent nature... Are you certain that she did not simply leave of her own accord? Perhaps she had a secret beau and has taken herself off to marry. Not of course, that such a thing would be desirable, but certainly it would be better than the alternative.

Another letter, dated nearly a month later.

As to that subject on which we were arguing, we will speak of it no more. I am sorrier than I can say, and wish only for your grief to fade so that you may be hale and hearty once more. I miss your bright merry eyes, and the laughter which we shared, and I am certain that she would not wish you to go on in such a wretched fashion.

I am, as always, your faithful and loving,
IDA

Rocking back on her heels, Augusta sat absorbing what she had just read. The letters felt heavy in her hand, substantial evidence of something very real that had happened long ago. They did not mention Margaret by name, but she was certain that they were referencing her. She did a quick calculation in her head. If the dresses mentioned in the ledgers were bought in 1858 when Margaret was perhaps four or five, then she would have been about twenty when these letters were written.

Augusta carefully put them back in order and pressed them into the compartment. She would have to tell Jill and Sharon about her discovery and how she had found it. They probably wouldn't be thrilled that she had gone ahead and opened the compartment, but she had to imagine that their excitement over the find would outweigh any disapproval.

Her playlist had long ago stopped, and outside it was growing dark. After she packed up her stuff and locked the carriage house behind her, she stood for a moment, letting the cool evening air wash across her skin. Aside from the occasional passing car, she might have been in the 1870s. "Margaret," she whispered into the dusk, "what happened to you?"

21

Margaret

My garden was planted well
With flowers everywhere,
But I had not the liberty then for to choose
The flower that I lov-ed dear.

—"The Seeds of Love," Traditional Folk Song

MY VISION BLURRED, my world spun. As soon as I had escaped from Main Street, I stumbled behind a stone wall and leaned over and retched.

I didn't want to go home. I didn't want to see Henry's smug face when he learned that Jack had betrayed me, that he had been right all along. I didn't want to go sit with people who had lied to me for years about who I was, people who had stolen me away from my mother. As I stood with my boots growing damp in the wet leaves and the cold wind pricking at my skin, I realized there was only one other place to go.

But the closer I got to Phebe's house, the more I could feel that something was wrong. I hastened my step as I approached the cottage. The usually tidy shell path was scattered and unkempt, Phebe's beloved wind chimes lay tangled on the ground, and one of the front windows was broken.

My problems momentarily forgotten, I rushed up the front steps. "Phebe?" I banged on the door until I heard footsteps inside and it opened a crack.

"Oh, it's you," Phebe said, stepping back, arms crossed. She looked tired. There were dark rings under her eyes, and her shoulders were tight and hunched.

"What's happened? Who did this?" I thought that Phebe would invite me in, put some tea on and explain everything. But she did not invite me in, and her expression remained stony.

"What happened? I'll tell you what happened. *You* happened, Margaret Harlowe. Word of your dark doings has spread throughout town, and who do you think has paid the price? Certainly not you," she said, pinning me with a disgusted look.

I stood there, my mind sluggishly working to understand, until it finally hit me like a cold wave. It had been weeks since the men had shown up at our doorstep, and I had all but forgotten about their threats. How could I have known that they were serious? They were all bluster and show, and I had assumed that was to be the end of it. Yet every word they had said had been true; they had found the person that I cared about the most and visited their rage on her.

"But they have no reason to accuse you! Jenny Hough came to me—she knows I acted alone."

Phebe leveled an exasperated look at me, her brown eyes flaring with impatience. "You really have no idea how the world works, do you?" She moved to close the door but I stopped her.

"Wait. Phebe, please. May I come in?"

"You've caused me enough trouble. This is the thanks I get for taking you under my wing, for giving you hospitality when everyone else shut their doors on you. Well, I'm not staying in this town a minute longer, not so long as *you're* here, walking about and causing me grief."

"You can't leave. People love you here," I said, desperately. "No one would dare lay a finger on you."

She gave me a hard, almost pitying look, and I felt like a child. "No, they might not dare lay a finger on *you*, being the rich white girl that you are, but no one would so much as blink an eye if my house were to burn down. They can come to me with their fishing nets and ask me for charms and spells, but it isn't me that they respect, it's the novelty of someone like me."

Was she right? I couldn't believe that she was. I had seen for myself how people revered her, sought her out. Everyone in Tynemouth lived in relative harmony, it seemed to me. But as my gaze swept anew over the jagged glass of the window, the muddy boot prints through the little herb garden, a disturbing sense of ignorance spread over me. I had always thought myself so above the rest of the townspeople; had I been too high in a tower of my own making that I had not seen the reality of life for others? Was I oblivious to the dramas and hardships that others endured outside of my front door?

Phebe was still watching me with unnerving scrutiny. "Mmm-hmm," she said, as if sensing my deepest thoughts. "You're beginning to realize you don't know as much as you thought. Well, you go muse on that somewhere other than my front step. I don't want to see you again."

And with that, she shut the door.

22

Augusta

"WOW. THESE ARE...AMAZING."

It had been a day since Augusta's discovery of Ida Foster's letters, and she'd barely been able to wait until Jill had come in that morning to show her. Jill carefully slipped the letters back into the Mylar sleeves Augusta had made for them and placed them on the desk. There wasn't any reason for Augusta to feel proud or protective of the letters—anyone who had opened the desk probably would have found them—but as Jill leaned over to look at them again, Augusta felt her heart tighten a little.

Sharon was standing behind Jill, reading over her shoulder. "Lori is going to be very excited. It'll be interesting to see if we have George's side of the correspondence in the archives."

Augusta wasn't holding her breath. If the letters indeed referenced Margaret and her disappearance, then she couldn't imagine that they were in the archives after she'd already been through everything with a fine-toothed comb.

"Speaking of the archives," Jill said, "I do want to touch base about your exhibit. We've got time, but it can't hurt to look ahead. Did your trip to Boston turn anything up?"

"Yes and no." Augusta filled her in on the ledgers and the entries for a girl's wardrobe, and her theory about what it might mean for proof of Margaret's existence.

"It is compelling," Jill agreed. "I'd like to get Lori's take on it before jumping to any conclusions, though. If nothing else, it should give you a good starting point for your exhibit. But don't get too wrapped up in just finding Margaret—I'd still like to see you broaden your scope a bit."

Augusta said she agreed, but she had no intention of abandoning Margaret now, not when she had just found such a tantalizing clue.

Sharon glanced at her watch. "I have to run to Boston, so I'll take these with me if you're all set?"

Augusta nodded, knowing that she didn't really have any choice, as much as she would have liked to keep the letters in her desk so she could pore over them again. She kicked herself for not taking any photos of them with her phone first.

"Will you be okay if I duck out early, too?" Jill asked. "My in-laws are coming from Beijing and Brian wants to meet them at the airport."

"Yeah, of course. I can arm the house and lock up when I leave."

"Great. Reggie is just across town at the hardware store, so if you need anything you can give him a buzz."

The old house was so peaceful when she was the only one there, and she was looking forward to making a mug of tea, turning up her music and getting some work done.

A storm was rolling in and Augusta grabbed her cardigan and settled in at her desk. On Main Street, the old-fashioned lamps were turning on, and the first raindrops started to patter against the windows. Chris had been texting her all day, so when she saw her screen light up, she turned off her phone. She wasn't going to let him steal her precious work time.

Opening a new tab on her browser, she scrolled the apartment listings on Craigslist and was surprised to find that she might be able to afford her own studio apartment in Tynemouth on her new salary. Maybe she would even get a cat. Or two.

A noise downstairs pulled her out of her search. Turning down the music, she strained her ear. She'd become used to the idiosyncrasies of the house and the constant background of creaks and groans. But this didn't sound like settling floorboards, the scurry of the mouse that was forever outwitting Reggie or even ghostly footsteps. This sounded distinctly human and very much in the present. Someone was banging on the door, trying to get in.

Sighing, she grabbed her phone and shoved it in her pocket. There was always a handful of people who either didn't see the sign or didn't believe it when it said they were closed and insisted on coming to the front door and pounding away until someone answered.

Augusta hurried downstairs to where the pounding was growing louder. "We're closed!" she called, putting her ear to the door. She waited for a grumble and the receding sound of footsteps.

"It's me," a familiar voice said curtly. "I texted you, but you didn't answer. Can you open the door?"

Augusta's heart sank. If only it were a belligerent tourist trying to get in. But it wasn't. It was Chris.

She hadn't seen him since the night of the breakup, and she'd left all his texts unanswered. They had vacillated between terse one-line messages like we need to talk or call me, and more sinister ones like: I'm standing on the pier. I don't know what to do without you. The guilt she'd felt had been almost unbearable, but she knew that that was what he was counting on and that she couldn't give in.

But now he was banging down the door to her workplace. She only waffled for a moment before unlocking the door and stepping back.

He looked surprised when the door swung open, his fist still half-raised in mid-knock. Behind him the passing headlights of cars illuminated him in flashes. "I texted you," was all he said.

It was pouring outside, so Augusta gestured for him to step inside, and closed the door behind him. They stood awkwardly in the front hall, surrounded by the artifacts of another era. They'd only been broken up for two weeks, but already he felt like he belonged to another chapter of her life, one she had been long overdue in ending.

"I'm working," she said tersely. She didn't like the collision of her worlds, his intrusion into her sanctuary.

"You didn't answer my texts," he said again. "You don't get to just toss me aside after five years and act like I don't exist. You owe me better than that."

For a moment, his words found their mark and she felt the familiar guilt. Maybe she did owe him a real discussion about where they stood. But then she thought of Leo and what he'd said in the car about feeling guilty, how she'd felt so light and happy just sitting beside him. "I couldn't answer you. I didn't want to give you false hope."

He stared at her, his fair features darkening. "You're such a phony, do you know that?"

"I am not," she responded, instantly feeling like a little kid baited into an argument.

He moved closer and she automatically took a step back. "You act like a victim, but you're the one who's always running away and leaving a mess behind you."

"Did you just come here to pick a fight?" There was something in his eyes, something about the way he was moving that wasn't right. "Wait. Are you...are you *drunk*?"

She had only ever seen Chris drunk once before, and it had

been at some after-work event of his at a bar. He'd mostly com-
plained and been a little surly when the bartender had cut him
off. Aside from that, Augusta didn't know what kind of drunk
he was, and she certainly didn't know what he would do in a
tense situation such as this one. "I think you should leave," she
said before he had a chance to answer.

"I'm not drunk," he said. His voice was so steady that she almost believed him, but the redness in his eyes and alcohol on
his breath gave him away.

Suddenly, she felt warning bells going off in her head. "Chris,
we can talk later over the phone, but I think you should go now."

"We won't talk later! You're just saying that. You're going to
keep ignoring me like you always do."

Why had it taken her so long to see how broken their relationship was? How had she let it get this far? Everything that
was happening in that moment confirmed that she'd made the
right choice in ending things.

"You made me think you loved me. Then you got this new
job and made new friends and decided that I didn't fit your
new life, so you just threw me out like trash. You use people,
Augusta."

It wasn't true, was it? *Had* she used him? He'd certainly been
a comfort to her in the aftermath of her father's death, and
perhaps she owed him more than how they'd left things. "I'm
sorry," she forced herself to say. "It's not you. I just don't think
I can be in a relationship right now. I just need some time to
figure things out."

"What things? Why do you need time all of a sudden?" He
narrowed his eyes and a truly horrified look crossed his face.
"You're seeing someone else, aren't you?"

"What? No, of course not." Yet Augusta could feel her cheeks
heating as she thought of Leo, and the way he made her feel
when they were together.

"It's that guy I saw you with that day, isn't it?" he asked, as if he had been reading her mind.

"I work with him, that's all." She hadn't done anything wrong, but her guilt only burned hotter. "He isn't anybody. I'm not seeing anybody. I told you—I just need some time to myself."

Chris took her by her shoulders, moving surprisingly quickly for someone who was drunk. "Look into my eyes and tell me that he doesn't mean anything to you. I want to see if you're lying."

She shrunk from his touch. "I'm not lying!"

It happened fast, yet it felt like slow motion. Chris was pushing her up against the wall, something she never in a million years would have thought him capable of. Maybe that's why she was so slow to react: she couldn't believe it.

"Chris!" Her head banged against the wall from the force of his push. Stunned, she just stood there, afraid to so much as breathe. She had only narrowly missed hitting the painting of a clipper ship that hung above her.

The room was deadly silent, Chris's breathing and her heart beating in her ears the only sounds. He still had his hands on her shoulders, but he was frozen, as if he couldn't believe it either. Above her, the painting rattled in its frame. Was that it? Was he going to hit her? Slam her back into the wall again? The eyes that looked back at her were those of a stranger, and she had no idea what he was thinking or going to do next.

It couldn't have been more than a second from when her body hit the wall, but it seemed to happen in one stretched-out moment that went on forever. Then, with the force of a boulder hurtling down a mountain, the painting came crashing down. It clipped Chris on the shoulder, sending him reeling backward. They both watched as it clattered to the ground, like a spinning top slowly coming to rest.

Augusta knew that she should have been scared for her life, but all she could think about was how much the painting was worth and how horrible it would be if it had been damaged because of her. Chris must have been thinking the same thing, because he took an unsteady step back and said, "I didn't mean to do that. Is that worth a lot of money?"

"You're more concerned for the painting than for me? Jesus, Chris, you could have killed me!"

For the first time since barging in, he looked genuinely stricken, as if just realizing what he'd done. "That's not what I meant. I—"

"Just go." She was shaking, and hardly registered the door shutting behind Chris as he slunk out. Slumping down on the floor, she pressed the palms of her hands into her eyes until her vision swam. What did she do now? Call the police? Jill? God, how would she explain this to Jill? Hefting herself up, she inspected the fallen painting. Though the painting and the frame were old, the mounting mechanisms were state-of-the-art, no doubt Reggie's handiwork. She ran her finger over the back of the frame, then studied the corresponding mount on the wall. It was intact. Those mounts were designed to withstand earthquakes, yet had come off the wall with the barest of impact from her.

The air in the hall had gone stale, and for a moment she thought she might be on the edge of a hallucination again. Because nothing about what had just happened made sense.

The painting hadn't fallen. It had flown.

23

Margaret

'Tis not the frost, that freezes fell,
Nor blowing snow inclemency,
'Tis not such cold that makes me cry,
But my love's heart grown cold to me.

—"The Water is Wide," Traditional Folk Song

I FEEL THE energy change as soon as he enters the house. The delicate balance of old and new, feminine and masculine, is disturbed by his presence. I might hate men for the wrong done to me, but hundreds of men have come and gone through my doorway over the years, and none have aroused my attention such as this one. No, this man carries a dark energy within him. He is the angry sea, and the young woman, my champion, the little boat upon which he releases his wrath. But more than that, he threatens to undo that for which I have been working.

Leaving books open, gently nudging her in the right direction is all fine and good, but soon I will need to do more. I watch her as she absorbs what has just happened, and I can see the confusion in her face, wondering what caused the painting to fly. Does she know whose blood runs through her veins? Does she know how I watch her, and why? She may not know she needs me yet, but she will, and I have need for her.

★ ★ ★

It had been nearly a month since I had learned the dark truth of my origins, a month since Jack had left my heart tattered and bruised. Tynemouth was suffocating with its smallness, every familiar building a reminder of what I had lost. I could no longer walk past Pryce's Grocery without Jack's betrayal piercing me anew, nor stand outside of Phebe's empty cottage and feel anything other than a guilt so heavy as to be unbearable. I needed a change of scenery. So when I received a letter from George in Boston saying that he needed to see me about a personal matter, I all but leaped at the chance to escape. I had not spoken with George at any length since the revelation about my family that night, and I missed him, even if he was not truly my brother. Any part he had played in the deception I could forgive, if only because I was so very lonely, and longed for some shred of normalcy and love.

It felt good to leave Tynemouth behind, even if only for a day. Though Boston could not boast of the same wild beauty as the coast, there was nonetheless a singular energy that pulsed through the city and bade me come take up my place among the tall edifices and bustle of people.

The Boston office was a grand building, much improved and expanded in the recent decades. Our home in Tynemouth was modest, and my frugal parents lived below their means, but Harlowe Mansion was a true beacon of commerce and industry. I found George in the large wood-paneled office downstairs, looking altogether out of place among the heavy account books and imposing brass lamps. He rose from the desk, where he'd been tapping his pen against paper, gazing out the window. "Maggie," he said, embracing me. "But aren't you a sight for sore eyes."

Indeed, his eyes did look strained and red, and immediately my anger at my favorite brother faded. No matter that we were truly cousins; he would always be my brother. "Come now," I told him, leading him to the deep window seat where we could sit together, "a world where you are sad and down is not a world I care to live in. What's happened?"

He fiddled with the end of his curled mustache. "It's Ida. She's having doubts. I told her that I had a voyage coming up after the wedding and she didn't take it well."

My first instinct was anger on George's behalf. Perhaps I could punish Ida with a spell, make all her hair fall out. Who was she to complain when she had the greatest prize of all laid at her feet, that of George's love? But I stayed my anger, folding my hands in my lap.

"And she is willing to lose a lifetime of domestic bliss because of a few short months at the beginning of her marriage? Bah," I said. "The girl is a fool."

George gave me a sad smile. "She's the best of girls, but I appreciate your loyalty."

"She just has to be brought round," I told him. "Shall I speak to her?"

He looked dubious. "I'm not certain that would be such a good idea."

"George, I say this with all the esteem I hold for you—you have had a golden life, untouched by tragedy or adversity. Things have come easily to you and—no, let me finish—you've not had to struggle. You love Ida and she loves you. This will be resolved, but you may have to fight. Are you willing to fight for her?"

"Of course I am!" he said testily. "Only I don't see how we can come to an agreement. I cannot give up my occupation and—"

I stopped him. "No one is asking you to give up your occupation, least of all Ida, I suspect. She only wants to know that you prize her above all else. You must show her how much you will miss her, how much it pains you to leave her behind. If you love her as you say you do, then you must let the love shine through each and every word you utter to her. There can be no room for her fears and insecurities to fester."

"And if she does not change her mind?"

"Then she was not the woman you thought her to be. But if she is all things good and kind as you have told me many times, then she will." I watched couples stroll arm in arm outside the window, oblivious to the bittersweet vignette within. "If I had someone worthy of such a love, I would do anything to keep them," I said, trying not to let the bitterness creep into my voice. "I would cross oceans for them. I would fight battles for them, would carry them broken and cold home, tend to them and keep them safe with me always. I would not rest until they were by my side, where they belonged."

The sun had sunk low into the sky, the dim light coming through the windows no more than a grim reminder of coming winter. "Maggie," he said softly, taking my hands in his. "If ever there was a woman deserving of such a love, it is you."

The office was very quiet, the only sound the faraway traffic of Boston. I looked away quickly so that he could not see the tears filling my eyes. Was I deserving of such a love? I had thought so, once, but now I was not so sure. Phebe's words sat heavy within me, and I wondered if she was right after all, that I was selfish and naive. "Well," I said briskly, whisking a tear from my eye, "I have kept you from your work long enough."

He rose with me. "Thank you for coming. Thank you for—"

I stopped him with a kiss on the cheek, my hand lingering on his jaw. "Do not mention it. You would do the same for me." We parted—him back to his work, and I back to Tynemouth. Little could I know that it would be the last time I would ever see my dear George.

24

Augusta

AUGUSTA'S KNEE BOUNCED under her desk, her mug of coffee untouched. She was supposed to be writing up condition reports, but all she could do was replay her encounter with Chris the night before over and over in her head. She needed to tell Jill or Sharon about the painting and what had happened, there was no getting around it. Even if she hadn't seen any damage, that didn't mean that something hadn't come loose within the mounting mechanisms, or that a miniscule crack hadn't formed in the paint. Besides, she was fairly certain she should disclose that someone had been on the premises after hours.

Pushing her chair back, she slowly went across the hall. All she wanted to do was forget about the hatred and anger in Chris's eyes, and now it felt as if she was walking to her execution. As upsetting as her encounter with Chris had been, she was mortified that she now had to relive it for her coworkers.

What would Jill think of her? Would she lose Jill's trust? Would she lose her job?

As it turned out, both Jill and Sharon were across the hall, and they looked up when Augusta hesitantly knocked on the door. "Hey, can I talk with you for a minute?"

"Yeah, of course," Jill said. Sharon was moving to leave, but Augusta stopped her. "Actually, I think both of you should be here."

She didn't miss the look that passed between the two women, and Augusta swallowed. Closing the door behind her, she pulled up another chair and perched on the edge, trying to keep her knee from bouncing. Jill's classical music was still playing softly in the background. Outside, a little sparrow flitted between the branches of the oak tree.

"So, um, last night when I was working in the house, my ex-boyfriend showed up. I didn't know he was coming." Augusta stared at her hands, swallowing before continuing. "He was drunk, and he got aggressive and he pushed me." Augusta could still feel the shock as her body connected with the wall, the fear of not knowing what would come next. She took a breath and continued. "The painting in the hall fell off the wall. It doesn't seem to be damaged," she hurried to explain. "But I thought you should know what happened, and that Shayna should probably look at it to—"

Sharon stopped her, leaning forward and placing her hand on her arm. "Augusta, are you all right?"

"Oh, yeah, I'm fine. I thought you should just be aware so you could take a look at the painting and in case there are any insurance or liability issues with having someone being on the property after hours."

Jill and Sharon shared another look, and Augusta's stomach dropped. They were concerned, not for the painting, but for her. And suddenly she realized that she was *that* woman. She was the woman who stayed with the wrong man, and even though everyone would hurry to point out that it wasn't her fault, they would wonder deep down why she really stayed when she *had* to have known who he was. She was the woman who everyone pitied.

Just when she thought it couldn't get any worse, there was a knock at the door, and then Leo was sticking his head in. "Hey, is this a bad time? I have the summer program applications if you're ready to go over them."

"Actually, could you give us fifteen minutes?" Sharon asked.

Even though she was staring down at her hands in her lap, Augusta could feel Leo's questioning gaze on her. If she could have disappeared into thin air, she would have. "Yeah, no problem, I'll be downstairs."

Jill waited until the door had closed behind him. "We'll take a look at the painting later and see if we need to pass it on to conservation." She paused. "What about you, though? Do you have somewhere safe to stay?"

It was the same question Leo had asked a couple of weeks ago, and she'd laughed him off. "I'm staying with my mom. I don't think he would come there."

Sharon nodded. They were both being so painfully nice, so gentle. "We need to have better procedures in place," Sharon said to Jill. "Tynemouth is a small, safe town, but we're still a mostly women–run place and I don't like the idea of someone being alone here and closing up. Not," she added quickly, turning to Augusta, "that this is your fault in any way."

Augusta didn't say anything, hating how small she felt in front of two women she admired. They were talking about safety training and having an emergency protocol, but Augusta hardly heard them. "I have to go do something," she said, standing abruptly.

Jill looked a little startled, but gave her a reassuring smile. "Thanks for letting us know, Augusta," she said. "If you need anything, you know where to find me. Can you close the door behind you, please?"

They were going to talk about her. She supposed she was lucky that they weren't angry about the painting and that her job was safe, but as soon as she was down the hall and out of earshot, she sagged against the wall. Downstairs, she could hear a tour moving through the house, the low ripple of laughter at something the guide had said. The thought of going back to her office and getting work done seemed impossible. She didn't want to be there, didn't want to sit at her desk and pretend that everything was all right.

Tears swam in her eyes, and before she knew it, her entire body was racked with sobs. The last few weeks had finally caught up to her and she felt as if she was being crushed from the weight of everything—the breakup, the hallucinations, the confrontation with Chris. Just as she was about to make a break for the kitchen, Leo caught her coming up the stairs. Wonderful, just what she needed. She could only imagine what she looked like with her makeup running and her eyes red, but she was too tired to care, too tired to try to put on a brave face.

Leo took one look at her, and before she could wipe her tears or stammer out an excuse, he was gently pulling her to him, as if it was the most natural thing in the world. He didn't say anything, just let her cry. He felt good and safe, the muscles of his arms that she'd spent weeks memorizing wrapped around her, his steady presence reassuring her.

But even as he held her, she had to wonder: Could he be like Chris? She had once thought that Chris was the most attentive, kindest man, and look how wrong she had been. It was bittersweet to have Leo stroking her hair and murmuring reassurances when he was only doing it because it was what any friend would have done in the situation. Yet, she couldn't seem to bring herself to break away.

25

Augusta

WHEN SHE'D SNIFFLED back the last of her tears, Leo gently held her out at arm's length and studied her. "I think we should go get some coffee. Sound good?"

Augusta nodded, grateful for the chance to get out of the building. Since the incident with Chris, Harlowe House didn't feel like the sanctuary it had once been, and she didn't want to chance breaking down in front of a group of befuddled tourists. Leo let Jill and Sharon know they were popping out, and he led her downstairs, skirting past the tour group and out into the sun-drenched day.

Except for a couple of locals with newspapers and a guy with headphones working on his laptop, the coffee shop was mostly empty. "Nitro cold brew with almond milk and an extra shot, right?" Leo asked her after he'd gently installed her on the sofa in the back.

"Oh, yes. Thank you," she said, surprised that he had remembered her order. She tried to pay but Leo waved her off, so she waited on the sofa. With yellow twinkle lights strung over it was cozy—borderline romantic. A few minutes later Leo returned, balancing their two drinks and a plate with two thick slices of chocolate cake.

"It looked too good to pass up," he said as he placed everything on the table. "So," he said, as he sat down beside her.

"So," she replied.

"You don't have to tell me—"

He'd barely had a chance to say anything when the words came tumbling out of her mouth. "My ex-boyfriend came to Harlowe House and attacked me," she blurted out. She'd already told Jill and Sharon, and she'd rather he heard it from her than second-hand through veiled references. Before she could talk herself out of it, she told him everything from Chris showing up drunk and angry, to the painting that had seemed to fly off the wall.

The words hung heavy in the air, the acoustic coffee shop music filling the silence. "Please don't look at me like that." She didn't think she could bear his expression of pity and concern. "And please don't ask me if I'm okay. I'm physically fine, and anything else is beyond my ability to process right now."

He nodded, his gray eyes clear and unbearably kind. "I'm glad you're okay," he said softly. "You know I'm here if you want to talk more, but there's no pressure. Or I can just sit here and eat cake while you vent at me, whatever you want." He paused, his ghost of a smile fading. "Or, if you don't want to be around men right now, I get that, and I can give you some space."

"No," she said quickly. "Please don't go." What she really wanted was to feel his arms around her again, to block out the world for a little while, but that moment had already passed.

"You got it." He stretched his legs out, settled deeper into the couch, and they sipped their drinks in silence. The air between them was warm, comfortable. Everything about Leo was comfortable, as if they were old friends picking up where they'd left off after a long absence. The only thorn intruding on their serene bubble was that she wanted to be completely honest with him.

She found the words slipping out before she could stop herself. "I know this is going to sound crazy, but I think Harlowe House is haunted. Or rather, I'm haunted."

To her surprise, Leo's gaze remained steady. "Oh, yeah? What makes you say that?"

"Well," she started, not sure how to piece together all the strange things that had been happening to her, "the painting, for starters. There was no way it could have fallen off the wall the way that it did. It literally flew straight off the wall and then hit Chris—my head never even touched it. Then there's the books... every time I sit down at my desk there's another book I don't remember pulling, open to certain pages about Margaret Harlowe." She took a deep breath; this part was going to be harder to explain. "Since I've come to Harlowe, I've had some...hallucinations." Leo didn't say anything, so she continued. "On my first day I was in the old kitchen and it was just a flash of what the room must have looked like in the 1800s. But since then, they've become longer, more vivid, almost like I'm seeing the past of the house through someone else's eyes."

Never in a million years would she have confided in Chris about something like this. But Leo wasn't making faces or interrupting her, so she kept going. "At first, I thought it was just me being light-headed because, well, because sometimes I don't eat enough and I get dizzy. But I've been trying to be better about eating breakfast before I come in and it's still happening."

Leo set down his cup and tented his fingers. He looked incredibly serious, and she braced herself for him to finally ask her just what the hell she was talking about. But he surprised her. "I think we should look for her."

"Look for who?"

"Margaret. That's who this ghost is, right? You said that you keep finding books open to pages about her. And," he said, giving her a meaningful look, "she clearly is looking out for you."

Augusta hadn't thought about that. When the painting had flown off the wall, she had assumed the timing was coincidental. But what if it really had been Margaret trying to protect her? The thought was at once comforting and unnerving. "So you believe me?"

Leo shrugged. "Of course. If you say it happened, then it did. What other explanation could there be?"

There could be lots of other explanations, though most of them involved Augusta not being in full possession of her mental faculties. But in that moment, it really didn't matter. All that mattered was she had told Leo, and he had believed her.

"We should hit the archives again, do interviews with locals, anything to try to find out what happened to Margaret. You said something about an urban legend about her disappearing... there's gotta be something more to that story."

Augusta sat up straighter. "The letters," she said in a breath. At Leo's questioning look, she hurried to explain the letters she'd found in storage, how they hinted at some family tragedy. "And in my interview with Claudia she mentioned that her ancestor may have been involved with Margaret in some way."

"We should look at cemetery records, see if she's buried somewhere in the area." He was animated now, his enthusiasm boyishly charming. "Or police records. Did they have those in the 1870s? Lori would know."

The barista came by to take their plates, the pretty one who always flirted with Leo. She stopped when she saw Augusta's untouched slice of cake. "Oh, are you still working on that?"

Augusta shook her head. "No, I'm all done, thanks."

"Could you stick it in a box for us?" Leo asked her, before turning back to Augusta. "You might change your mind later and need a chocolate hit."

She didn't have the heart to tell him that she'd probably throw it out before it could become a temptation in her refrigerator at home. She watched the barista scoop up the plates and disappear, then changed the subject.

"Are you sure you want to take this on? I mean, it's kind of outside the scope of your job description."

"Do I want to go on a historical scavenger hunt for a ghost?" He shot her a devilish grin. "Hell, yeah, I do."

Taking a long sip of her coffee, she tried not to let herself be distracted by how adorable he was when he was excited. He was usually so laid-back, almost careless in his demeanor. But then he suddenly grew serious, the smile fading, the crinkles around his eyes smoothing out. "What happens if you have another… episode? I don't want to pursue this if it's going to put you at risk or under too much stress."

She hadn't thought of that. Since the last hallucination, that melancholy ache in her chest hadn't gone away. If anything, it had grown, leaving her restless and desperately curious. Her interest in Margaret had grown into an obsession, and she couldn't rest until she had figured out what had happened to her. "I guess that's a risk I'm going to have to take."

26

Margaret

If you don't love me,
Love whom you please,
But throw yore arms round me,
Give my heart ease.

—"Down in the Valley," Traditional Folk Song

I TOOK THE overnight coach back from Boston, drifting in and out of a fitful sleep as the horses plodded along the muddy roads. I had hoped that some fresh scenery would have numbed the pain, but as soon as we approached the familiar roads of Tynemouth, I knew that it was not to be the case. I no longer had Phebe to run to for guidance, and it struck me too late that she had been right. I had only ever sought her out when I needed something, whether it was company, a sympathetic ear or her wisdom. Now she was gone, and it was too late for apologies and realizations.

The coach deposited me on Main Street in the early hours of the morning, right in front of Jack's store. Mercifully, I did not see him as I hurried home with my head down. I avoided my family for most of the day, lying in bed. I hated that I felt weak and listless on account of a man, and it was only the thought of the babe in my womb that induced me to drag myself to the dining table and take tasteless nibbles of the roast.

Dinner that night was a silent affair, aside from the too-loud scraping of forks on plates, the gurgle of water pouring from the decanter.

It was only Henry, Father and Mother, and me. They were not my parents, though, I reminded myself as I took small sips of water. There was nothing in my life that was true: not my family, not my love for Jack, not even who I had thought I was. I had only myself, my baby and a burning anger deep within me.

Henry was the only one who seemed oblivious to my dark mood. My parents treaded around me as if I were a venomous snake that might strike at the slightest provocation. They must have heard by now of my scene with Jack in the street, but if they still thought to send me away, they had not broached the subject again. But Henry was extra solicitous, making certain that my glass was always filled, reserving the choicest cuts of meat for me. I suppose he thought that I would come to Boston now with him, that we would be some sort of family, he, the child, and I. We were cousins after all, but I still found the thought repugnant.

After I had chewed and swallowed as much tasteless food as I could bear, I made my excuses and slipped outside. I needed to feel the briny air on my neck, the cooling ocean breeze in my hair. For all the tinctures and potions I had concocted for others over the years, there was no remedy for the fissure in my heart, the crack in my armor. In the woods, at least, amidst the whispering trees and melancholy cries of the night birds, I was part of something larger than myself and my earthly troubles. Neither the graceful deer that watched me with large black eyes nor the scurrying mice cared who I was.

I walked over roots and leaves and rocks until the soil turned sandy and I came to the rocky promontory overlooking the ocean. I was standing on the rocks, letting the icy ocean spray roll across my bare feet when I sensed him. He had not come for weeks, and I had thought that he would have at least given me that one last consideration—to not show his face again, to let me mend my broken heart in peace. But no, I was to have no respite from the man who simultaneously made my blood boil with anger and my heart throb with desire. "What do you want, Jack?" I asked flatly.

He stopped a few paces behind me, silent. I thought he would beg for forgiveness or try to explain everything away with pretty words; it would be more than a little satisfying to see him on his knees begging. But instead he surprised me.

"When I was little, I was so envious of the sailors and merchants that headed out to sea for adventure," he said, his voice soft and clear over the crashing waves below. "I cursed my parents for being mere grocers. When I was nine years old I resolved that I would stow away on the next ship to Santiago and make my life as a pirate."

I couldn't help the snort that escaped my lips at the thought of Jack as a stowaway boy, tall and lanky and sunburnt, throwing his weight against the mast of a ship. He had come up beside me and out of the corner of my eye I saw his lips curve in a faint smile. "Just as well that I got hungry and came home before I ever so much as stepped foot on the docks," he said. "I would have made a terrible pirate."

Silence fell between us, the waves lapping hungrily below on the rocks. The wind tugged at my thin shawl, but I refused to submit to the shivers that were building in my spine. As if sensing this, Jack moved to drape his coat over my shoulders. I stiffened and stepped away.

"If you think to soothe me with stories in the dark or play gallant knight, you vastly misunderstand my character. I would sooner push you over these rocks than listen to such tripe."

"I believe you would," he murmured, a hint of amusement in his voice.

I gave a weary sigh, finally allowing myself to shiver in the sharp wind. "Why have you come, then, Jack?"

He didn't say anything, and for a moment I thought that he hadn't heard me. But then he spoke. "I'm not the villain you think me," he said softly. "It was sport for me in the beginning, perhaps, but it was for you, as well."

I opened my mouth to contradict him, but closed it just as quickly again. He was right. It had been sport for me, too, a hunt, and I had thrilled at the chase as much as he had, if not more.

"What we have..." He paused, clearing his throat. "What is between us is..." Sighing, he kicked a pebble off the rocks and watched the sea swallow it. "I've not the way with words that you have, Maggie."

I nodded. I knew what he meant, regardless of his words. What transpired between us when we were together was magical; it transcended our bodily pleasure. I might have wished him dead, I might have never wanted to see him again, but I could not deny that I felt the spark that existed between us.

"I'm with child," I said before I could stop myself. "I am keeping it."

I heard the sharp intake of his breath, felt the air ripple with his shock. But when I readied myself to defend my choice, he again surprised me.

"I can't marry you, Maggie," he said, his voice weary and a little sad.

"And did I ask you to?"

"Well, no, but..."

"It is not my intention to ensnare you in matrimony with me. I shall get on very well without you," I snapped.

"You hardly need me for anything, it seems," he said dryly. "I will provide for the child—you need not worry on that score."

"I don't want your assistance." I couldn't imagine that Jack had enough money to provide for a wife, let alone a child.

He let out a long, slow breath. "You didn't ask why I can't marry you."

"I don't care, but I suspect it has something to do with the question of your inheritance, and the lack of my suitability as compared to a girl like Lucy Clerkenwell."

"You're wrong," he said, his voice holding a hard edge. "I can't marry you because I am already engaged."

I stared at him, at the beautiful high cheekbones, the muscles and bones and flesh that made the man I loved. The salt air sharpened at his revelation, yet I felt as if I was a thousand miles from the rocks. I had been wrong to think that I didn't care, that I could live without Jack. I suddenly realize I cared, I cared very much that I could never have him.

He spared me the need to ask who, though of course I already knew. "Lucy Clerkenwell," he said. "It was a foolish, rash decision, made in the haste of youth after we had lain together when we were sixteen years of age. She was not with child, thank God, but I made her the pledge all the same."

"You've been engaged to her for *years*?" I couldn't have felt like more of a fool if he'd informed me that he lived on the moon. "You pursued *me*. You lay with *me*. You told me you were going to speak to my father, to your parents. Was it all a ruse? Did you ever have even the slightest intention of marrying me?"

His jaw was tight, his eyes downcast and wet, and I realized with horror that he was fighting not to cry. "I thought that if I ignored it that it might simply go away. I prayed that Lucy might let me go once we were older, but she has no wish to sever our engagement, and I am honor bound to marry her."

A laugh escaped me. "*Honor*. What a fine word to bandy about in a situation such as this. There is nothing honorable about your conduct, toward me *or* Lucy. You're weak. You wanted to travel the world, yet you gave up your dream so that you could stand behind the counter at your parents' shop. You love me, but you would rather placate Lucy Clerkenwell and stay despite your changed feelings. You're a coward."

At this, he took me roughly by the shoulders, yet I was still not afraid of him. He was strong, and he could have easily pushed me over the edge, could have dashed my bones amongst the rocks below. Taking my chin in his hand, he forced me to meet his flashing gaze. "I am not a coward," he said hoarsely. And then, as if to prove his point, he claimed my lips in a savage kiss. My body responded, betraying me by pressing against him. Pulling back, I slapped him and he stopped, but he was grinning now. "This," he said. "This is what I will miss."

"Wretch," I hurled at him. But my blood was pumping, my heart afire. I would be lying if I said that I would not miss the passion, the danger that I felt when I was in his arms.

I turned on my heel and left him there still panting with desire. He was a coward, and I had nothing to fear from him except breaking my heart. Or at least, that was what I thought. As the night creatures stole on soft feet and the cowering moon slid behind the clouds, I made a pledge: Jack Pryce would pay for what he had done, for the fool he had made of me. If not in this life, then in the next.

I would raise my child, live on my own, and I would be the disappointment and curiosity that I had always been destined to be. I cared not a button for Jack Pryce or the people who had all these years pretended to be my family. I would not deign to live with Henry in whatever taboo relationship he had schemed up. I would go my own way and I would harden my heart somewhere that Jack could never find me.

27

Augusta

THE HOUSE WAS RESTLESS, expectant when Augusta came in Monday the next week, a quiet energy stalking through the empty rooms. Silk flowers quivered in their vases, the barren hearths yawned, hungry. How had she never realized how alive the house was, how it pulsed and clenched and waited, waited, waited? All of the bravado and determination Augusta had felt while seated in the safety of the coffee shop next to Leo faded as she sat down at her desk, a pensive aura wrapping itself around her.

With her spreadsheet of object catalog numbers open before her, Augusta eventually fell into the rhythm of updating the objects that needed to be assessed for conservation. Usually the monotonous task was the last thing she wanted to tackle on her to-do list, but today it was a license to let her mind wander all the familiar, well-worn paths: Leo, her mother and their fights, and, of course, Margaret.

Was Margaret some kind of guardian angel? If she really had come to Augusta's rescue and knocked the painting off the wall, then she must be. It was still hard to wrap her head around the fact that she was now someone who apparently believed in ghosts, but if she understood her episodes for what they were—visions of the past—maybe accepting the existence of ghosts was the next logical step.

The fact that she had been anticipating it made it no less frightening when the columns of numbers began to blur and fade. Closing her eyes, she let herself fall into the vision, no less scared than she had been the first time. But she was here now, and there were answers, if only she could find them.

It was the air that changed first, a clean sharpness with the faint scent of lemons and grass, spreading and swirling like milk poured into coffee.

Forcing herself to get up from her seat, Augusta moved as if in a trance through the now-familiar shadowed halls of the house. She found herself outside, a mild autumn breeze lifting the curls at her neck, coal smoke hanging in the air. The distant murmur of the ocean carried to the rocky garden—gulls crying, boats alerting one another of their presence with baritone horns. But there was another sound, closer, softer. The sound of human breath and footsteps.

Aside from the dream of Margaret in the mirror, she had never seen another person in her episodes before. Would they be able to see her? Would they speak to her? The idea was both thrilling and terrifying. If she was truly in the past and it wasn't just a hallucination, could her interaction change the course of the present? Watching the past unfold as if a movie was one thing, and it was strange enough, but being a player in it was another thing altogether.

As the figure loomed closer, her heart began to hammer against her ribs, her hands clammy and cold. This was it. She felt as if she was staring down Death himself.

But the face that came into view wasn't that of Death, or even that of a stranger. It was a pleasant face, with dark eyes and hair that was greased and parted. It was a face she had seen before, she was sure of it, but she couldn't place him. The man looked as if he had walked off a movie set, dressed in a single-breasted coat with striped trousers and a loosened ascot. Every pore, every bristle along his jawline was sharp and hyper-focused. Swallowing, she waited for him to either walk through her or to demand to know who she was. Instead, he stopped short, peering at her. "Maggie, are you all right? You look like you saw the devil himself."

"George," Augusta said in a breath. It was Margaret's brother. He looked just like the portrait of him in the sitting room, and a younger version of the photographs Augusta had seen of him as an old man in the 1920s.

"The one and only. You always know how to make a fellow feel wanted. Come, sit with me a moment."

Before she could do anything, he was taking her hand in his, and leading her to a wrought iron bench overlooking the terraced garden.

Full skirts swished around her ankles, and the tight laces of her boned corset molded to her ribs. Her full hips swayed, her posture fluid and easy despite the constraints of her dress. It was Augusta's body, but Margaret's movements, Margaret's confidence. Why didn't he realize that she was not his sister, but a stranger from another time?

"I know how you like this spot," he said, pulling her down with him so that she was practically in his lap. "Remember when you were little and you used to sit out here, throwing apples down the terraces? Our old nurse—what was her name?—she used to have a fit trying to gather them all up again."

Augusta didn't know what he was talking about, but felt herself nodding.

"Now," he said, taking her hand in his and gently rubbing

her wrist with his thumb, "will you tell your favorite brother what is troubling you?"

She could feel the feather-soft touch of his finger on her skin, his dark eyes gentle and warm as they searched her face. What were they seeing? Someone unsure of her place, of her own body? Or a beautiful woman who moved with the rhythm of cresting waves and spoke like the moonlight shafting through pine needles?

Augusta opened her mouth to tell him that there was something wrong, that this was all a mistake, but the words that came out were not hers. They were soft and husky, musical. "Oh, George, if only all men were half so good as you."

"Has some blackguard trifled with you?" George's eyes darkened, his jaw tightening, and for the first time Augusta realized that this was a man who might look gentle and kind, but could be capable of violence. A man like Chris.

Augusta waited for her own answer, as if she were waiting on a cue for the next line in a play. The source of her words were somewhere just beyond her grasp, like a vague memory. But no sooner had she opened her mouth then it all vanished again: the cold bench beneath her, sweet-smelling apple trees and George's hand on hers. She was sitting in the parking area behind the backyard, the buildings of Main Street just visible through the thinned trees.

She blinked rapidly, trying to regain her bearings. She hadn't just witnessed the past, she had *been* Margaret, seen the world through her eyes, felt an unspoken understanding between herself and George. Had anyone witnessed her strange journey from her office to the parking area? She must have looked like a sleepwalker, moving through the house without paying any heed to her surroundings.

For a long while she just sat with the lingering memory of George beside her, the sharp, salty air curling between them. If she waited long enough, would it all come back? Did she *want* it to all come back? There was only one thing that was certain, and that was her hallucinations were becoming more intense, more vivid and all-encompassing, building to something. But what?

"So, where should we start?"

Augusta looked up from her work, half expecting to find George lounging in the doorway instead of Leo. Her mind was still sticky, full of cobwebs, like she still had one foot in the past.

"Where should we start what?"

"Looking for Margaret." He came in and sat in her extra chair. "You didn't think I'd forget, did you?"

"Right," she said. She hadn't thought he'd forget, but she hadn't really been certain if he was serious or not. "I was just doing some data entry."

"Must be some serious data entry. I think I was standing there for about a full minute before you noticed. Not," he added, a tad sheepishly, "in a creepy way."

Part of her wanted to tell him about the hallucination, but the tender moment between her and George had been so private, and she couldn't bring herself to share it with him. "I might have been thinking about Margaret, too," she said, in an attempt to at least partially tell him the truth.

Leo didn't press the matter, and she turned her mind toward the search, tapping her pen against her desk as she thought. There were plenty of places where Augusta knew to look for Margaret, but she and Leo couldn't very well interrogate her dreams or penetrate her hallucinations. "Hmm… Office of Vital Records?" she suggested, although she wasn't holding out hope. If there was any record of Margaret there, someone would have probably found it long before now. But she was looking forward to spending the hour with Leo, and maybe she would turn something up for her exhibit.

"Sounds good to me." Leo waited while she saved her work

and gathered up her notebook and water bottle. "So," he said, "everything going okay since last week?"

It took her a moment to realize he was talking about Chris, her nasty encounter with him. At first blush Leo looked casual and unworried as he leaned against the doorframe, waiting for her. But then she noticed his hand at his side, curling and uncurling into a fist, and the tightness in his jaw. She wasn't used to seeing him look anything other than laid-back, and while she was flattered that he was upset on her behalf, she didn't want him to think of her as a victim.

"Yep, everything is great," she said in a tone that didn't invite further comment. She didn't want to think about Chris; it was bad enough that the fight played over and over in her head—the feel of his hands digging into her shoulders, her back slamming into the wall.

"He hasn't come around anymore?"

"Nope."

Leo seemed to get the message, and when she had all her stuff together, they left, making small talk until they reached the town hall a block away.

The binders of yellowing paper were almost as ancient as the clerk who pulled them and set them down on a rickety table for them. "No phones, no pens and keep your voices down," she instructed Augusta and Leo before returning to her desk and picking up her knitting needles.

"So, what are we looking for exactly?" Leo asked in a whisper.

Augusta let her gaze roam the overwhelming collection of binders in front of them. She had no idea what they were even looking for, let alone where to start. "Wasn't this your idea?"

He raised his brows. "Yeah, but you're the expert."

"I'm hardly an expert," she said. "But maybe we should check all the family names first, like Harlowe and Foster, just to make sure that there's nothing obvious we're missing." It was a long shot, but it was possible that Margaret was hiding somewhere in these binders, perhaps with a different last name. Or maybe there was a record of a marriage that had previously been overlooked.

"See, you say you're not an expert, yet you always come up with these great ideas." Already pulling the first binder toward him and scouring the pages, Leo added, "I think it's time to admit to yourself that you're kind of amazing."

"Voices down!" the clerk called from her desk before Augusta could fully process what he had just said.

"Busted," Leo whispered.

They worked quietly, but it was hard to concentrate when she could hear Leo's soft breathing next to her, see his rolled sleeves and open collar from the corner of her eye. As she suspected there were no Margaret Harlowes, so she flipped to the Ms on the off chance that Margaret might show up with her first name listed as her last. It was a long shot, but they were here and there was nothing else to do. Tracing her finger down the names, she stopped as one jumped out at her.

Montrose, Louisa. b. 1829 d.185?

She racked her brain trying to remember where she'd come across the last name. She could see it in her mind, printed neatly on cream-colored paper. Then it came to her. It had been on her family tree, on her mother's side. It was probably a fairly common name, but she made a mental note to check her family tree again when she got home and see if the name and dates were a match. She was about to tell Leo when he leaned over and said, "Jill just texted me—she and Reggie are going to The Sea Dog for drinks after they close up and asked if we wanted to meet them there."

Demoralized by their fruitless search as well as not really wanting to return home to a night of TV reruns on the couch, she said, "Yeah, I'd be up for that. Should we go over and meet them now?"

"Oh," he said, as if just remembering something, "shoot. I actually have dinner plans with Lisa tonight."

Of course he had dinner plans. He had a whole other life outside of work and she wasn't part of it. She didn't know who Lisa was, and she was pretty sure she didn't want to know. "Next time," she said with a weak smile.

As Augusta walked through the darkening town to the bar a few blocks away she thought of Margaret's portrait, her knowing green eyes, the challenging tilt of her chin. Something told her that Margaret hadn't been one to wait around for a man, or anyone else for that matter. Margaret would have taken what she wanted and to hell with the consequences. How freeing that must have been, how intoxicating. For just one night, Augusta wished she could know what it would be like to be someone like Margaret.

The next morning, head throbbing from a hangover, Augusta gingerly set her stuff down in the staff kitchen and plugged in the electric kettle to make some tea. Despite Leo not coming— or perhaps because of Leo not coming—she'd let go the night before and enjoyed herself to the fullest. It had been freeing to forget everything from her unrequited crush, to Chris, to Margaret, even, but now she was paying for it. Every time she thought she might be on the verge of a hallucination, it turned out to just be the effects from a night of too much drinking. So as she climbed the narrow steps to the third floor of Harlowe House, she was half holding her breath, wondering if she was once again going to slip into the past, or vomit all over a historic carpet.

She rarely came up here—there was little reason to—but she needed to check the insect traps. Kneeling down, she fished the glue trap out from behind an empty bookshelf. She recorded the assortment of feckless moths and unlucky spiders and put out a fresh trap. But as she was walking her hands back to stand up, the floorboard wobbled under her. Frowning, she leaned closer to inspect it. If there was something wrong with the floorboard, Reggie would need to know so that he could address it.

Since she had her condition reports with her, she took a quick picture and jotted down a note. It was getting hot up there, but something made her kneel back down and test the edge of the plank again. To her surprise, it came up in her hands. There were probably dead rodents and decades' worth of dust, but she couldn't help leaning down and peering in.

The flashlight on her cell phone illuminated something that didn't look like it belonged under a floor. She drew in her breath, leaning closer. Two books, wrapped in brittle fabric, were nestled in the cavity.

She sat there, motionless. If she had thought that taking the letters out of the desk was borderline unethical, these books would be like lifting the Holy Grail from its resting place. It didn't even matter what lay between the covers—though she couldn't help the wild speculations that raced through her mind—just the fact that someone had hidden books in the attic was hugely significant. Opening and inspecting them was a job for a curator or an archivist, someone who could take them to a sterile environment and do it properly. But everything she knew and respected about museum protocol seemed to fly out the window as she gently lifted the first book and thumbed it open.

It was bound in soft leather, a simple gilded embellishment on the spine. The first page was titled in cursive "My Common Book" and underneath was the inscription:

To Louisa Montrose, from her mother, Catharine.

Her mouth went suddenly dry. Montrose. That name again. This was the third time she'd seen it: first, on her family tree, and the most recently just the previous day in the vital records. Again, Montrose wasn't an uncommon name, but something inside her jumped in recognition, and she knew that whoever this Louisa Montrose was, they had to be related in some way.

She gingerly turned the pages, her eyes scanning the hand-written entries, dated from the 1840s. Who was Louisa Montrose? And why had she hidden her book in the attic beneath the floorboards where no one would ever see it? Most of the entries seemed to be recipes, little songs and some sketches, though they were difficult to make out. Placing it gently on the cloth, Augusta turned her attention to the second book. This one was bound in a much simpler paper binding, the entries written in a different hand. She didn't need to see the name on the first page to know to whom it belonged: it was Margaret's. It read more like an account book, people's names listed with little shorthand entries next to them.

Alice MacKay—husband takes his hand to her when inebriated. Hattie Mason—three miscarriages. Gave her instructions to drink a tisane of willow bark and mint. Her brother controls her finances and I do not trust him.

She flipped forward. It was all women that Margaret had apparently advised or treated in some way. Had Margaret practiced medicine of some kind? There could have been female midwives back in the 1870s, though Augusta couldn't imagine that a wealthy family such as the Harlowes would have allowed their daughter to have a vocation. And if she had, surely there would have been some record of it somewhere else.

Downstairs, a phone ringing reminded her that she couldn't stay up here all day. Quickly, she put both books back in the hollow space, replacing the board. She would not take them, but neither would she tell Jill or Sharon. These were hers, a secret between her and Margaret; Margaret had led her there, she was sure of it, and to lay them bare under the eye of an archivist or the public would be a breach of trust.

She was still sitting on her elbows and knees when her phone buzzed. She jumped, Leo flashed across her screen. Call? it said.

She groaned, suddenly remembering some very drunken texts she'd sent to him the night before. The books were instantly forgotten as Augusta called him back, her heart beating a little faster as she waited for him to pick up. "Hey, what's up?"

"Not much, what's up with you?"

Twirling a strand of hair around her finger like a high schooler, Augusta switched the phone to her other ear. "You wanted me to call just so you could tell me you're not up to anything?"

"Maybe, would you be mad if I did?"

"I'm livid," she said, biting her lip to keep from grinning. If she'd made a total ass out of herself the night before, then he was too gentlemanly to say anything about it.

She could hear the smile in his voice. "Yikes, okay. Then I guess I better tell you why I really called."

Her breath hitched, and for a stupidly drawn-out moment she thought he was going to say something about how he'd been waiting to ask her out. But of course, he was dating the mysterious Lisa. "So I was talking to Lori in Boston, and she said that she was looking through the Ida Foster letters you found."

Augusta was only disappointed for a fraction of a second. "Oh, yeah?"

"She says that they could go a long way in helping not just our interpretation of the house, but also the community in the 1800s." He paused. "Well done, you."

"That's awesome, I'm glad they'll be helpful. No Margaret sightings, though?"

"No Margaret sightings," he confirmed. "But I was thinking of cross-referencing some of the names in the letters with documents in the archives. That's a thing right, cross-referencing?"

He was too adorable. "Yes, that's a thing. And it's a really good idea," she added.

"Lori sent me home with some photocopies and a list of the

names that show up." She could hear the rustle of papers as he started to rattle off names. "You have a better grasp of the history of Harlowe House than I do, so tell me if any of these are familiar. Let's see…there's a Mullins, a Montrose, a Crenshaw, a—"

Augusta sat up straighter. "Wait, go back. What was that name?"

"Which one? Crenshaw?"

"No, before that."

"Um, let's see. Montrose?"

Augusta's mind whirred. It couldn't be a coincidence. The universe was all but throwing the name at her, making certain that she understood without a doubt that she was connected in some way to the Harlowe family, to Margaret.

"Hey, you still there?"

"Yeah. Yeah, I'm here," she said quickly. "It's just that name… I think I know it. Can you read me the context it appears in, in the letter?"

The rustle of papers again. "It looks like she might have been a member of the extended family? Ida references Jemima's relatives being in town for a visit. It was her maiden name."

Augusta's ears buzzed, her heart beating faster. How had she missed it on the Harlowe tree? Margaret's mother was a Montrose, which meant that Margaret was a Montrose.

"Are you okay?"

She came out of her thoughts. "Yeah, I just think that I… I think I might be related to Margaret?"

Now it was Leo's turn to be stunned into silence. "Really? Is your family name Montrose?"

"Way, way back apparently."

"Damn. That's huge." They were both digesting the significance of this when Leo suddenly spoke again. "Not to change the subject, but while I have you on the phone…" He trailed off and Augusta waited expectantly. "I—I was wondering if you were free after work next Friday? Maybe we could grab a bite to eat?"

She must not have heard him right because it sounded like he was asking her out. When she didn't say anything, he hurried on. "I know that you just went through a breakup, and I totally get if you aren't ready to go out or whatever. It can just be two friends having dinner if that's—"

"No, I mean, yes. Yes, I would love to go."

"Oh, yeah?"

"You sound surprised. Did you think I wouldn't want to?"

"Not surprised, just, glad."

She almost asked who Lisa was, but thought better of it. Augusta was trying to think of what to say that wouldn't make it sound like she'd been pining for him almost two months, when she heard Jill calling her from down the steps. "I'm glad, too," she said. "Hey, I have to run, but see you next week?"

"Wouldn't miss it for anything, Miss Montrose."

When Augusta came in on Monday, she was surprised to find Leo working in the ballroom. With their date on Friday, Augusta had a new feeling of butterflies when she saw him sitting cross-legged on the floor, a nautical tattoo she had never noticed before peeking out from his shirtsleeve.

At her footsteps, he turned, his face brightening. "Hey, Jill said you were working in the carriage house today so I figured I wouldn't see you. Lucky me," he added with a crooked grin.

"Just needed to grab something," she said, waving a notebook she'd forgotten the day before. "I'm heading to the carriage house now, but give a shout if you need me." *Please need me*, she added to herself.

It was quiet in the carriage house with the late autumn rain pattering on the roof. Augusta set herself up to work, putting a new playlist on her phone. Most of the boxes left were uninteresting, hardware and rusted knickknacks. There were some musty old mattresses that would probably be documented and then disposed of. Augusta got into a rhythm of taking photos, jotting notes and then moving on to the next object on the shelves. She was clipping along, taking a photo of some old lawn ornaments, when her phone slipped from her hand.

She scrambled to catch it, but it clanked to the floor, skidding under the dusty shelf. Crouching, she groped to find it, only to push it farther back by accident. Damn, she would have to find a broom or something so she could fish it out. She stood up, but was hit with a wave of light-headedness. Wincing, she braced herself against a shelf, blinking against the stars in her eyes. She'd forgotten to bring her water bottle with her and was probably a little dehydrated.

She shouldn't have been surprised when, on clearing her vision, she was met with a very different view of the carriage house than when she'd closed her eyes. She shouldn't have been surprised when she smelled the sweet scent of hay, or the musk of old leather either. Yet as her gaze wandered over the carriages and horse tackle, she caught her breath.

What had she been looking for? Her phone? The concept of a phone itself grew fuzzy and indistinct. No, she had been looking for an herb, that's right. Thyme. Well, she wasn't going to find it in the carriage house. Wiping her hands off on her apron, she went out to go to the stillroom.

Molly was outside hanging linens on the line. When she saw Augusta, she scowled. "I caught that dog of yours in the root cellar," she said, her Irish accent heavy with distaste. "Mind he doesn't eat something that might not agree with him."

Augusta nodded, but she had no intention of reprimanding Shadow. He was a good dog, and her truest friend. As she went to let herself into the house, she caught her reflection in the glass panes of the door and couldn't help but admire how fine her long, dark curls looked, how her complexion glowed.

In the stillroom, she just stood for a moment, inhaling the

comforting scent of herbs and dried flowers. She took no joy in the charm she was about to make, but it had to be done. Jack would pay for his falsehoods.

He had stopped coming to their meeting place the last few weeks, but if she sent for him, he would come. She was sure of it. After that, it would simply be a matter of persuading him to ingest the concoction.

When she'd ground and measured the herbs, she went off in search of a vial, but stopped short at the sight of Henry lounging against the pianoforte in the ballroom. He always seemed to be haunting the house these days, doing nothing in particular except getting underfoot. Before she could backtrack, he'd turned around, his gaze locking on her.

"Cousin," he said, his dark eyes brightening. "You look pale. Are you well?"

For a moment Augusta couldn't find her tongue, but then words not quite her own came out of her mouth. "What do you want, Henry?"

"Not this tired old conversation again," he said, with a dramatic sigh. "I want you to be happy, as I always have, and I always will. I worry for you, especially in your condition."

"Well, I am quite happy. Your concern is unwarranted."

"Are you?" He tilted his head to the side, regarding her. "You are a most patient woman, then. Most women would not be so *happy* to learn that their lover was already engaged."

She stilled, her hand resting on the pianoforte. Henry had known. He had known that Jack was already betrothed to someone else, and he had said nothing to her. She resisted the urge to slap him clean across his face, but then he gave her the most patronizing, pitying smile and she lost all restraint. Before she knew it, she had her hands on his lapels, shaking him as if her life depended on it.

"You miserable excuse for a man! You've known all this time and said nothing in the hopes that what... I would be your mistress? Your *wife*? We're cousins, raised as siblings—it's unnatural!" He pushed her off him, holding her at arm's length while she beat at his chest.

"Augusta! Stop!"

Henry was looking at her with the strangest expression, but she kept hitting him, her anger boiling over. Why did he not defend himself? Why was he just standing there with his hands on her arms? "You brute!" she cried, but still he did not move.

When at last she had exhausted her fury, she let her forehead fall against his chest. But instead of the wool of his waistcoat, the fabric was soft, thin. When she looked up, it was not Henry's pale face that was peering down at her, but a brown-skinned face etched with concern. The name Reggie floated through her mind, though she was sure she had never met a Reggie in her life.

"Jill? Leo?" he called over his shoulder, his hands still firmly locked onto her arms. She struggled against his grip, but her anger was leeching out of her, leaving her weak and exhausted.

"Augusta, hey. It's okay. It's okay."

"Reggie?"

Blinking, she looked around the ballroom for the pianoforte, for Henry, but all she saw were a few folding chairs and the half-erected exhibit. A moment later Leo came jogging into the room. "Hey, what's going on? Is everything okay?"

"I'm okay," Augusta mumbled, though she felt as if she might throw up.

"She was shouting at someone named Henry, and then started hitting me," she heard Reggie explain as Leo guided her to a chair. "I think she's having some kind of manic episode or a nightmare or something."

"Here, drink this," Leo said gently, handing her a plastic water bottle.

She took it from him with shaking hands and lifted it to her lips. It tasted like chemicals, but it was cold, and she drank until it ran down her chin.

"Is there someone I should call?" Reggie was asking Leo. "I don't know if she's on some kind of medication or something or—"

Leo shook his head. "No, I think it'll be okay. Can you go let Jill know that we need a few minutes in here? Thanks, man," he said as Reggie nodded and left.

When they were alone, Leo took Augusta's cold hands in his and rubbed them warm. "Was it a hallucination again?" he asked in a murmur.

She nodded. It had been a hallucination, but it had also been so much more. Just like in her last episode, she had actually *been* Margaret. But unlike the last time, she'd had access to Margaret's thoughts as well—her knowledge, her feelings.

Leo was studying her face, trying to find an answer, though she already knew there wasn't one. "Was it worse than the other ones?" he asked softly. When she nodded again, he swore under his breath.

"I… I *was* Margaret. I saw her brother, Henry and me—I mean, they—were having an argument about someone named Jack. I think he was her lover." Augusta drew in a soft breath. "She was pregnant," she whispered, that detail resurfacing in breathtaking clarity. Margaret hadn't said anything about being pregnant, but Augusta could feel the absence of life in her stomach now, and it left her strangely empty.

Leo nodded, but she could tell that even he was having trouble believing everything she was saying. "All right," he said soothingly. "What do you want to do? I could call your mom, have her come pick you up maybe?"

Augusta gave a vigorous shake of her head. "No, I'd rather stay here." There was an unexplainable tug in her chest that tethered her to Harlowe House, and besides, there was no way her mother could even begin to understand what had happened. "I think I should just get back to work and try to forget it."

Judging from his expression, Leo didn't agree, but he gave her hands a squeeze. "Okay," he said, "I'm going to grab my stuff and bring it in here and work, so if you start to feel woozy or anything, let me know." He hesitated, as if trying to find the right words. "I know it's none of my business, but I have to ask… Are you using any drugs that might—"

"No," she said sharply, taking her hands back from him.

"Okay," he said, not in the least bit perturbed. "Sorry, I had to ask. It's just that…well, it doesn't matter. I'll be right back."

Augusta watched him leave. She couldn't help but be a little insulted that he thought she would lie, though if she were on some kind of drug that would at least be an explanation. They worked in silence for the rest of the day, only occasionally exchanging the barest of words when work necessitated it.

That evening, as Augusta was curled up on the couch watching game show reruns with her mother, she got a text from Leo. Hey, I hope you're feeling better and that I didn't cross a line with my question earlier today. Are we still on for Friday? Totally understand if you want to cancel, but I hope you'll still want to go.

She texted back that they were still on and she was looking forward to it. But that night, when she closed her eyes and drifted off to sleep, it was of an intense young man, tall, with dark hair and piercing blue eyes, of whom she dreamed.

28

Augusta

THE DAYS LEADING up to her date with Leo—was it a date? Or were they just hanging out as friends?—were long and exhausting. Work was a minefield; every time Augusta so much as blinked, she was afraid that she would slip into another waking dream. Yet whenever it did not happen, an unaccountable sadness welled in her chest, that feeling of homesickness, of loss. Nights were likewise unrestful, full of dreams that were not quite hers.

But as soon as Leo pulled up in front of her house, she pushed aside all the unpleasantness and decided that she would enjoy tonight. God knew she needed a night out, and she still couldn't quite believe that she got to spend it with Leo. Sliding into the passenger seat beside him was like coming home.

"So where are we going?" she asked when they'd pulled away from the house, both pretending like they couldn't see her mother peeking out through the blinds at them.

"There's this outdoor food festival going on tonight... I thought we could grab a bite to eat and walk, if that sounds good?"

They pulled up to a park filled with food trucks, lights strung all through the autumn trees. Families strolled around the lit-up green, and a folk band was playing on a small stage in the middle. It was perfect. She could get whatever she wanted to eat and not have to worry about being self-conscious while they meandered the illuminated paths.

Leo got something from a Mexican stand, and Augusta got a mango lassi and a savory pastry. There was an outdoor art exhibit, and they wandered the park, hunting for all the sculptures that had been tucked into the winding paths.

"Hey, so I feel like I should explain myself," Leo said suddenly.

"About what?"

"The other day, when I asked if you were on something—"

She shook her head. "It's fine. I understand, it's hard to believe. I probably wouldn't believe me either."

"No, it wasn't fine. I believe you, and anyway, it's not any of my business." They'd gradually slowed until they were standing in front of a sculpture of birds taking flight, a small pond their backdrop. In the twilight, their black silhouettes looked so real, like they had simply been frozen in time on their ascent. "I think I mentioned that my ex-girlfriend died. I can't remember if I told you any more than that."

He was looking past her, at the glassy surface of the pond, but he seemed to sense the shake of her head. "Well, she died shortly after we broke up. It was an overdose, though it was never clear if it was accidental or not. She would threaten to hurt herself a lot, and after a while I stopped taking her seriously." Shoving his hands in his pockets, he kicked at a rock, sending it splashing into the water. "I thought she was trying to guilt me into coming back, but she was serious."

The full implication of this and what it must have felt like for him pierced her right through the heart. In the aftermath of their breakup, Chris had made veiled references to hurting himself and Augusta had been worried, scared. How terrible it must have been for Leo to be saddled with such a sense of guilt. "Oh, Leo. I'm so sorry," she said, wanting to reach out and take his hand, but stopping herself.

"That's why I don't drink, in part," he said. "I never want to be in a situation where I'm not in control of myself. Not just because of accidentally taking it too far, but also in case I have to drive someone to the hospital or do CPR."

She'd never put it together that Leo didn't drink. He rarely joined her and the others for after-work drinks, but if he did, he usually had a club soda or something. She hadn't thought anything of it.

"Anyway, when I saw you..." He trailed off, his jaw tightening as he quickly looked away. "Well, I'm just glad that you're all right."

It didn't seem quite appropriate that she was flattered he was so concerned for her—after all, it was born out of a terrible experience for him—but she couldn't help but feel glad that he'd shared. "I get it," she said. "No harm done in asking."

They continued walking, leaving the birds in flight behind until they found a bench. There was plenty of room, but Leo sat near her, and she could feel his warmth even in the cool evening air. Leo, visibly brightening, asked, "So, where are we in our Margaret search?"

"I guess that depends," Augusta said cautiously. "I haven't had much time to do research, but I feel like I know so much more about her now since...since my last episode."

"Like what?"

Augusta gazed out at the modern scene before her, feeling a million years out of place. Two children with balloon animals ran ahead of their parents, who were pushing a stroller. The light strain of folk music drifted from an outdoor speaker on the main green. It all seemed so impossibly far away from Margaret's life. "I think she got into some kind of trouble with her lover. She was pregnant, and the man she wanted to marry turned out to have betrayed her. He was already engaged." She remembered the bone-deep sense of betrayal, could feel Margaret's hurt. "Her brother—or rather, cousin—the youngest one, Henry, he had worked against her in the hopes of…well, I'm not sure of what. I have the impression he might have had some kind of feelings toward her. Like, romantic feelings."

Leo raised his brows. "Oh, wow, that's fucked up."

"No kidding." She shuddered, remembering the way her skin had crawled when Henry had turned his gaze on her. "That's not all. Remember when you found those family names and Montrose was one of them?" He nodded. "Well, I think Margaret was adopted."

"What do you mean? Why?"

How to explain this. Somehow, she'd just *known* that Margaret had been adopted by her aunt and uncle's family, the same way she'd known that Margaret was pregnant; it was just part of her. "Think about it," she said. "There's no evidence of her birth anywhere in the Harlowe archives. The first thing that shows up that could even maybe be related to her is the expense for girl's clothes. Before that she would have been just a baby. You said that Louisa Montrose was related to the Harlowes on Jemima Harlowe's side. I think she was Margaret's mother. She got into trouble, or died in childbirth, and the Harlowes adopted her daughter." She didn't tell him about the book with Louisa Montrose's name in it. After she'd found it, she'd gone back to look at her family tree, and sure enough, there was Catherine Montrose and her daughter Louisa, born of an unknown man. After that, the line went dead.

Leo seemed to digest this. "So your common ancestor was Margaret's grandmother?"

"I think so."

He gave her an appraising look that made her skin tingle. "Maybe that's why you're able to see all of this," he said. "Maybe there's some kind of... I don't know, some kind of genealogical memory passed down."

It seemed crazy that she would be able to see things as her ancestor did, but was it any crazier than the hallucinations? "I was poking around online, trying to find information about reincarnation and stuff like that, anything that could explain it. It's hard to know what to believe when it comes to all this, though."

"Hmm," was all he said. He leaned back on the bench, rubbed at his jaw as if thinking of something unpleasant, then looked away uneasily.

"What is it?"

He grumbled something that sounded an awful lot like "God help me for what I'm about to do," and then leveled his gaze back on her. "You should talk to my mom," he said.

Augusta blinked. "What?"

"My mother," he repeated. "She's into all of—" he broke off, gesturing vaguely "—all of that stuff. Crystals, angel cards, past life regressions... New Age stuff."

Augusta absorbed this, then gave him a sly smile. "Are you saying you want me to meet your mom?" She still wasn't sure if this was a date, and now she was going to meet his parents. So much for her big plans of taking some time for herself and getting some distance. It was impossible to keep her feelings tamped down inside of her when he was sitting so close to her that she could have rested her head on his shoulder.

"Yeah, I am, though I hope I don't regret it," he muttered. "She can be...a lot. But she'd like you," he added quickly. "That's for sure."

"I'd love to meet her," Augusta said. "I need all the help I can get."

"It's almost a three-hour drive up to Maine," he said, as if hoping this might dissuade her after all.

"I love road trips," she countered brightly.

He slanted her an amused look. "Well, in that case, I guess I have no choice but to bring you up."

Exceedingly pleased with herself, Augusta took a long sip of her drink. Not only did she have an excuse to soak up some more one-on-one time with Leo, his mother might actually be able to help her. For the first time in what felt like months, she allowed herself to hope. She was free of Chris, free of the limitations she'd placed on herself for so long, and soon she might be free of the hallucinations, as well.

Being out in the fresh air with the faint pulse of music made her brave, hungry to take her ranks among adventurous souls who followed their hearts on crisp autumn evenings. She allowed herself to tilt her head just a little to the side, enough that she could rest her head on Leo's shoulder.

She held her breath, her heart beating fast as she felt Leo shift a little, and then he was finding her hand and lacing his fingers through hers. The music had ended, and the only sounds were the shrieks of playing children. It was almost perfect, except for one thing.

She flicked her tongue over her lips. "Leo?" she asked.

"Augusta?"

"Is this a date?"

There was an almost imperceptible stiffening of his shoulder, and it took what felt like an eternity for him to answer. "Well, let's see," he finally said. "I picked you up at your house and brought you to this ridiculously romantic food fair, we're sitting on a bench and your head is on my shoulder, and I was just getting ready to kiss you." He paused. "Sure seems like a date to me."

He was going to kiss her. Augusta tilted her face toward him as he cupped her jaw, her eyes drifting closed. Warmth buzzed through her body, anticipation mounting until it was almost unbearable.

But the kiss never came. Blinking her eyes open, Augusta drew back. Leo's expression had hardened as he stared past her toward the path. "Do you know that guy? He's staring at you."

She followed his gaze and her whole body went rigid. What were Chris and Doug and Gemma doing there? And why did she feel like she'd been caught doing something wrong? Beside her, heat practically radiated from Leo. "That's him, isn't it? Your ex?"

Before she could fully process what was happening, Leo was pushing up from the bench, striding toward the path. "Leo," she warned, trying to catch up to him. "Don't say anything. It's fine."

He didn't even slow his step. "He assaulted you. It's not fine."

"It wasn't assault," she pleaded. "It was just…" But she trailed off. It *had* been assault. Why was she so eager to dismiss it as such? But that still didn't mean that she wanted Leo going for blood on her behalf.

By now, Chris was saying something to Doug, who shrugged and wandered off in the direction of the festival. Gemma looked as if she wanted to stay and watch what happened more than anything, but eventually turned and followed Doug.

Augusta finally managed to put herself between the two men. Chris looked obnoxiously good, like he hadn't even been through a breakup with his long-term girlfriend. He was probably hitting the gym even more now that she wasn't around to complain about all the time he spent there, and he'd finally gotten the haircut that he'd been putting off for so long. "What are you doing here?" she forced herself to ask through gritted teeth.

"Doug and Gemma wanted to meet up with some friends. I'm allowed to go out places, too," he added with a sneer. An unwelcome pang of jealousy shot through her, hot and sharp; when was the last time Chris had taken her out to do anything like this when they were dating?

"You should keep walking," Leo told him in a dangerous

growl that stirred something hot and deep within her. She'd never had two men fight over her honor before, and while it might have been a romantic fantasy, she wasn't exactly eager to see it play out in real life.

Ignoring him, Chris craned his neck to see around Leo. "Augusta," he said. "Now that you're here, I need to tell you something. I've tried texting you but you never answer."

"There's nothing to talk about," she said, amazed that her voice came out as steady as it did. "Remember what happened last time you 'just wanted to talk'?"

Color crept up Chris's neck, proving that at least he was still capable of feeling *some* shame about the incident. "I was drunk and things got kind of out of hand—" at this Leo let out a snort "—but I'm sober now and I want to talk to you. To apologize."

Augusta gave a stiff nod. She didn't really want an apology; she just wanted Chris gone so she could move on with her life. His guilt was his own problem. Why should she have to carry it, too?

"Okay. Apology accepted," she said flatly.

But instead of finally leaving, Chris was shoving his hands in his pockets, looking like a guilty kid trying to come clean about stealing cookies from the cookie jar.

"Yeah?" Augusta prodded him. "What?"

"I don't really know how to say this," Chris said, shooting her a nervous glance and looking suddenly unsure.

"Say it," ground out Leo. "And then go."

"That night, when…well, you know. I saw something."

Augusta waited for him to go on.

"When the painting fell. I saw…" He hesitated. "I saw something. There, in the hall with us." There was something in his tone that told her this wasn't just about him and her and their fight. Suddenly, goose bumps were springing up on Augusta's arms.

"Margaret," she whispered.

"Who?" He shook his head as if she wasn't making any sense. "No, it wasn't a person. I don't know what it was. But when you were against the wall, there was this…light."

"Light?"

Chris gave a miserable nod. "It was…coming from you."

Rather than vanishing, the goose bumps only spread further. "What are you talking about?" she forced herself to ask.

"There was something happening to you when that painting fell. It wasn't… Look, I know I was rough and what I did was wrong. I feel like shit, believe me. But there was no way that I pushed you that hard."

"You were drunk," she said pointedly. "You're probably not remembering clearly." All the same, she got the feeling that he was telling the truth. Why would he lie about something he clearly felt like he needed to get off his chest? All the same, she didn't want to think too much about what it might mean. It was hard enough to accept that she was able to see things through Margaret's eyes in the past, never mind that Margaret might be somehow visible to others, here in the present.

"Look, I didn't have to apologize, and I didn't have to tell you any of this. Believe what you want, but something fucked up happened and I thought you should know."

"Yep, that's it," Leo said, rolling his sleeves up and stepping forward. "Time for you get the fuck out of here."

"This is the thanks I get for being the bigger man in this situation. Fuck you, Augusta. And fuck you, random dude that my ex-girlfriend is fucking."

Blood rushed to Augusta's face. She couldn't decide if she wanted to smooth things over or if she wanted to wallop him. Leo, probably sensing as much, took her firmly by the hand. Chris spat on the ground and stormed off, nearly barreling into a gawking bystander. Relief welled in her chest as he walked away. But with his receding back went all the romance, all the magic of the evening.

"Asshole," Leo muttered. With a light hand on the small of her back, he steered them back to the parking lot. Augusta stole a sidelong glance at her knight in shining armor, his sleeves rolled to the elbow as if still ready to fight. "Have you ever actually punched someone?"

He shot her an amused look. "I might have in some of my wilder days. Definitely never in defense of the honor of such a beautiful woman, though."

A little thrill ran through her at his words. For all the drama and disappointment of the night, she was leaving with the right man, and nothing really mattered besides that.

29

Augusta

IT WAS ONLY a week before Leo made good on his promise, and Augusta found herself on the way to Pale Harbor, Maine. They'd stocked the car with snacks, coffee and music, and the three hours flew by. Plugging in the adapter, Augusta scrolled through her phone and put on a new song.

Leo glanced at her. "What is this?"

"It's an old folk song I heard somewhere," she told him, even though she couldn't remember where she'd heard it or even how she knew all the words.

Come, all you fair and tender girls
That flourish in your prime
Beware, beware, keep your garden fair
Let no man steal your thyme
Let no man steal your thyme

For when your thyme is past and gone
He'll care no more for you
And in the place your time was waste
Will spread all over with rue
Will spread all over with rue
A woman is a branchy tree
And man's a clinging vine
And from her branches carelessly
He'll take what he can find

The haunting melody filled the car. Only occasionally did they fall into silence as Augusta remembered why they were going to meet his mother in the first place. Leo wasn't her boyfriend, and he wasn't introducing her to his family because she was someone important to him. He was taking her to meet his mother because he thought she might be able to help Augusta with her dreams and hallucinations. They had gone on one date, and it had kind of been a disaster thanks to Chris. She could only hope that the incident hadn't completely scared Leo off from wanting a second date.

The town of Pale Harbor was ridiculously quaint, with saltbox houses perched around a picturesque harbor, and lobster traps and signs for a harvest festival decorating the little town green. She could see why Tynemouth would remind Leo of his hometown, and why someone would be homesick for a place like this. It was hard to imagine the families living in the single-family wood-sided houses with charming gardens ever having to worry about watering down a gallon of milk to make it last a week, or hoard food from school lunches when the grocery budget ran out early.

Turning off the main street, they pulled up in front of an inviting wood-shingled house with a rambling, cottage-style garden. Leo slowly got out of the car and stretched. "Here we go," he muttered.

Fragrant lavender and other herbs poked through the old rail fence, and wind chimes tinkled gently in the breeze. A yellow placard warned them to beware of "the guard cat." Leo shook his head as he rang the bell.

An older man with long, gray hair, wearing an old T-shirt and Birkenstocks, opened the door. "Hey, Leo," he said. "Come on in, man."

"Hey, Dad. Is Mom around?"

"I think she's reading in the living room. You brought a friend!" he exclaimed, as if just noticing Augusta. "I'm Terry," he said, sticking out his hand. "Welcome to Casa Stone."

"Thanks, nice to meet you."

Terry waved them back into the house, so they followed him down the hall, past crystals hanging in windows and framed posters of Jimi Hendrix and the Grateful Dead.

"Leo, I think your parents might be hippies," she told him in a whisper.

"I think you might be right," he whispered back, leaning down. "They met following The Dead on tour. They're basically walking stereotypes."

In the living room, they found a woman in a flowy, linen dress embroidered with flowers sitting in an armchair, book in one hand, petting an orange tabby cat with the other.

"Hey, Mom," Leo said, bending down and brushing the older woman's cheek with a kiss. "You look good."

"Thanks, honey. This must be Augusta," she said, with a warm smile that creased her tan skin. "So nice to meet you, dear."

"Hi, Mrs. Stone."

"You can just call me Ellen," she said, unseating the cat and rising to clasp Augusta's hand. "You have a lovely aura, such a soothing shade of lavender."

"Mom," Leo said in a tone Augusta had never heard him use before.

She ignored him. "Please, make yourself comfortable. Leo,

there's some iced tea in the fridge if you want to grab us some glasses."

Leo dutifully went to the kitchen and Augusta tried to discreetly take in all the details of the room that was the polar opposite of her own childhood home. Pat Podos would have described the succulents hanging in macramé plant holders and silk turquoise curtains as "crunchy granola," but Augusta liked it. It was homey.

After Leo had come back and poured and passed around glasses of homemade peach iced tea, he lowered himself beside Augusta on the couch. "So," Ellen said, settling back into her chair. "Have you called Lisa lately?"

"I will," he said, a little testily. "I've just been busy."

Augusta darted a curious look between mother and son. There she was again—the mysterious Lisa.

"My daughter is getting married," Ellen told Augusta, her voice brimming with pride. "She and her girlfriend have been living together for what, seven, eight years? We've been waiting for this forever and are so happy they are finally making it official. I gave her my blessing the day I met Kira. I only don't know why they waited this long."

"Mom, she's almost forty, she doesn't need your blessing," Leo said.

His sister. Augusta almost groaned out loud. Here she had been working herself up into a panic thinking he was seeing someone. Her heart immediately felt a little lighter.

Ellen waved him off with a fluttery hand, her copper bangles clinking. "So," she said, turning back to Augusta, "what exactly has Leo told you about his eccentric mom?"

Leo started to say something, but she stopped him with a raise of her brows that said she knew exactly what he had told Augusta about her. "No, no. It's fine." She looked at Augusta expectantly.

"He told me that you might be able to help me with ah, um, a problem I'm having."

"Mmm," Ellen said, as if she was used to being sought out for advice. "Well, depending on what your problem is, I might be able to help you. I'd like to think I'm handy in a few different areas. Leo, why don't you go see if your father wants some help making dinner, and Augusta and I will have a chat."

Leo started to protest, but Ellen shot him a look that would have made Pat Podos proud. Sighing, he stood up. "I'll be in the kitchen. If you need me, just give a shout," he said. He hesitated, then leaned down and added in a whisper, "Don't let her push you into anything that makes you uncomfortable. She means well."

Ellen leaned back in the armchair and the cat jumped up again and started purring. It circled in her lap three times before it settled, gazing at Augusta through narrowed yellow eyes. "Leo is a wonderful cook," Ellen said when he had left. "We're in for a treat. But that's not why you came, so what brings you all the way up to Pale Harbor for help?"

There was something comfortable and nonjudgmental about the older woman, and Augusta found herself telling her everything from the strange dreams to the hallucinations that grew more vivid each time. She'd already told Leo, so the words came easier. Ellen never interrupted or so much as batted an eyelash at some of the stranger details; she just nodded knowingly and stroked the cat, while the sounds of Leo and Terry moving around in the kitchen drifted in.

When Augusta had finished her story, she studied Ellen for her reaction. "That must be very hard," she said gently. "Not just the episodes, but reliving it all. Thank you for trusting me with that."

Augusta's shoulders sagged and she felt like a huge weight had been lifted. She still hadn't given herself permission to think too deeply on everything, but Ellen was right: it *was* hard. She felt like two different people, neither of whom were in the right place or the right time. When she was in the present, she was yearning to see Margaret's world again, to understand her and what had happened to her. When she was in the past, she worried that she would lose herself, that she might never come back.

"Don't mind me," Terry said, setting down a tray of vegetables and hummus. "Just bringing in some refreshments for you ladies."

"Thank you, dear," Ellen said with a warm smile. She offered the plate to Augusta, who shook her head.

"So, what should I do?" she asked after Terry had shuffled back out, humming a song under his breath. She didn't really think the woman sitting across from her could fix all her problems, but at least she was a good listener. Would she tell Augusta to put a crystal on her forehead and say an incantation? Or was there some kind of ceremony that involved burning herbs and sprinkling holy water? Augusta was willing to try anything, but Ellen's answer still surprised her.

"I don't know that there is anything you *can* do," she said. At Augusta's crestfallen expression, she continued. "Everything that you've told me makes it seem like you haven't done anything to bring this on. If anything, this outside entity, this Margaret, is the one who is instigating the episodes."

Well, that wasn't what she had wanted to hear. She still wasn't convinced that it all wasn't just in her head, and that there wasn't something seriously wrong with her. "I guess it's not worth asking Margaret to leave me alone?" Even as she said it, she realized how ridiculous it sounded. But more than that, she realized she wasn't quite ready for the visions to end. She wanted to know what had happened to Margaret after that fight with Henry, how she had disappeared into thin air.

Ellen tilted her head in consideration. "You could. She clearly wants you to know something, and I wonder if, once you know what she's trying to tell you, if she'll stop on her own. I think you need to set some boundaries, though."

"How do I do that?"

"Well, for starters, you could try to open communication with her, ask her to show you a vision when you're ready. That way you aren't unprepared when an episode suddenly begins. She obviously chose you for a reason. Maybe it's because you're related, or maybe she sees in you someone who would understand her and fight for her. She might not be speaking directly to you, but she's certainly making sure you see what she wants you to see. The next time you feel an episode coming on, see if you can beat her to the punch and ask her what she wants. I know it's not the solution you were probably hoping for, but I think it's your best chance to gain a little control."

Augusta mused on this. Sitting in the cozy living room, with the smell of dinner wafting in from the kitchen, Harlowe House and its ghosts seemed far away. She and Ellen chatted more about work, and she was even able to get some embarrassing stories about Leo from when he was younger. The golden evening light was starting to fade when Leo stuck his head in and told them that dinner was ready.

They sat down in the homey dining room and Terry turned on some quiet jazz in the background. As Leo brought the food to the table, he leaned down next to Augusta's ear. "I hope you'll try it. I made it with you in mind." She flushed at the warmth of his breath on her neck, the words settling over her like a comfortable sweater.

How could she not try the mouthwatering vegetarian feast in front of her, knowing that Leo had made it, and for her in particular? She could worry about the calories later, but for now, letting herself indulge in the food that he had cooked for her was the most intimate thing in the world.

Eating with Leo's family was warm and lovely, and never once did Augusta feel like an outsider, even as they discussed past family vacations or his sister's upcoming wedding. When was the last time Augusta had had a family meal? Even before her dad had died, Augusta had been away at college, and then her parents had separated. In a way, eating with the Stones felt like coming home.

After a dessert of blueberry pie and homemade vanilla ice cream, Leo collected the dishes and said that they should be going.

"At least stay for some tea," his mother protested.

"It's a long drive back, and I don't think Augusta wants to hear about another Grateful Dead concert from before she was born."

Ellen gave a little pout, but wrapped her arms around her son, who stood at least a head taller than her. "Okay, sweetie. You have a safe drive home, then. And call your sister!" she admonished him. "You don't need a reason to just talk with her once in a while."

The tips of Leo's ears turned delightfully pink, but he nodded. He dropped a kiss on his mother's head, and his dad pulled him into a big hug.

"It was really nice to meet you," Augusta said, sticking out her hand. But Ellen ignored it, instead wrapping her in a hug.

"It was nice to meet you, too, sweetheart. Come back anytime, and good luck with Margaret. Let me know how it goes."

Stars were peeking through the cloud cover as they climbed back into the car, dusk falling around the little Maine town.

"So, did my mom have any useful advice?" Leo asked once they had turned onto Main Street.

Augusta thought back over her conversation before answering. "I think so. I think she wanted me to feel empowered by the whole situation. Either way, though, it was good just to talk about everything with someone who isn't involved."

Leo nodded, but didn't ask her specifics. "That's good."

There was something about being in the car that made talking to him easy. Maybe it was that they were both looking ahead, so she didn't get her words tangled up under his attentive gaze. As they wound through the labyrinth of narrow streets, Augusta couldn't help but smile.

"What?" Leo asked, glancing at her.

"Nothing, really. I was just thinking how most of our conversations have been in this car."

She thought Leo might laugh at her for making such a strange observation, but she should have known him better by now. "Huh. You're right," he said, before pulling a U-turn. "Let's change that."

"Where are we going?"

He shot her a lopsided grin. "To the place where I spent most of my wayward youth in Pale Harbor." He nodded in the direction of a hill winding away from the main road.

A few minutes later, they pulled into a small gravel lot and Leo turned the car off. "Are you up for a little hike?"

She wasn't much of a hiker, or really anything that required being outside in the elements without massive amounts of bug repellent, but she probably would have followed Leo into a volcano, so she nodded.

It was a short, steep climb up. The gravel kept slipping out from under her flimsy shoes, and she definitely heard more than one kind of animal skittering through the overgrown brush. Leo stopped to help her up several times, and Augusta was glad for the dark so he wouldn't see how much she was struggling.

"Here we are," Leo said, as he helped her scramble up the final incline.

Augusta caught her breath. They were on a grassy overlook with endless views of the moonlit ocean in one direction, and the wooded town in the other. In the distance, a lighthouse winked at them as it threw its beams of light out into the dark abyss. It was cool and breezy and breathtaking, and totally worth the scratched ankles and aching lungs.

"Isn't it something?" Leo asked.

"It is," she agreed, glad that she had taken the risk to climb up with him.

"There's a great spot to sit over here." He gestured and she followed him to a natural dip in the ground that faced out over the water. They sat down, side by side, their shoulders just touching. A little thrill of anticipation rushed through her, as if she was sixteen again and had found herself outside the school dance alone with her crush.

"I'm surprised there aren't more people out here," she said. It seemed like the perfect place to come and watch the stars come out.

"This technically isn't public land," Leo told her. "See that house over there?" Augusta followed his finger to the faint outline of an imposing estate. "That's Castle Carver. It's a museum, kind of like Harlowe. I think you'd like it, actually."

In the dark, she could just make out a set of large windows that overlooked the water, and a turret. From what she could see, it was unlike any other house she'd ever seen. "I'd love to see it in the daylight."

"Maybe the next time you need some spiritual guidance from my mom I'll take you back here and you can go on a tour."

She couldn't quite make out his face in the dark, but she could hear the smile in his words.

"Thank you again for bringing me here," she said. "Not just for this view, but for meeting your mom. Talking with her really did help."

"Of course."

Biting her lip, she chanced a sidelong glance at him. The moon was casting him in tender shades of marble, a work of art that begged to be touched. If she was a little braver, she might have traced the line of his jaw, explored the contours of his face. But it wasn't enough to be physically close to him; she needed to know everything that made him the man she was developing feelings for. "You're really close with your family, aren't you?"

If he heard any of the envy in her voice, he didn't show it. "Yeah, it wasn't always like that. My mom had breast cancer a few years ago, and her prognosis was pretty bleak. Luckily, she was able to beat it, but going through something like that really puts things into perspective fast. We've come a long way." Pushing the thick layers of his hair back, he flashed her a little smile. "Anyway, I'm glad it was helpful. They're good folks, even if things are still strained between us from time to time."

She couldn't help but ask. "Strained how?"

"They trip and smoke a lot of pot, especially my dad. Which is fine," he hurried to add. "It's nowhere to the level of what Rachel was into, but they know about her overdose, and sometimes it's hard for me to be around them when they're high. It puts me on edge, like something terrible could happen at any moment."

Her heart broke all over again at the thought of what he'd gone through, the weight of the guilt that he carried on his shoulders.

"That must be tough. What was she like?"

Leo looked surprised. "Rachel? She was…" He broke off, as if searching for the right words. "She was like a firework—bright, loud, demanding attention. You couldn't help but be in awe of her. Even though she was always slammed with work at her nonprofit, she still had time for everyone who came through her door. But she also had a dark side, and in the end, her demons won."

Augusta bit her lip, not sure she wanted to know the answer to her next question. "Do you think about her a lot?"

"It's hard not to. I think more about what could have gone differently. I try not to get caught up in a cycle of what-ifs, though. For a long time, it was all I did—what if I'd been with her when she OD'd? What if I had believed her when she said she was in a bad place instead of brushing it off as her trying to get my attention again? But what's done is done and what-ifs won't bring her back."

They were silent as Rachel's ghost drifted from the starry sky and settled between them.

"What about you?" he asked, turning toward her so the moonlight caught the vulnerable glint in his eye.

"I was never super close with my family, but I don't have any siblings or cousins. I thought when my dad died that my mom and I would grow closer, but it was actually the opposite. We drifted further and further apart. It's actually kind of bullshit," she added, her own anger surprising her. "For some reason my mom seems determined to act like nothing happened. I don't know if it's because she and my dad were on the outs toward the end of his life because of the separation or what, but she acts like he never existed."

Leo was quiet while she spoke, but she felt his hand find hers and squeeze. "I'm so sorry, Augusta."

They sat like that, the cool breeze washing over them, the lap of the ocean in the distance. Having his fingers laced through hers felt like the most natural thing in the world, and another little piece of her slotted into place.

"Can I ask a question?" There was something in Leo's tone that put her on guard, a promise that he wanted to go deeper. But he'd opened up to her, so she resolved to do the same for him.

She nodded her assent, steeling herself for whatever he was about to ask. But his question, when it finally came, surprised her. "Do you think you're ready for a relationship so soon after everything that went down with your ex?"

"It's funny," she said, struggling to find the right words. "Those episodes...when I'm experiencing the world through Margaret's eyes... I get this feeling in my chest, like this clarity about what really matters and how short and special life really is." Her cheeks were burning and she could feel Leo's gaze on her through the dark, but she continued. "I guess I had this picture in my head of how my life would go, and since I broke up with Chris, I've had to reimagine what that picture would look like. I wanted to be single and find myself and all that stuff. But what I'm beginning to realize is that I don't need to find myself. I've been here all along." She scratched her fingernail in the dirt, suddenly wondering where she was going with this. "I met you, and I—I like you a lot. I understand if you don't feel the same way," she hurried to assure him, "or if it's too fast. I just wanted you to know that—"

But she didn't have a chance to finish. Leo was gently turning her chin to him, leaning into her. Instinctively, she closed her eyes as his lips met hers. His breath was warm and tasted of vanilla and peppermint, the gentle touch of his fingers awakening every part of her body. The moment she had been dreaming of for weeks was happening, and it was everything she had imagined and more. The lean muscles of his arms tightened under her palms as she explored the glorious shape of him. His fingers found her hair and a tingle of pleasure ran through her. "Is this all right?" he murmured as he pulled her closer.

It was more than all right—it was heavenly, her whole body warm and liquid from his touch. But she just nodded, afraid that if she tried to speak, she might break the spell.

"Good," he said, between light kisses on her throat, "because I've been dying to do this for weeks now."

She faltered, surprised at his words; she hadn't realized he'd been feeling this way for as long as she had. But she wasn't about to question it. Leaning deeper into the kiss, she savored the warmth of his hands on her back and neck, feeling both completely safe and more alive than she could ever remember.

But even he couldn't keep the ocean wind from picking up and winding around them, making her shiver. "You're freezing," he murmured, pulling away slightly.

"I'm fine," she said through chattering teeth. She had finally found out what it would be like to kiss him, and now the changeable Maine weather was thwarting her. "You're keeping me warm," she added.

He gave her a look that said he didn't believe her for one second, his hand still cupping her cheek. "Come on," he said, standing up and helping her to her feet. "I should be getting you home."

"I'm not a teenager, you know. I can stay out late."

"You're not? Well that's good to know." He flashed her a grin as he helped her climb back down.

When they'd made it back down to the car, he pressed her back against the car door and stole another long kiss that left her weak in the knees. Could it be this good all the time? She'd thought that she'd just needed a taste, a little glimpse of what life could be like with someone like Leo, but now she realized how good it was, and what torture it would be to have to go back to being near him but not with him. Some people liked having crushes, enjoyed flirting and the back-and-forth dance of a will-they-or-won't-they relationship, but she was decidedly not one of them. Why waste time if your heart knew what it wanted?

"Hey, will you do me a favor?" he asked, when they'd pulled apart and she was resting her head on his chest.

With his heartbeat strong and steady under her ear and his arms loosely around her waist, she would have promised him anything. "Yeah, of course."

"Will you promise not to try anything with Margaret at the house until I'm there?"

Surprised, she looked up and found that there was apprehension in his eyes.

"I know you can handle it," he said quickly. "I'd just feel better if I was there in case something went wrong. Humor me?"

"Sure," she said, more touched that he was concerned than worried that something actually might happen.

"Right," he said, clearing his throat, as if coming out of some private thought. "Let's get you home."

The highway was empty when they merged on, and Leo rolled down the windows so the cool air whipped in around them. Augusta leaned her head back, closing her eyes. Was this what it felt like to get what you wanted? Was this freedom, being able to be yourself and finding that you were accepted, wanted, even?

"Leo?" she found herself asking.

He gave her a quick, sidelong glance. "Yeah?"

"I want to go fast."

"You sure?"

She nodded. He didn't say anything else, just smiled, and shifted gears. Soon they were flying down the highway, hands clasped over the center console, music drifting through the night.

30

Margaret

Love is the centre of all we see,
Love is the jewel that guides us true,
No matter what, love, you'll stay with me,
No matter what, my love, I'll stay with you.

—"The Water is Wide," Traditional Folk Song

HERE IS WHAT I know to be true: we are part of something larger,
something more beautiful than we could ever comprehend. During our
brief tenure on this earth, we see but only a glimpse of the world around
us. But I have been denied this enlightenment, doomed to prowl this in-
between place until my story is known, my earthly remains paid their
proper due. I see but am not seen. I hear but am not heard. I cannot
forget, yet I am not remembered.

Do not judge me. I do not wish harm on my champion, who has
been so good to me and cleared away the dust from my name. But it is
hard, so very hard. I am a song that ended on an unresolved chord, a
story without an ending. So when I see my chance, I take it.

My little champion comes into the house, a faint smile playing at her
lips as she goes about her work. Ah, but I know that smile all too well.
It is the telltale sign of a heart light and in love.

She moves through the house, quiet and reverent. She cares for this place, and well she should. It is her home, too, in a sense. I let her linger in front of the place where my portrait should hang, contemplating the empty space.

I wait until she is in my stillroom. I have played little part in her discovery of her bloodline; that has been her own doing, like wiping the dust away from a mirror and seeing the reflection beneath. Now I must reach through the mirror.

It begins as a whisper. She pauses, tilting her head as if straining to hear. Come this way.

Her hand stills, the hairs on her neck rising. She lifts her gaze, searching for the source of her disquiet, and oh, but I can almost taste the air that passes through her parted lips.

It is said that youth is wasted on the young, but I believe that it is life that is wasted on the living. If I had a body, I would not starve it or deny myself any pleasure. I would fill it with food, savor each and every little miracle that the universe saw fit to bestow on me.

And so I shall.

31

Augusta

AUGUSTA HAD NEVER really been one to hum before, but as she let herself into Harlowe House the next day, she realized she was humming. It wasn't one of the tunes that seemed to haunt her dreams, but a song from the car ride with Leo last night. Even though it had been well after midnight when she'd finally gone to bed, she was feeling light and alive and full of hope. She waved to Reggie, who was making coffee in the kitchen, then headed upstairs.

Jill was in her office with the door open, and Augusta paused outside for a minute, debating going in and talking to her. Would she and Leo have to disclose their relationship to everyone else at Harlowe? Were they even *in* a relationship? She was getting ahead of herself. All they'd done was share a couple of kisses, albeit steamy, beautiful, perfect kisses. They weren't dating or anything. Yet somehow, she knew that what was between them was more than just hormones flaring under a romantically starry sky.

It would have been easy to push everything else out of her mind in favor of just reliving the previous night over and over, but if she was going to face Margaret, she wanted to get it over with. The sooner she could go back to normal and focus on her job and Leo, the better. He wouldn't be happy when he found out that she'd gone ahead and contacted Margaret without him. After all, he'd specifically asked her not to. But then, she had a feeling that Margaret wouldn't come if there was anyone besides Augusta. Continuing past Jill's office, she grabbed a flashlight from her desk and headed to the place where she'd had her first vision.

Augusta felt her as soon as she walked into the old kitchen and snapped on the flickering light bulb. "Hello, Margaret," she whispered into the musty air.

There was no answer, but she hadn't really been expecting one. Setting down her flashlight, she kept Ellen's words in mind. Margaret wanted only to be heard, to have her story told. Augusta had nothing to fear from her, even if the episode was surreal and made her feel as if she wasn't in control. Making sure that the door was closed behind her so she wouldn't be interrupted, Augusta sat in the middle of the room on the hard dirt floor and closed her eyes.

Nothing happened. Blinking her eyes open, she looked around. If Jill or Reggie came in and saw her, she was going to have an interesting time trying to explain what she was doing. Since the previous episodes had all begun at innocuous moments, Augusta instead forced herself to do some work.

No sooner had she picked up her pen, then she felt the hairs on her neck all the way to her scalp stand up. "Margaret," she whispered. In answer, the room shifted and blurred, taking her back to a different time.

32

Margaret

She became a corpse, a corpse all in the ground
And he became the cold clay and smothered her all around.

—"The Two Magicians," Traditional Folk Song

SEE WHAT I SEE. Feel what I feel. Be what I am.

I am not a gentle tide ebbing and flowing, but a violent undercurrent, sucking and grabbing and dragging down until I get what I want. And oh, how sweet is my reward. I am many things, but I am not your friend. I have been weak before, and I paid with my life. I will not be weak now.

She does not fight this time. She comes meekly and gladly, as if a lamb to slaughter. Good heart, gentle heart. Perhaps I should, but I can feel no guilt for one who lives only a half a life.

"Show me, Margaret," *she says. And I am only too happy to oblige.*

Jack was at their old meeting place on the rocks, and broke into a hesitant smile when he saw her. She had sent him a note, telling him to meet her there. And while she hated having to swallow her pride to send for him, at least it would be for the last time.

The air hung heavy with mist and the rasping call of crows.

What little remained of her broken heart throbbed at the sight of him, dark and handsome and belonging entirely to another woman.

The charm burned the skin beneath her bodice. She imagined feeding him the concoction of deadly nightshade, the color draining from his face as his jaw locked, his eyes went wild. She imagined cradling his lifeless body in her arms, the moon casting him pale and beautiful in death. It was no less than he deserved, yet she could not bring herself to say goodbye quite yet.

"Are you all right?" he asked, moving toward her.

She stepped out of his reach. "What a question! Of course I am not all right. Where did you tell Lucy that you were going tonight?"

He pressed his lips, and a dark look crossed his face. "You know that we don't live together."

"I know nothing about you or your affairs, clearly." If she was to give him the poison, then she had to at least make an attempt at luring him into a sense of security. She could not be angry, brash. But her fury burned too bright.

"Let's not speak of it," he said. Pulling her toward him, he wrapped his arms tightly around her waist. She could feel every inch of his long body against hers, the heat of him searing her with desire.

She let him kiss her, and before she could help herself, she was returning his kisses with equal vigor. She vowed that this would be the last time she allowed him such liberties, that it would be the last time she allowed him to breathe, but for that moment, he was hers.

His hands roamed her body, cupping her breasts through her dress, pressing his leg between her thighs. Pleasure shot up through her core. But then he pulled back suddenly, his lips swollen, his eyes dark. "What is that?" he asked.

"What is what? Jack!" she exclaimed as he plunged his hand into her bodice and drew out the satchel.

It looked harmless enough—a little burlap pouch bound with twine and filled with herbs, but he must have seen the guilt in her eyes because he drew back.

"What, did you mean to poison me? Or is this some witch work, a curse perhaps?"

She didn't say anything.

Jack fingered the little knife that he always kept in his boot. "I would be well within my rights to defend myself," he said. But there was no emotion in his voice, no conviction. He looked tired, defeated. "I would be well within my rights to fan the flames of the rumors and expose you for the dark work you do."

"But you won't," she said, tilting her chin defiantly.

He rakeed his hand through his hair, sighing. "No, I won't. Just like you will not kill me, as much as you may like to."

That was the problem, with such a love as theirs; they knew each other too well.

She was just about to tell him that perhaps he didn't know her as well as he thinks, when the sound of clumsy footsteps in the underbrush rang out. Was it the town boys again? How long ago that meeting in the woods seemed now. Jack must have thought the same thing, because he moved closer, putting himself between her and the noise.

She didn't know who she expected it to be, but she nearly lost her footing when her brother appeared in the clearing, his face pale, his eyes alive with fury. "Henry?" she asked, stepping around Jack. "What are you doing here?"

But he didn't even look at her. "Pryce," he said, staring daggers at Jack. The two men sized each other up like wolves circling each other. "I do hope you weren't threatening my dear cousin with that knife."

"Your cousin?" Surprise flickered across Jack's face and she almost laughed. He didn't know that Henry was not her brother! She never told him of her heritage, of the truth about her fam-

ily. What did it matter now, though? What did anything matter? Soon it would all be over.

"Go home, Henry," she ordered him through gritted teeth.

"I am not yours to order about," Henry said in a voice that she
had never heard from him before—older, mature. "I've come to
collect you and bring you back to Boston with me. This tryst
with Jack Pryce is over. I won't have my cousin lowering herself in such a way."

He grabbed her by the arm but she shook him off. "I'm not
going with you," she spit. "I would rather die than live as your
mistress or whatever it is you think to make me."

Jack finally seemed to snap out of his shock, and he reached
for her other arm. "Listen to her, Henry," he says. "She doesn't
want to go with you."

"It doesn't *matter* what she wants," he snapped. "She is a fallen
woman, and you are in no position to make her respectable. I
will care for her and the child, and she will be safe and out of
your reach."

She should have at least pretended to placate him, but they
shared the same blood that was so easily stirred to passion.
"You're mad," she told him. Grabbing the knife from Jack, she
brandished it, hoping it would convince him that there was
nothing for him there but danger.

But he didn't move, only gave a humorless smile. "Don't be
ridiculous, Margaret. Do you want to end up like your poor
mama? Broken and used and without a friend in the world? Do
you really think that our parents will allow you to live alone
with a bastard child? They may have raised you like their own,
but they have limits, especially when it comes to the good name
of the family and the business."

She could not stand to hear her dead mother spoken of in such
a way. She could not stand the pitying, condescending look on
Henry's face. It was not really Henry who was at fault, though;
he spoke no more than the truth, though she shuddered to hear

it. No, Henry was merely the vessel for all her rage, all her hatred, all her hurt and betrayal. It was not fair that she should have been denied the love she had found, nor made to live in shame for the natural consequences of that love.

The knife grew warm in her hand and she realized how foolish the notion of poison was then. Henry was still speaking, but she could not hear his words, nor that Jack was imploring her to put the knife down. All she could think of was how unfair it all was. It should have been her walking arm in arm with Jack down Main Street. It should have been her who held him close at night in their shared bed. It should have been her who owned his heart for all eternity. Henry thought that he understood her, thought that he could replace Jack. Well, he was a fool. She lunged at him as Jack called out her name, but it was too late. Henry stumbled backward.

Their bodies met, the jet buttons of her bodice pressing hard against his chest, the clandestine embrace that Henry had always craved. It was short-lived, however; something hot and sharp pierced her and, as quickly as they met, she pulled back.

She saw the shock on Henry's face first. Then she looked down. The silver knife she had just held was sticking out of her chest, her hand still wrapped around the handle, Henry's wrapped around hers. She jerked her head back up, still not fully understanding. The baby, had the knife touched the baby? Was there a spell to staunch the crimson flow of blood? Her head was light and, suddenly, she knew she was dying. It did not matter if the knife had pierced her baby or not, because her baby would die with her. She fell, first to her knees, and then to her back on the cold, rocky ground. No spell could save her now.

Above her stood Jack, his face twisted in anguish. Hot blood ran down her body, but she was too cold, colder than she had ever felt in her life. The scent of pine needles and mud filled her nostrils. The part of her tethered to the physical plane grew smaller and smaller, the rocks, and the tall, creaking pines expanding around her.

"What have you done?" The voice was tinny and sounded like it was coming through an old pipe. "Dear God, what have you done?"

But Henry didn't say a word. She could not see his face, but she could imagine only too well the look of shock, the horror in his eyes. He couldn't have meant to do it, he loved her. For all his faults, Henry had always loved her. If only he had not, then she might have still been breathing in the salt air, might still have felt the life growing in her belly.

Jack fell to his knees, his face filling her rapidly shrinking field of vision. "Margaret, can you hear me?"

Henry finally broke his silence, striding over and pulling him off her. "Get away from her, you scoundrel!"

She had never known Jack to cry before, but he cried then, his tears rolling down his cheeks and splashing onto her hands. They would be the only cleansing ritual her body would know.

Everything had gone black, but still their voices, the vibrations of their energy, surrounded her. She was in her body, but she was above it. She was dead, but she was still there. Air rushed around her, catching her up in its stream, and suddenly she was dancing in the leaves above them. She could feel the mist that hung heavy in the clearing, every damp particle fusing with her very soul. She was everywhere and nowhere, a ship drifting without a port, a starling swept up in a storm with no perch in sight. She was the dolphin caught in the fisherman's net, a vibrant life force with no body to call home.

"She's dead." Jack's voice choked with emotion. "You've killed her."

"I saved her," Henry lashed back. "She would have killed one of us, and then she would have been a murderess. A pregnant murderess, no less. Would you really see her name splashed across the newspapers? Have her stand in front of a judge and jury and sentenced to death? And besides, you are party to this."

She could practically hear the color drain from Jack's face.

There was a long silence, and when Henry spoke again, there was a tremor in his voice. "We—we need to bury her."

"Bury her—! Henry, you're mad."

"No," Henry said coolly. "I am the only one who is thinking clearly. We cannot leave her body here for anyone to find."

"She deserves a proper burial. We owe her at least that much."

"Well, aren't you a Samaritan? You didn't seem particularly concerned about what she was owed when you were fucking her."

Jack started to say something, but Henry was not finished. "I saw you, taking my sister against a tree like she was a whore, your hands all over her. Deny it all you want, but you're an engaged man, and you've been seen cavorting with a woman who is now dead. Who do you think people would believe—a Harlowe, or the son of a small-time grocer?"

"I loved her," Jack said quietly.

"You got her with child, knowing you would never marry her. You didn't love her. You used her."

A choke escaped Jack's lips, and soon they were lifting her, moving her. Then cold, grainy dirt cascaded over her.

That was my end. At least, that should have been the end. But now I have the chance to finish things, the way they should have been finished. I only need to go a little deeper, root myself a little firmer inside of her. But before I can, we are interrupted.

33

Augusta

"AUGUSTA? AUGUSTA!"

Augusta cracked open one eye, expecting dirt to come cascading down onto her face. Her head was pounding and it felt as if someone had poured cement in her lungs. But instead of a shallow grave, she was in the old kitchen, light spilling in from the doorway. She was herself. Not Margaret, not a ghost. And it wasn't Jack nor Henry who stood over her, but a very pale and very agitated Leo.

"I know what happened," she breathed. "I know what happened to Margaret."

"You don't look good. I think we should find you somewhere to sit down," he said, but she was barely listening. The light bulb above them buzzed; everything was too vivid, too harsh.

"It wasn't Jack. It wasn't Jack! It was her own brother, Henry. He was jealous and he killed her." She could still feel the knife slicing through her, hot and sharp, and she automatically put her hands to her stomach. The baby. The grief she felt at losing a child that wasn't hers—had never been hers—cut deeper than almost anything she had ever known. She fought back tears. "Then they buried her somewhere, but I don't know where." She shuddered at the memory of the light dimming around her, the cold earth opening up to swallow her.

She might have been back in the present day in her own body, but she still felt the acute loss echoing through her. Margaret had lost the child, lost her life, but it was Augusta who felt as if she was grieving. She had seen Margaret's sad story play out, and yet she was desperate to go back.

"This ends now," Leo said grimly, helping her up. "I should never have encouraged you or taken you to see my mother. This isn't good for you. You can barely walk."

She brushed aside his concerns. Now she would be able to curate an exhibit and tell Margaret's story. Not just an exhibit, she could publish a paper. It wasn't every day that a historic mystery was solved, and she had a secret weapon of firsthand knowledge. Of course, she could never divulge what had happened to her, but she would know what information to research, would know the answers before she even started.

"I'm telling Jill you're sick and taking the rest of the day—no, the week—off," Leo said as he took her hand and led her out to the staff kitchen.

This snapped Augusta back to attention. "No!" She jerked her hand away from him, almost losing her balance. "I want to stay. You don't get to make decisions for me."

There was some surprise in Leo's face, but mostly disappointment. "All right," he said with infuriating calmness. "It's all right. Why don't we go for a walk, then? Get some coffee?"

Normally she would have leaped at the chance, but she didn't want to leave Harlowe House. She belonged there. Carefully, she made her way out of the room, bracing herself against the wall as she went. "No, thanks. I'll be in my office."

"Augusta." He reached for her, but she pulled away.

She sat in her office, staring straight ahead, numb. When she and Leo had kissed, everything had seemed so bright and promising, but now she could barely think of anything except for the feel of the knife piercing her, the cold earth swallowing her up. It felt as if she had left a piece of herself—an important piece—back in the ground with Margaret.

On a whim, Augusta picked up her phone and scrolled through her contacts before hitting Call. It rang several times before a woman's low, rich voice answered.

"Gussie? Why are you calling me? Phones have this amazing feature now where you can just type your message." Maureen paused, Augusta's former coworker's flirtatious energy permeating through the screen. "Unless you just wanted to hear my voice?"

Augusta launched right into it. "Have you started your criminology program yet? Do you know anything about body decomposition or how to find a body?"

There was silence on the other end of the line, and then: "Augusta Podos, do I need to be concerned?"

"Hypothetically."

"Uh-huh. Well, if you're planning on body hunting you better invite me."

"It's hypothetical. I'm just curious."

"You know Google is a thing, right?"

"Maybe you were right the first time and I just wanted to hear your voice." Augusta couldn't help herself; her inhibitions were falling away faster than her nerves could catch up.

"Gussie. Stop it. You're going to make me blush." Maureen gave a dramatic sigh. "Okay, fine. Tell me what you want to know."

Giving an account of being buried without including the firsthand experience of her episode turned out to be harder than she thought, so she opted for vagueness. "I'm trying to figure out where someone might be buried. Someone from a long time ago."

"Okay," Maureen said slowly. "Most towns have records of that kind of thing. Have you tried that?"

Augusta shook her head impatiently, even though Maureen couldn't see her. "It wasn't recorded, and I'm pretty sure it was an unmarked grave somewhere other than a cemetery. I know that there are trees around the area, and I don't think it's a very deep grave because...well, it doesn't matter why."

Maureen mused on this. "If it's not a deep grave it could mean that whoever did the digging was planning to move the body later to another location. Skulls are the first thing to appear in dirt when it's disturbed by human activity or erosion, so if someone really knew what they were doing they could have buried the corpse head-down—foot bones are small and harder to see. But if it was an amateur or they were scared of being caught in the act, they could have just done a sloppy job." There was a drawn-out pause on the other end of the call. "I can't believe I'm saying this, but—maybe if you have this kind of information about a burial, you should call the police?"

"I'm not calling the police. It's a historical murder, and it's been forgotten for over a century. Besides, it's all hypothetical."

"Hypothetical. Right."

There was silence. Her mind was spinning. Margaret wanted to be found—why else would she have shown Augusta everything that had happened to her?—but she had never shown Augusta where she was buried. Was it possible that Margaret herself didn't know? Would Augusta just have to go out into the woods and hope to stumble on a skull? It was like searching for a gruesome needle in a haystack. "I have to get going, but thanks for the info."

"Sure. But before you go—are you doing all right? You sound...different."

Augusta hadn't been aware that she sounded anything other than like herself. Was it because she wasn't the same shy, insecure girl that had worked at the Old Jail? Or was it because she hardly had the time or patience for anything besides Margaret anymore? "Yeah, I'm fine."

The pause that followed was a heavy one. "I miss working with you, Gussie," Maureen said softly. "We should hang out sometime."

If she hadn't been so single-mindedly focused on Margaret, Augusta would have been touched and relished the chance to spend some time with Maureen. How many times had she felt alone and friendless, when there were people right in front of her who had just been waiting for her to let them in? But she had Margaret now, and even Leo was proving too much of a distraction from what was important.

"Yeah, definitely," Augusta told her. "Let's set something up." But as she said it, she knew that the time had passed.

Augusta could feel the critical gaze of her mother on her at the dinner table that night. She didn't want to be sitting in the linoleum-tiled kitchen or pushing around microwaved lasagna. She didn't want to be making small talk about her job or listening to her mother recount the neighborhood gossip. All she wanted to do was be with Margaret again. To *be* Margaret again. Margaret had unfinished business, and she felt the restlessness, the urgency in her own bones.

With a huff, her mother put her fork down and gave her a hard look. "So, how long are you going to sit there ignoring everything I say?"

Augusta hadn't even realized her mother had been speaking. "What?"

"What's going on? You've been in a foul mood since you got home."

"I am not in a foul mood."

"Yes, you are." Her mother crossed her arms, giving her a look that usually would have sent Augusta running. "You're like a sulky teenager."

"How come we never talk about our family? How come you're so afraid of facing the fact that Dad died, and we never do anything to remember him?"

"What are you talking about? Of course I remember your father."

"That's not what I mean."

Her mother drew in a ragged breath. "Because it's not my place to sully my daughter's memory of her dead father." She gave Augusta a pointed look. "Okay? So enough of that."

"What is that supposed to mean? Because you guys didn't get along, I'm just supposed to forfeit any sort of memories of him?"

"I swear to God, Augusta, this is not a conversation I'm having with you, especially when you're acting this way."

Her mother's words rolled off Augusta's back. If she didn't want to talk about Augusta's dad, fine. There were plenty of other questions that needed answers. "How come you keep all our family stuff hidden away? Why do I have to go digging just to learn who I am?"

"You're not making any sense—you know exactly who you are. You are Augusta Jean Podos and right now you're being a serious pain in my ass."

But Augusta wasn't giving in. "I want to know about where we come from, about all the names on the family tree. How come we never visited anyone for the holidays? How come—"

Slamming her hands on the table, Pat cut her off. "Fine. You want to know about our family? I'll tell you. Our family is a disaster. There are feuds, rifts, tragic deaths and more divorces than happy marriages. My own grandmother told me we were born under a bad sign and that if I cared about our family at all that I wouldn't have any children to continue the curse. I wanted to protect you from the bad luck and sadness that seems to follow every generation, but it looks like you want to go down that road, too. You had a good relationship, job and place to live, and you threw it all away to come live here and start over again—and for what?"

"So it's just superstitions? That's it?" She had expected some big dark secret, *something* concrete about their origins. "Of course we have divorces and deaths—every family does. You could have told me the truth all along. I'm not a child."

"You're *my* child," Pat retorted.

There had to be something more. Her mother was down-to-earth and eschewed all things occult and supernatural. Augusta couldn't believe that Pat would accept the idea of a family curse. "You didn't want me to know about our family because you're suddenly superstitious? Jesus, Mom, you never even let me believe in Santa."

"It's not just superstition," Pat mumbled, not quite meeting her eye. In all her twenty-eight years, Augusta had never heard her mother mumble. Pat always had something to say and knew exactly how to say it.

"*What?*" Augusta demanded, afraid that she'd already heard the gist of it.

Her mother shot her a peevish look. "I said, we're descended from one of the Salem witches."

Augusta blinked. It was a running joke in Salem that everyone was a descendant of one of the dozen or so convicted witches, and it seemed like every tourist who came through the Old Jail was also convinced that they were a descendant. Some probably were, but mostly it was their own family lore or wishful thinking. Was her mother really one of those people? Why had she never mentioned anything about this before? It wasn't impossible that her family really did have some tenuous connection to one of the witches; after all, her family had lived in Salem for generations.

A fog that she hadn't known was clouding her mind suddenly lifted, and Claudia's story about Phebe and the mysterious girl who had gotten her mixed up in some kind of trouble came back to her. Margaret looking after Augusta, choosing her to see Margaret's story. The books she had found in the attic, filled with what she had thought were recipes but now realized were herbal charms, spells. Margaret had lived two hundred years after the infamous trials, but she had been a witch all the same. Of course, she wouldn't have been a witch in the way the tourists who came through The Old Jail envisioned witches with pointy hats and broomsticks; she would have been more of a healer than a witch.

"Augusta? Did you hear what I said?"

"Yeah, I heard," Augusta muttered. "You lied to me and isolated me from our family, all because of some dumb superstition." It didn't matter if Margaret had been a witch in the true sense of the word or not. It was ludicrous to believe that their family carried a curse because of one eccentric ancestor. But then again, what if Margaret really *had* possessed some sort of power? Wouldn't that explain Augusta's visions? Her head spun. Everything she thought she knew about her life turning upside down.

Pulling out the box of family documents from under the bed, she let herself get lost in the web of names. Podos, Gennetti, Bishop, Cooke, Barrett, Montrose, Hale. Why had no one ever told her who she was? Who had all these people been, and how had they shaped her? She refused to believe that her family was cursed, or had some dark, tragic roots. But what if there was some truth to it, even just a little? She thought of her interview with Claudia, and the way certain stories were passed down by families. If she was truly related to Margaret, then maybe there was some grief that ran through her blood, passed down generation to generation, manifested in untimely deaths, broken hearts and melancholy dispositions.

She had always been lonely, adrift. Maybe that was why she had clung to Chris for so long. Older parents and no cousins or siblings or really any extended relatives to share their family history. With Margaret, she made sense. She was descended from a powerful woman, a woman who had been wronged.

Without really knowing why, Augusta threw on some shoes and grabbed her car keys.

"Now where are you going?" her mother called from the kitchen, where she was elbow deep in the dishes with which Augusta would usually help.

"Out," she answered, slamming the door behind her.

As soon as she pulled up and turned off the car, she felt better, like she could finally breathe again. This was right. This was where she belonged. Somewhere, deep down, she knew she was being impulsive, but it felt good to give in.

She punched in her code and let herself into the house. Jill or Reggie might see that she had come in at night, but really, who cared? All that mattered was that she was where she was meant to be. She alone was steward to Margaret's legacy, and thus the legacy of Harlowe House. Inside it was quiet and still, and she closed her eyes, breathing in the familiar scent of old wood.

"I'm here," she whispered to the empty house. "Just because you finished showing me your story doesn't mean you have to leave."

Such welcome words I never heard. I would have come regardless, but to be invited, well, that is no small thing. It makes my work infinitely easier, lessens the energy I must expend to complete the magic. This is what I have been waiting for all these years. My champion, my blood, my vessel. This time there will be no interruptions. This time we shall finish what was started.

I feel her stiffen in surprise, then give a little sigh as I make myself at home.

Margaret, *she says in her mind.*

Augusta, *I answer.*

We are together, her and I. A host and a guest. A body and a soul.

34

Margaret & Augusta

WHEN I OPEN my eyes, my old stillroom greets me, though it is empty and stale now, a musty fug hanging in the air. A spiderweb tickles my face and instinctively I swat it away. I marvel at the way the sticky silk clings to my fingers; I have never felt anything so wonderful.

An electric torch rests on the ground, but I don't need it; I can find my way in the dark as well as any cat. I have seen my house from afar all these years, but now I move through it as I once did. I pick up a crystal vase, reveling in the satisfying weight of it in my hand before placing it down again.

In the kitchen I pour myself a glass of water and stand there, letting it dribble down my chin and stain my shirt. Glorious, it is so glorious. Then I go to the lavatory and turn on the light so that I might see my reflection in the mirror.

The face that gazes back at me in wonder is not me, but I

know it so well that it may as well be. My curls are lighter and shorter, and freckles dust the bridge of my nose. I frown. The clothes do little to flatter the female form. No matter, I shall make do. Somewhere deep in the brown eyes I see fear, but I cannot dwell on that. I am free, and that is all that matters. Though I inhabit her body, I am not privy to her thoughts, her memories, her fears. Just as well—I have no interest in them.

I move through the house like that for hours—exploring, touching, experiencing. There is a whole world outside that door, but for now, I just want to rediscover my home. I have time now. I can do all the things that were denied to me. All that is missing is Jack.

When I showed Augusta what became of me, I learned something, as well. I had always thought that it was Jack who delivered the fatal blow. But it was Henry. All these years I saw the knife in the wrong hand, felt the blade slice into me from the wrong direction. It might not have been Jack's hand, but if not for him and what he did, I would not have been on those rocks that night, and Henry would not have come to defend my honor.

Sunlight filters in through the museum curtains and I am soon to lose my solitude. "Oh, Augusta! You're in early." It's the woman named Jill. She looks startled to see me, her cherry red lips open in surprise. I give her a wide smile and try out my voice.

"Just wanted to get started on some research!" I say. My words come out chipper and higher than I intended.

Her gaze lingers on me a moment too long, and I know that she can sense a difference, but cannot put her finger on it. "Okay. I hope you're feeling better today," she says. "I'll be in my office if you need me."

When she's gone, I resume my inventory of my house. Aside from my portrait, which used to hang in the dining room, it is as if I never lived here. Perhaps I should have let Augusta make her exhibit first, but I suppose I can tell my own story now.

I watch as tours of people come stomping through my house, loud and oblivious. When I can no longer stand the sight of unwiped shoes on my carpets, I take myself outside. As soon as the salt air touches my face, I am reborn, my new body baptized in sunlight. I shrug out of the cardigan and let more of the air caress my skin.

My tether has snapped and I am free from my prison at last, a butterfly taking flight from its chrysalis. For the first time in over a century I can see outside the walls of my house, experience the world beyond. Tynemouth has changed, and it is harder to see the ocean now from the front lawn. Technology of which I was only vaguely aware before now hurtles down the street in front of me. Instead of fish carts and horses trudging by, cars clog the air with their exhaust, and there is an unpleasant tinge to the air that I cannot quite place. Just like my new body, I feel a surge of anger that those charged with stewardship of such a gift should squander it so.

I catch my reflection in a shop window as I walk down Main Street, and I cannot but help admire it again. When I catch the eye of a young man, I wink, then throw my head back and laugh. Such freedom! But my joy is short-lived, and I turn melancholy when I pass the building that used to be Pryce's Grocery, now a shop selling knickknacks and souvenirs. Jack. The sands of time have long since claimed him. I do not know what became of him, but I have often wondered. He never got his just deserts. Did he return to Lucy? Did she bear him children? Did they grow old together? Did he ever come to the spot on the rocks again and think about what might have been?

All the strangers in my midst are from an unfamiliar time and place, and loneliness washes over me. I would give anything to have George swing me up in his arms again and pepper me with compliments. I would give anything to have Shadow at my heels. Someday I may very well meet them on the other side. This mortal vessel can only bear me for so long. This time, though, I will leave the earth when I am old and wrinkled, and on my own terms.

I pause in front of Phebe's cottage, or rather, where it used to stand. No trace remains of the oyster shell path or the wooden gate. I strain my ear, trying to hear the shells tinkling in the wind, but they are gone now, their chaotic melodies nothing but a forgotten memory. I wonder whatever became of Phebe, if she ever forgave me. She is a regret that no time can erase.

My stomach rumbles and I laugh. Another reminder of my body! I swear I shall never tire of it. Though I long to stand on the rocks and feel the ocean spray on my feet, I turn back toward home to find something to eat.

The refrigerator yields a bounty of food. Such wonderful things I have never tasted! I sink my teeth into a peach, letting the juice run down my chin as my mouth explodes with sweetness. I am eating my fill when I sense a male presence behind me, and turn. Leo, in the flesh.

"Augusta?" He watches me as if he's never seen the girl in front of him before. "Jill said you were in early. Are you sure you want to be here today?"

I let my gaze run over him, making no pretense of hiding my interest as I lick the sticky peach juice from my fingers. He is fine looking with his frank gray eyes and an open, almost boyish face. Not as tall as Jack, but well-built and cutting a fine figure nonetheless. He takes a step closer, hesitant, and I can smell the decadent scent of him, all cedarwood and soap.

"Go on," I tell him, holding out the peach so that he might try.

He could not look more wary yet desirous if he were Adam and I Eve, offering him the forbidden fruit. The peach sits in my hand between us, the artificial kitchen light glinting off the soft flesh. "I—I'm glad to see you eating," he finally says, his gaze moving from the fruit to my mouth, where it lingers. "I never wanted to say anything because...well, I worry and—"

He breaks off as I set aside the peach and close the small distance between us, placing my hands flush on his chest. Through the thin material of his shirt, I can feel his heart beat faster under my fingers. I don't know of everything that has transpired between them, but I do know that Augusta was a fool for not seeing the way he looked at her, the way he hung on every word she said, like she was a goddess to be worshipped. I trail my fingers down his chest, reveling in the muscles that tighten beneath them.

"What—what are you doing?" he asks, though he does not step away.

"What would you like me to do?" I reach up, dusting his jawline with kisses. His skin is warm, soft. Alive.

"Augusta," he says, his breaths coming hotter and deeper. "I don't think this is a good idea. Not when you've been—"

I stop his words with a kiss, deep and probing. His body softens just a little into mine and oh, what heaven. This is what it is to be truly alive. A body on its own is just a vessel, but a body infused with love is to taste all the universe has to offer. And I have hungered for so long.

Augusta watched in horror as her body moved of its own accord.

Leo was kissing her, but not her. *He was wrapping his arms around her, but not* her. *All of the sensations—heat, happiness, arousal—she had felt kissing him on the hill were gone. It was like eating food but not being able to taste it. Claustrophobia pressed in around her, but she had no body to fight it, no voice to scream. She was like a fishing bob, tethered to her body, but floating above, separate. Trapped.*

Leo, she screamed fruitlessly. It's Margaret, not me! It's not me! Help! *But no words came out of her mouth.* Margaret, *she thought desperately.* Please, let me out. I'll tell your story. I'll do anything you want—just please, let me out!

There was no answer. This was just a bad dream, it had to be. She would wake up with a lingering sense of nostalgia, just like all the other dreams. Even during the height of her episodes she'd never felt so help-

less. Now there was no more hiding from the truth: she'd fallen victim to something much darker, something far beyond her control.

Leo pushed away. He leaned against the wall and drew his hands over his face, looking as anguished as if he'd just hit a dog with his car. "I can't. I'm sorry, but I can't. Not when you...when you haven't been feeling well."

Margaret gave a fluttery laugh. "Oh, very well. Later, perhaps."

Augusta watched as Leo shot her a lingering look of misgiving before beating a hasty retreat from the kitchen. What did Margaret want? What would she do? She didn't know where Augusta lived or any of the details of her life outside of Harlowe House—did she? Did Margaret simply want to live in her old house again? If she did, then someone would surely have to realize that she wasn't Augusta. But how could they help? She felt as if she were in a speeding car with the brakes cut, her hands tied behind her back.

Margaret ate her fill from the fridge, then returned to her office upstairs. Her only hope was that Margaret had as little control as Augusta had had during her episodes and would soon slip away. But she had a horrible, sinking feeling that told her Margaret was here to stay. Augusta had, after all, invited her in. How could she have known Margaret's dark purpose? How could she have known that Margaret would betray the bond, the alliance they had come to form at Harlowe House?

35

Margaret

MY BOOKS, BOTH of them, are where I left them. I wait until the tourists and staff are gone before I take a little file up to the attic and shimmy it under the floorboard. There, among a blanket of dust and dead insects, I find the bundle that I hid over one hundred and fifty years ago. The only other person who has laid eyes on them has been Augusta. The thought makes me smile. Her eyes. My eyes.

I rock back on my heels, savoring the weight of them in my hands. They are softer, more fragile than when I left them here, but memories rush through me as I hold them. All my knowledge, all my power, preserved for such a moment as this. I pause, my fingers dancing to turn the pages, but I stay them. What I read, *she* reads. I may be in control for now, but my position is tenuous. Any knowledge in these books that I seek to use, she will also be privy to. The only part of Augusta's life I know of, is that which has played out within this house. And though she can see through my eyes since our fusing, I must remember, she is of my blood, and latent though they may be for now, she still possesses powers. Who do you think caused the painting to fly, whether she knew that she was doing it or not?

Standing, I let the blood rush back into my legs. I don't know where Augusta went when she was not at Harlowe House, and I do not care. Her old life is not my life. All the same, considerations must be made. I cannot very well sleep here and attract undue attention, nor wear the same clothes continually. Eventually I will have to find somewhere to live, have to attend to all those little details that fill her life.

Downstairs, the clock reads eleven. I have hours yet before I must give over my house to the tourists. I have seen Augusta disarm the security system hundreds of times, and I easily enter the code and let myself out.

My next stop is the carriage house. Jack never gave me lover's tokens. He was not rich enough to buy me precious things, nor yet clever enough to fashion me anything with his hands. I had no need of such trinkets, though, for I had his heart. Or so I had thought.

The only thing that remains of him in this house is a little tin box that once held sewing pins and that he used to bring me a pressed flower once. You would not know that it was anything special, that it once represented all my hopes and dreams, mottled with rust as it is. It is a miracle that it has survived so long unnoticed. Tracing my fingers over the faded rose design, I give it one last look before slipping it into my pocket.

It is a fine November evening, a hint of sweet-smelling dried grass mingling with the ocean brine. The pavement under my shoes is hard, but the path is familiar. By the time I reach the old cemetery, I am perspiring from the humidity. I always loved the cemetery, even in my own lifetime. Perched on a hill overlooking the harbor, its marble stones glow like lost souls in the night. It has fallen into disrepair, though, and the gate is rusted, the overgrown grass threatening to swallow up the stones. I pick my way through them to the older section in the back where crooked crosses and crumbling cenotaphs jut drunkenly out of the ground.

There is the Harlowe plot. The wrought iron fence that once gleamed black is now peeling and flaking, the marble stones weather-beaten and faded. I have heard enough tours over the years to have memorized the death date of each and every one of my family members, yet seeing the engraved numbers that cap the end of each life still tugs unexpectedly at my heart. Where is my body? I wonder. Under what anonymous tree do I lie, and what is left of me? I remember Jack above me, a cascade of cold dirt and mud, but where? Did they leave me in the clearing, or take me somewhere else? Even if I knew, could I bear to see my own bones, jumbled and rotten? I shiver in the cool night.

When I have paid my respects at George's grave, I stand, brushing the dead grass from my knees. I am just leaving when a name on a simple grave nearby catches my eye.

JACK PRYCE
REST IN PEACE

A hundred emotions run through me, emotions I haven't felt in years, never even felt during my own lifetime. No dates, no carved cherub or weeping willow. Just a name nearly eaten away by lichen. When did he die? How? For all that the history of my family has been immortalized in the museum, Jack is as lost to time as I was.

Kneeling, I place my palm against the mossy stone. "Jack," I breathe into the night air. "We shall be together again. And soon. I have not forgotten my pledge."

Let no man steal your thyme. The old lullaby runs through my head as I leave the cemetery. I smile to myself. No man shall steal my time, not again.

★ ★ ★

I wait for Leo the next day, having spent the night sleeping under the stars in my old woods. It was invigorating to breathe in the fresh air and bathe myself in the light of the moon, but I cannot sleep in the woods every night. I crave the comforts of hot baths and soft pillows that I have so long gone without.

"Hey," I tell him, coming into the ballroom. He gives me a wary look before quickly dropping his gaze back to his work.

"Hey." Pink is creeping up from his collar, a remnant of shame or desire from our encounter the previous day.

"I hope that I didn't upset you yesterday. I've just been under a lot of stress lately and I suppose I acted strangely." The words slip out easily; I have been watching Augusta for months and can mimic her as well as any parrot.

He had been kneeling on the floor with his papers spread around him, but he gets up and crosses the room, stopping an arm's length from me. "Let's just pretend it didn't happen, yeah? I think we both could have handled that better." He gestures to his computer, which is sitting on the folding chair. "My laptop is acting up again and I have a presentation tonight at the community college." Pausing, he gives me a shy look through his dark lashes. "I hate to ask, but do you think you could take a look at it again and see if it's something obvious that could be fixed?"

I glance at the machine on the floor. Augusta may have known what to do, but I don't. I give him a helpless shrug. "I wish I could help. I need to get some work done upstairs." I give his arm a friendly squeeze so he knows that there are no hard feelings, then leave him.

Augusta

MARGARET! If she could hear Augusta or understand, she gave no indication. Hurt and confusion flashed across Leo's face when she left him standing there, humming a song under her breath.

Augusta had watched as Margaret had taken the books out from the floorboards in the attic the night before, then gone traipsing through the cemetery. There was something in those books that Margaret didn't want her to see, because she'd quickly closed them up and put them back. But Margaret must have forgotten that Augusta had already seen the books, already knew what was inside of them. Not that she had been able to make much sense of the spells and notes that filled the second one.

Margaret sat at Augusta's desk, flipping through papers and occasionally examining the computer. If only there was some way to get a message out, to send the alarm that something wasn't right. But how? Augusta had no control over her body, and everyone thought she was right there, sitting at her desk like she was supposed to be. Her only hope was that Margaret would grow tired of her new body and leave on her own.

Just then there was a knock at the door and she—Margaret—looked up to see Leo.

"Hey, sorry to bother you." Augusta's heart clenched at the sight of him, looking vulnerable and unsure.

"You're never a bother," Margaret said, sitting up and giving him a bright smile.

Leo hesitated for a second before continuing. "I was wondering if you were around this weekend? I'm driving up to Maine to visit my parents, and I would love the company."

How could he not see that she wasn't herself? But then, how well did he really know her to begin with? They'd only known each other for a couple of months. There'd been the promise for something more, but just when they'd been about to explore it, Margaret had stolen everything from her.

Setting aside the papers, Margaret gave him an apologetic smile. "Oh, I wish I could, but unfortunately I have plans this weekend."

Plans? What plans could a one-hundred-fifty-year-old ghost-witch possibly have?

Leo didn't seem put off. "Oh, yeah?" he asked casually. "What are you up to?"

"Oh, family obligations. You know how it is," she said. "My parents need me at home."

Augusta watched Leo's reaction carefully. Would he catch Margaret's mistake? Did he realize that it pointed to something sinister? But more important, did this mean that Margaret didn't know everything about Augusta's life outside of Harlowe House?

But he showed no sign of it. "Sure, totally understand," he said. He was about to turn away when he paused, turning back. "I'd really like it if you could come. We can talk more about Margaret and your exhibit. And look, I know that it's not really my place or anything, but I have to say, I'm worried about you. My sister is going to be in Pale Harbor this weekend, and she's a psychiatrist. I thought maybe you could...that is..." He trailed off, looking almost embarrassed. "Well, if you're not feeling well, maybe she can refer you to someone who could help."

He thought Augusta had a split personality or something and wanted his sister to check her out. First, he had thought she had a substance abuse problem, and now he thought it was mental illness. Why couldn't he see that it was something that went beyond all logical explanations?

Margaret tapped her pen against the desk, and Augusta could sense her irritation. But then she brightened. "You know what, maybe I will. Why not? It could be fun. Though I assure you, there's nothing wrong with me."

Lingering a moment longer, Leo nodded. "Great, it's a date, then."

Whatever little hope Augusta had evaporated with Leo's words. Even if he had realized there was something wrong, what could he have done to help her? What could anyone do?

Margaret

Jill's office was once my brother Clarence's bedroom. The lovely damask wallpaper is now painted a bland creamy white, and the window is shut tight against the fresh summer air. Tamping down my irritation, I paste a bright smile on my face and knock.

"Come in!"

Jill is seated behind her desk. She looks up and smiles. "What's up, Augusta?"

Perching on the edge of a chair, I let my fingers run over the smooth wooden arms. "Oh, nothing much. Just doing some research." I pause, as if thinking. "How would I go about finding someone who lived in the 1870s in Tynemouth?"

Jill's perfect eyebrows lift in surprise. "Is this about Margaret again? I thought you said you turned up some good information in the archives?"

My name coming from her mouth causes me to tighten. But of course, she doesn't know anything. "Did I? That's right. This is about someone else, though, someone who would have been tangentially related to the Harlowes."

"The best thing to do would be to ask Sharon or Lori, though they might just point you to the Office of Vital Records."

I had been hoping not to have to rely on someone who works here, but I nod, as if this perfectly answers my question. "Of course. Thank you."

I rise to leave, but Jill stops me. I can hear the hesitation in her voice. "Augusta, how are you doing? I want to make sure that you're comfortable and feeling safe here after everything that happened."

Surprised, I sit back down. I know that I am not Augusta, that I cannot grasp every nuance of this modern life. But Chris, that miserable excuse for a man, has at least given me an excuse. "Truthfully," I say, "it has been hard. I feel as if I'm not myself sometimes."

Jill nods sympathetically. "Please take care of yourself. And if I can do anything, reach out whenever. I'm here for you. You deserve to feel safe."

A bubble of emotion rises in my throat, and for a moment, I think I might cry. Aside from Phebe, I never had the confidence of a close female friend, never mind one my age. Swallowing back the unwelcome emotion, I remind myself that she is not *my* friend, but Augusta's. None of them are my friends, especially not Leo.

Augusta

The last time Augusta had been at the Office of Vital Records, she'd had Leo at her side and was filled with excitement. Now she watched as Margaret climbed the old stone steps up to city hall and she felt hopeless and helpless, but curious. Who was Margaret looking for, and what did she plan on finding?

With all the grace and dignity of a queen, Margaret employed the old woman working behind the window to find birth and death records from the late 1800s and seated herself at a table to wait for them to be brought to her.

Margaret flipped through the binders with amazing speed, her finger tracing over the typewritten names. She let out an exasperated huff when the first binder didn't yield whatever result she was expecting.

It was nearly four binders later when Margaret caught her breath. Her finger rested reverently over a line, her lips silently mouthing the name.

Pryce, Jack. b. 185? d. 1877

Augusta should have known; Margaret wanted to know what had become of her lost lover, the man who had not killed her, but who had broken her heart and led her down the path of destruction. He had only lived a year longer than Margaret, and it was hard not to wonder if his death had somehow been related to losing her. It was a tragic story, a doomed romance, but Augusta couldn't bring herself to feel truly sorry for either of them. The room had gone very still as Margaret sat there, staring at Jack's name.

Then Margaret spoke, and again Augusta was reminded that, though both their souls inhabited one body, Margaret was still somehow able to keep at least a part of her thoughts veiled from Augusta. "Jack," she said. "Soon."

Her words came out in a whisper, almost as if she hadn't meant to speak at all. Then she sat up straighter and called to the clerk. "Excuse me, but how would I find out the manner in which someone died?"

The old woman raised her brows behind her reading glasses. "You don't," she said shortly. "You would need to find the death certificate for that, and we don't have those here."

Margaret scowled, slamming the binder shut. Pushing back from the table, she stalked back outside, leaving the angry clerk yelling at her to come back and clean up all the binders she'd left everywhere.

On the steps, she paused, squaring her shoulders and looking up at the gray sky. "Yes, you begin to see my aim now," she said, and Augusta realized that Margaret was addressing her, Augusta. "But know this—none of this will have been in vain if my plans come to fruition. You are part of something bigger than yourself now."

A small smile played on her lips, and despite Margaret's reassurance, all Augusta heard was a deep note of foreboding.

It was dark and Harlowe House had been long closed for the evening by the time Margaret returned from walking through town. Her step was determined as she made her way around the back of the house to the garden shed. Margaret rattled the chained handles. This was where Reggie kept most of his tools and landscaping supplies. What was Margaret looking for?

But Margaret wasn't deterred. Picking up a rock, she smashed it against the chain until it was mangled and eventually splintered. She pulled the doors open and rifled through the tools until she found a shovel. As soon as her hand wrapped around the handle, Augusta knew. There were only two things that Margaret would be using a shovel for: either putting something in the ground or digging something up.

Shovel in hand, Margaret left the shed standing ajar and set out down the sidewalk. Humming a song under her breath, she drew sidelong looks from the few people she passed on the dark street.

It was only when the old cemetery came into view that a cold panic spread through Augusta. Margaret was going to dig somebody up, and Augusta had a sinking feeling she knew who.

Margaret made her way to the back of the cemetery, found the small grave and began to dig. This couldn't be happening. It might have been Margaret's dark desire that was guiding, but it was Augusta's hands that were plunging the shovel into the gravelly soil. It was Augusta who would have to answer for the desecration of a grave, and who would be haunted for the rest of her life by these actions if she ever escaped from the prison of her body.

A car rumbled past the street beyond the gate with a brief flash of headlights and then the receding sound of an engine. Would anyone see Margaret? Would anyone stop her? Maybe if she was arrested there would be a trial, some sort of psychiatric evaluation, and a doctor would realize there was something wrong. But no one stopped, and Margaret was free to continue with her gruesome task.

It felt like days had passed by the time Margaret ceased her digging, the shovel having finally reached something solid. But it was still dark, the only light coming from the moon and a buzzing streetlamp. The ragged walls of the grave rose up around her like a clay prison. Tomorrow or the day after there would be headlines in the local paper: "Old Grave Desecrated in Historic Tynemouth Cemetery" or "Vandals Hit Cemetery in Belated Halloween Caper." But tonight, it was just her, Margaret, and the dark magic that bound them together.

Crouching down, Margaret felt the edges of the old coffin and began clawing at the dirt, bringing up fragments of rotten wood and sending worms slithering.

It was the smallest of mercies, but the remains that came up were small, barely identifiable as bones. There was no gaping skull with hair, no rotted clothes clinging to bits of flesh. Just the crumbling remains of old bones. Was this what Margaret had been expecting to find? Or was she disappointed, hoping to have been able to gaze upon the countenance of her dead lover?

Margaret made no indication either way. She carefully collected the smallest bones and slipped them into a little drawstring pouch.

The first light of dawn was touching the sky when Margaret clambered out of the grave and hastily filled it half back in. The careless job wouldn't fool anyone, but it would probably be at least a few days before someone found themselves in this section of the cemetery and realized that something was amiss.

With the bones of her lover in her pocket, Margaret returned to Harlowe House where she made use of the change of clothes Augusta kept in her desk, and Augusta was forced to wait and wonder what was to become of her.

36

Augusta

THE HORROR OF the night spent digging in the cemetery
faded into the background over the next few days, and Augusta
almost wondered if she had dreamed the whole thing. But of
course, she didn't dream anymore, didn't even sleep; her entire
life was a waking nightmare of being trapped in her own body.

The drive to Pale Harbor was quieter than any trip Augusta
and Leo had ever taken before, but Margaret didn't seem to
notice. She was polite and good-natured whenever Leo spoke
to her, but she didn't offer anything, never attempted to keep
the conversation going. She must have been trying not to say
the wrong thing to alert Leo of who she was. Good, Augusta
thought, at least she wouldn't further tangle things with him.

It was odd that Leo was so eager for her to come to Pale Harbor again, and so soon. Augusta had gotten the impression that
he hadn't exactly approved of his mother's theories and that he

didn't have the best relationship with his sister. He shot her a crooked smile as he opened the passenger door and helped her out. "Watch your step, it looks like my dad was watering the garden and forgot to turn off the hose again."

Lightly placing his hand on the small of her back, he guided her around the puddles and up to the front door. His hand was probably steady, and Margaret could probably feel his warmth radiating through her clothes. She probably didn't even care.

It must have been Leo's sister, Lisa, who greeted them this time. A tall woman with a light brown bob and the same kind yet probing gray eyes as Leo's. "Baby brother," she said, giving him a side hug, "it's been too long. This must be Augusta." She gave Augusta an appraising look, that left her wondering if she was being tested, and if so, if she had passed the test. "Leo's told me so much about you."

"He's too kind," Margaret said, surveying the small foyer. "He's told me all about you, as well."

Most of what Augusta had gleaned from Leo about his sister was that she was older, lived in Portland with her fiancée and was a successful psychiatrist. Her wedding colors were going to be navy and silver, and she ran marathons.

"Lisa's getting married in December," he reminded her.

"Of course," Margaret said. "How exciting. Congratulations to you and your lucky man."

"The lucky woman, actually," Leo said quickly, as Lisa pressed her lips together.

"Oh! How lovely."

An unreadable look passed between Leo and Lisa. "Well, come on in," Lisa said. "Mom is waiting for you."

Leo installed her on the same sofa draped in quilts as last time. "I'm just going to go see if Lisa needs any help in the kitchen and then I'll send my mom in. Do you need anything?"

"No, thank you."

Augusta willed Margaret to look at Leo as he disappeared

out of the room, but she seemed quite content to just sit there and study her surroundings. The cat strolled in, took one look at Augusta, hissed and then fled. A few moments later Ellen breezed in, wearing a silky caftan and dangly turquoise earrings.

"Augusta," she said, extending her arms and pulling her into a motherly embrace. "So good to see you again, dear."

Margaret was all manners and warm smiles. As Augusta watched her easily conversing with Ellen, she had to wonder: Was Margaret truly evil? After having experienced Margaret's life and sorrows through her eyes, it was hard to label her as such. Yet she had stolen Augusta's life, her body, her hope. It felt like the worst sort of betrayal after Augusta had done everything she could to learn about Margaret and tell her story.

Ellen arranged the folds of her caftan as she seated herself on the opposite chair. "You're probably wondering why I invited you back to speak with me so soon after our last chat."

Augusta was wondering. Ellen's insight had been somewhat interesting, though clearly misguided. But Margaret only gave a little shrug. "You are a very gracious hostess, Mrs. Stone," she said. "Besides, I believe I am here to see your daughter—Leo thinks that I am in need of a diagnosis."

Ellen's eyes narrowed almost imperceptibly, but Augusta caught it. "Thank you. As I said before, please call me Ellen."

"Of course."

"Do you feel that you need to see a psychiatrist? Last time you were here you seemed quite certain that what was happening to you was not something that could be treated by a doctor."

Margaret just gave a shrug again. "If it will put Leo's mind at ease then I suppose it is the least I can do."

Though she couldn't see him, Augusta could sense his presence nearby, and somehow it was comforting. She would have given anything to be able to feel the soft couch cushions beneath her, and to have Leo sit beside her, his leg brushing hers. Margaret was plotting something to do with him, to do with

Jack. With the bones that still sat in her pocket. Augusta wasn't sure how, but Leo was in danger and she was powerless to help him. She didn't like the way Margaret watched him, appraised him. Just as she could sense Leo's presence nearby, Augusta wondered if Ellen could sense that something was wrong with her, that she wasn't herself.

"So," Ellen said, leaning back into her seat. "Did you take my advice from last time? Did you try to initiate contact with Margaret?"

It seemed an eternity before Margaret spoke, though it couldn't have been more than a fraction of a moment. "Yes, I did. It was very sound advice, thank you. She showed me just what I needed to know."

Ellen's response took even longer, and then all she said was, "Mmm." Was it Augusta's imagination, or was there something knowing in the older woman's eyes? "I wonder," Ellen continued slowly, "if that might not have been the best advice after all."

Margaret held herself a little stiffer. "Why do you say that?"

"I was operating under the assumption that she was a benevolent spirit, that she only wanted her truth told so that she could move on. But maybe that isn't the case."

"What does her supposed benevolence matter? Perhaps she was wronged and deserves more than just having her story known."

It was like watching a tennis match, Ellen scoring a point and then Margaret deflecting it, back and forth.

"A witch who practices vengeful magic invites that energy to come back to her. To avenge a wrong against a party that committed no wrong against you, well…" Ellen let her words hang. Her hand fluttered in a careless gesture, but her blue eyes were hard.

Margaret was perched on the very edge of the couch, her fingers tapping by her side. "Perhaps. But this is all hypothetical of course. We may never know what truly happened to Margaret or what she wanted," she said with a sad smile. Point: Margaret.

With impressive speed for a woman her age, Ellen was off her seat, her finger jabbing into Margaret's chest. "Listen to me, Margaret. I know what you've done. I know dark magic when I see it, and what's more, I may have only met Augusta once, but you most certainly are not fooling me with this charade."

Margaret blinked, then tipped back her head and laughed. "Oh, Ellen. I might have known that I was speaking to another witch. How good it is to shed this pretense and speak frankly. You will understand my plight and the trials that I have suffered. You will understand how our kind is forced to live in the shadows at the risk of being ostracized or even killed. And what of your daughter—would you have turned the other cheek if her life was taken at the hands of your son? Would you rest if she died in obscurity?"

"I would fight until my dying day for justice," Ellen hissed. "But I would never entangle an innocent in some dark plot or steal their life away."

The match seemed to have reached a stalemate, and the two women stood in tense silence, studying each other. For the first time since waking up in this nightmare, Augusta felt a flicker of hope. Ellen knew the truth, and if she was a witch as Margaret claimed, maybe she could actually do something to help Augusta. There was light at the end of the tunnel, and it was possible that Augusta could be back in her own body before the evening was over. Would Ellen tell Leo, explain everything to him? For all the unbelievable problems Augusta was facing, it was Leo not knowing the truth that was the hardest to bear. Every time Margaret so much as looked in his direction, a smile on her lips, a little of Augusta's soul dimmed, her hope dwindling.

37

Margaret

SO, THE WOMAN standing before me fancies herself a witch. She might be harmless, but she might also be more powerful than her homely demeanor would suggest. How can I be certain that she is not a threat? My spellwork is proven and my magic old, so I cannot imagine that this soft-spoken woman with the silver hair and keen blue eyes would be able to undo that which I have wrought. But appearances can be deceiving, and there is so much at risk if I fail.

I can see Leo hovering just beyond the doorframe, practically tripping over himself to try to hear what we are saying. I wait to speak until I hear Lisa call for him, and he reluctantly disappears back into the kitchen.

Ellen and I circle each other like two dogs before a fight. "Well?" I ask her. "What do you intend to do?"

Judging by her expression, she was not expecting so frank a

question. "I will do everything in my power to banish you and bring Augusta back."

"Mmm. But what exactly *is* your power?"

"My power?" Her gaze flicks around the room, as if seeing what I see—the framed family photographs on the mantel, the potted geraniums, the mundane comfort of it all. I raise my brows, waiting for her to answer. "My power is love," she says, straightening her back a little and jutting her chin.

"Love," I repeat, certain that I'm not understanding.

"That's right," she says, the waver in her voice evening out. "Love is the strongest magic of all. It can conquer anything."

Laughter bubbles up in my chest and I whisk a mirthful tear from my eye. She really believes that! "Oh, if only love were enough to solve my problems and send me on my way."

She scowls. "I wouldn't expect someone like you to understand. You don't appreciate what being a mother does to you, the fierce love for your children that will drive you to do anything—*anything*—to protect them."

Heat climbs up my core, red seeping in around the edges of my vision. She thinks that I do not know what it is to be a mother, that I cannot understand love without a living child of my own. Well, she is wrong. I know very well what it is to be a mother, perhaps more so because I lost my unborn child. I know what it is like to carry the heaviest burdens, to have to make impossible decisions for a little life that you would gladly sacrifice your own. How easy it would be to teach her a lesson about power, real power. I could send her crashing through the air like the man in the woods or put something in her tea that would stiffen the blood running through her veins. But I cannot risk upsetting Leo, not when I am so close to everything I have been working for. As much as I burn to see her convulsing and begging for mercy on the floor, a small show of skill will have to be enough.

I let my anger build and build and build, not just for her, but for the child I lost, the love that betrayed me, the world that forgot me. When I can no longer contain the energy jumping in my hands, I send it hurtling right past Ellen's ear and across the room. The lamp in the corner pops, and the air goes still.

Ellen stands rooted to the ground, her face colorless, her eyes wide with fear.

"Can love do that?" I ask her, delighting in my triumph.

I doubt she has an answer, but we are interrupted before she can say anything. The air is still crackling with tension when Leo comes in.

"Everything all right?" he asks, eyeing us warily. "I thought I heard something."

"Just—just having a little chat," Ellen says with a tight smile.

Her poor playacting is amusing. "Your mother is very perceptive," I tell him. "I always enjoy our conversations."

Ellen ignores me, instead turning toward Leo. "Can I talk to you for a minute?"

Lisa has emerged from the kitchen and is watching us with crossed arms. She and Leo share a look before he nods and joins Ellen in the hallway.

Making myself comfortable on the sofa again, I watch as Lisa tries to take my measure. She lacks Ellen's softness, and judging from the way she is piercing me with daggers, she does not like me very much. I don't care a fig if she likes me. These women are beneath me with their questions and suspicions. I give a yawn for her benefit.

"My brother seems to think that you have a split personality or some kind of disorder," Lisa says without preamble.

"Oh? And what do you think?"

"I think you've done a number on him, but I told him I would at least talk with you, see if there was anything I could tell him in my professional opinion."

"So you think to diagnose me? That doesn't seem very professional. You hardly know me."

"I don't think I need to know you, to be honest. Leo's told me everything and there is nothing that even remotely suggests a personality disorder. I think you're just out to have a good time and Leo can't see it because of his infatuation. And this is *not* my professional opinion—this is my sister opinion. Leo is my little brother and I love him to death, but he has *awful* taste in women. I'm not going to stand by and let him become collateral damage again by someone who is on a destructive path."

"My, my. I hope you don't speak to your patients so flippantly." I take my time examining the elegant ovals of my fingernails, each with a perfect moon crescent, while Lisa glares at me. "What will you do?" I finally ask her.

She blinks. "What will I do about what?"

"You don't think there's anything wrong with me from a medical stance, but Leo is worried for me, and you are worried for Leo. So," I say, spreading my palms, "what will you do?"

The look that Lisa levels at me is so caustic that it confirms everything I already suspected about her. Ellen may see me for what I am, but this woman is a doctor, a scientist. She would never believe the truth about me, would never even fathom it. She can posture all she wants, but I have nothing to fear from her. Leo is mine.

When Leo returns with Ellen, his face is ashen, his gaze erratic and unfocused. He looks like a man who has just received a death sentence. I sit through a silent dinner with both his parents and his sister, his father the only one oblivious to the tension stretched around the table.

After an abbreviated dessert, Ellen embraces her son. "Goodbye, sweetie," she says. "Remember what we talked about, and be careful."

Leo flicks an uneasy glance in my direction before nodding and returning his mother's kiss.

His bearing is stiffer as he guides me down the steps and out to the car, and I have to wonder: Just what did they talk about?

Just what kind of love does Ellen think will save her son and Augusta? Whatever it is, it is no match for my powers, forged in the blood of generations of women before me.

38

Augusta

THE RIDE BACK to Massachusetts was a silent one. This time there was no stop at the hill, and definitely no kissing. Augusta guessed she should be grateful for as much, but she was having difficulty mustering anything other than a numb sort of hopelessness.

She had thought that Ellen would have done something once she realized what was going on, but she hadn't even tried. And Leo's sister had only believed Augusta was out to take advantage of Leo. Of the two women, she had to assume that Leo would believe his sister over his mother, which meant that she was doomed.

The passing headlights illuminated Leo's profile in flashes. He was beautiful, truly beautiful. How could Margaret sit next to him and not want to reach out and take his hand in hers? Glancing sideways at her, he seemed to be trying to land on what to say. "Do you remember what music we listened to on our first car ride?" he finally asked.

How could she forget? They'd listened to Fleetwood Mac. But Margaret didn't seem to know that. She seemed to only know of things that had transpired in Harlowe House. Augusta filed this revelation away for later.

Margaret gave him a withering look. "Shall we drop this charade?" she asked him. "I'm not Augusta, and I don't have a brain tumor or anything of that nature. You must know that by now. Didn't your mother tell you as much?"

Leo did a double take, barely able to keep his eyes on the road, and Augusta was afraid he would veer into oncoming traffic. But he righted the car, his knuckles tightening around the wheel as he muttered something.

"What was that?"

"I can't believe that my mom was right and I'm talking to a fucking ghost or spirit or whatever."

Margaret arched a brow. "You are speaking to a very living, very human, Margaret Harlowe," she said. "And I think that you have some questions you'd like to ask me."

Leo took his hands off the wheel long enough to scrub them through his hair and mutter a curse. "What do you want?" he asked from gritted teeth.

"Leo," she said gently. "I'm not a monster. I only want the life that I was denied. I want to see the world beyond the walls of Harlowe House. I want to eat and drink and sleep and swim."

"And what about Augusta? What about all the things she'll never get to do now?"

Margaret cocked her head at him. "You really don't know, do you?"

"Know what?" His voice was wary, tired.

"That Augusta asked for this! She invited me, no, she begged for me to come to her."

"My mother said that she invited you, but—"

Margaret cut him off. "Augusta knew, Leo," she said. "She knew what she was doing when she summoned me. She wasn't happy, and she saw a way out."

She's lying! Leo, she's lying! I never would have agreed to this, Augusta screamed fruitlessly.

At Leo's dubious expression, Margaret continued. "She didn't eat, she didn't enjoy anything. She could barely stand up for herself."

"I don't believe that," Leo said. "Augusta might have had her demons, but I never would have let her do this if I'd known."

"But it wasn't your decision, was it? It was Augusta's. She is my blood, and I am hers. She lives through me now."

"So that's it? You're just going to live her life now? What are you going to tell her family?"

Margaret pursed her lips. "I don't know. I suppose they'll think she moved away."

"I see," he said curtly. "Can she hear me? Is she in there some-where? Augusta," he said, raising his voice as if he were trying to yell at someone over a poor phone connection, "if you can hear me, you have to stay strong. My mom said you have to keep yourself separate." He gave her a stony look. "Did she hear that?"

"Oh, Leo, I don't know," Margaret said, even though she knew very well. "Would you really like to speak to her? To say goodbye?"

What was she talking about? Would she do that? *Could* she do that?

Leo had the same questions. "What do you mean? What does that entail?"

"Bring me back to Harlowe House. You'll see for yourself that this was what she wanted, and you'll be able to say goodbye."

"How will I know that it's her?"

"You really don't think you'll know the woman you love?"

Even in the dark, Augusta could see his face flood with color. "I never said I—"

Margaret let out a laugh. "Please. Why waste your earthly breaths on denying it?"

Oh, Leo. She had no heart to be bruised or broken, but she felt her very soul crack open. The rest of the ride was silent until they pulled up outside of Harlowe House. Thick cloud banks obscured the moon, throwing the house into sinister profile. She couldn't believe that Margaret would really let her speak to Leo, not when she would just scream for help and refute everything that Margaret had said. Which meant that whatever was about to transpire was not going to be good.

39

Margaret

MY HOUSE LOOMS into view, the silhouette which has withstood the decades with grace and dignity, comforting in its timelessness. I may have a body now, but my house will always be home to my soul, my pain and love and life painted into every wall, my being reflected in every window.

Phebe warned me against the darker shades of magic, but there can be no light without darkness. It will be better this way. Augusta and Leo, together, and Jack and I together at last.

The rustling of paper-dry leaves in the wind guides me up the steps. The air crackles with electricity, cold and sharp. A storm is coming. Behind me, Leo's footsteps are slow and heavy. I turn, giving him a reassuring smile. Like a lamb led to slaughter, he follows.

Any guilt I might feel is quickly eclipsed by apprehension. I have never attempted anything on this scale before. What if it doesn't work? What if it does work, but not in the right way? The promise of coming face-to-face with Jack sustains me, and I usher Leo inside and up to the third floor a little faster.

I remove the books from their hiding place and pat my pocket, making certain that I still have Jack's box and the pouch with his bones. I briefly consider performing the ceremony in the attic, but think better of it. My powers will be stronger outside in the woods with the ocean at my back and the moon in my hair.

"Come," I tell Leo, as I lead him back outside.

"Where are we going?" he asks.

"Just a little farther. We need the moonlight to perform the ceremony."

Leo plants his feet in the ground. "Ceremony?"

"Yes, it's nothing to be frightened of. I just need to be able to concentrate, to make certain that I can channel her."

"And you swear that I'll be able to talk to Augusta?" I can hear the doubt in his voice.

"I swear."

He doesn't want to trust me, that much is plain. But his feelings for Augusta must win out, because he grudgingly falls into step behind me.

We reach the rocky promontory. The trees are not so thick here as they used to be, and lights from the town spill in through the twisting branches. "Here," I tell him.

In the dark, I can almost pretend that he is Jack. He is not quite so tall, nor lean, but the warmth from his body close to mine is exhilarating. Soon I'll be able to say all the things I was never able to say to him, do the things that should have been done the first time.

Rain is starting to fall, as Leo watches me form a circle of quartz on the ground. He's uneasy, shifting his weight and pacing about. But he is quiet as I make the necessary preparations.

When I am finished, I hold my hand out to him, smiling. "Come. We'll stand in the circle and I will channel Augusta for you. You may ask her anything you please, and you shall see that I was right."

He hesitates, but then he places his hand into mine. A jolt passes between us, some remnant of his regard for Augusta, no doubt.

"Hold this," I tell him, as I place the little tin box in one of his palms, the bones in the other. He opens his mouth to say something, but I stop him, closing his fingers around them. "Trust me."

"I don't trust you for one minute."

I shrug. It doesn't matter if he does or not, so long as he keeps still and does as I instruct him. Shivers run up my spine as I realize how close I am to seeing Jack again. Even if it is just for a moment, it will be enough.

The wind works itself into a frenzy, whipping and tugging at my hair. With Leo in place and Jack's token, it is time for the book. Clouds race, and the pale light of the moon is just enough to illuminate the words of generations of women before me. Even in my first life I never attempted such a feat of magic, but I feel more powerful now than I ever have before, with the damp earth beneath my feet, the storm in the air, and my new body ready and willing. Leo is saying something, but I am already incanting the words that will bring my errant lover back to me.

Augusta

Rain came down in heavy sheets as Margaret read from the book and Leo stood in the circle, looking more and more apprehensive. Although Augusta didn't know what was going through Margaret's mind, she knew well enough that Leo was in mortal danger. Margaret was holding a knife—where had she gotten a knife?—and with sickening clarity, Margaret's plan all came into focus. She was going to bring Jack back. She was going to somehow bring him back using the bones and Leo's body.

But why would she want to bring back the man who had betrayed her? Another woman might have forgiven Jack, but Augusta had seen the world through Margaret's eyes, felt her anger. She was not one to forgive. She craved revenge.

No! The realization of what Margaret meant to do came too late as she finished her incantation, her head thrown back as the rain drenched her. Lightning flashed, and Augusta saw Leo's eyes glaze over as he sagged to his knees. For a terrible moment she thought that he had been struck by lightning. He was just lying there, a dark, helpless form in the night. But then he was struggling to his feet, blinking and looking around the rocky clearing as if he couldn't remember what he was doing there.

Margaret held her breath, her hands clutched so hard around the knife that her knuckles were white.

"Where am I?" His voice came out cracked, uncertain. "I... Who are you?"

Margaret let out a long, slow breath of relief, and stepped forward, cupping her hand on Leo's jaw. "Jack," she said in a whisper. "Do you not recognize your true love?"

"You're not Margaret. I'm not..." He looked down at his hands. "I was sleeping. I was sleeping somewhere beautiful."

"Ah, my love. Of course you were. But I called you back. We have unfinished business. Do you really not recognize me?"

At this, she drew his face the rest of the way toward her and pressed her lips to his. Augusta could see him hesitate, but then he returned her kiss, first soft and questioning, and then with ardor equal to her own.

"Margaret? Is that you?" It was Leo's voice, but there was something foreign and unrecognizable in his tenor. "You forgive me, then?"

"I've thought about you these one hundred and fifty years," she murmured. "I thought of what we shared, what we had." Her words took on a hard edge. "I thought of how I gave you everything, and how you took it all."

Leo—Jack—didn't notice the tip of the knife nudged up against his wet shirt. He had his chin tucked over her head, his eyes closed, murmuring something indistinguishable over the driving rain.

Margaret was going to kill him. Augusta was going to kill him. She had seen inside the book, seen all the spells and drawings, but it had only been for a few minutes when she'd found the books. Which spell was responsible for bringing Jack back? Even if she remembered, how could she reverse it, trapped as she was in her own body? If she could have screamed, if she could have cried and called for help, she would have. But all she could do was watch helplessly as Margaret tightened her grip on the knife, pulling Leo down to her by his neck for a final kiss.

And then something strange began to happen. It started as a tingling, as if Augusta's entire body had been asleep and was awakening, starting from her toes all the way to her scalp. Anger built in her, a gathering torrent that threatened to erupt through every tiny crack. It wasn't just the danger Leo was in, but every pent-up emotion that she had buried over the years. Every time she'd bowed her head, every time Chris had made her feel small. Every time she'd taken the easy way out to avoid confrontation. It built and built and built until she was nothing more than a trembling leaf, ready to be torn from the branch and borne on a hurricane of her own making.

Margaret must have felt the shift deep within her, because she jerked backward, the knife loosening in her hands. Maybe it was because Margaret was distracted, or because her energy was weak from bringing Jack back. Whatever the reason, there was a window and Augusta could not risk it slamming shut before she'd climbed through.

Augusta had heard stories about divers who got the bends coming back to the surface too quickly. She was coming back into her body, but every muscle screamed as if she'd run a marathon, and every nerve ending was raw and alive. And all the while Margaret was fighting back, doing everything in her power to stay.

She could feel the knife now, could feel the metal warm and slick in her hand. It trembled, Margaret struggling to thrust it forward, and Augusta fighting just as hard to keep it back.

It felt like an eternity, but it must have only been a matter of seconds. Jack had been running his fingers through her hair, his eyes closed, but now his gaze snapped back to Augusta. "Margaret?" he whispered as he finally noticed the knife in her hand. "What is this? What's happening?"

"Undo the spell, Margaret," Augusta managed to say aloud. "Bring Leo back."

There was no answer, but she could feel Margaret now, their beings dovetailed together in one body. To an outsider, she must have looked like a broken marionette, fighting with herself, jerking and swaying back and forth.

Amidst all the fighting with herself, she and Leo had inched closer and closer to the edge of the clearing. It was a gradual slope to the beach, but it was rocky and covered in scrubby vegetation. The gravel beneath her feet shifted, and she teetered on the edge of the slippery rocks, feeling as if she might be lost to the wind at any moment. Was this it? Would she come back to her body just to find that she died from a broken neck?

"Margaret!" Jack lunged, fumbling, too, with his new body to catch her hand. A flash of lightning turned the world bright blue, illuminating his eyes, round with shock, as he overshot the distance between them, his feet going out from under him.

A cry escaped Augusta's throat that might have come from either her or Margaret. Scrambling down after him, her foot caught on a rock, twisting at an unnatural angle. Sprawling, she landed on her shoulder, hard. The knife went flying, clattering onto the rocks, and disappearing into the darkness.

Margaret had taken everything from her—her body, her life and now Leo. The anger that she had felt at her impotence was nothing compared to the rage that coursed through her now. Trees danced and snapped in the wind, singing to her. *Let no man steal your thyme, your thyme. Let no man steal your thyme.* Red built behind her eyes, climbing and climbing, turning the world into a bloody facsimile of itself. And then, just as suddenly, it all went black.

Turning her head, a weed brushed her cheek, sending a ripple of sensation through her body. She blinked her eyes open. *She blinked her eyes open.* They were her eyes again. She closed them just to make sure, letting the rain slide down her lids before slowly opening them. Pine needles and rocks bit into her back, the chill night breeze lifting the hair from her temples. Beyond the weeds, she could just make out the profile of Leo's body lying on the gravel below her, waves lapping hungrily mere inches from him.

Fighting against the throbbing pain in her own body, she scrambled up and tumbled the rest of the way down to him, crumpling onto the wet gravel beside him. "Leo. Leo!" His shirt was soaked, the rain and mud making it impossible to tell if he was bleeding. "Leo, please wake up."

She fumbled in her pocket for her phone, but it wasn't there. They were in a barren stretch of coast in the middle of the night; she would never be able to yell for help. She was tired, so tired. Maybe this was how it would end: her life force slowly seeping away into nothingness, Leo bleeding out below her just out of her reach. Then it hit her: Leo's phone. She clumsily searched his pockets until she found it. By some miracle it wasn't too wet, and with her last ounce of energy, she was able to hit the emergency button before collapsing again, the storm clouds spiraling above her into blackness.

40

Augusta

"EXPLAIN THIS TO me again," Lisa said, rubbing the bridge of her nose in a gesture so like Leo's that Augusta's heart clenched. "You and Leo were hiking in the middle of the night in a rainstorm and he somehow fell off a ledge?"

The fluorescent hospital lights burned Augusta's eyes, the beeping of machines grating her ears. Her throat was hoarse and her ankle was throbbing, but after being given some fluids and having her ankle put in a brace, she'd been released.

She didn't want to be sitting in the tiny hospital room, staring at the man who had come so close to death at her hands. She didn't want to be answering Lisa's questions or waiting for Leo's parents to come and learn what had happened. All she wanted was to be far away, sitting on a windswept hill under the stars, with Leo healthy and awake beside her.

At Lisa's question, she finally tore her gaze away from Leo. "I can explain it again, but you'll either believe me or you won't."

There had been a brief inquiry into what had happened, and Augusta had had to give her statement to the police. She'd told them that they were taking a night walk on the rocks and had slipped, with Leo taking the brunt of the fall. Since there was no evidence of foul play, they'd quickly released her with a warning about trespassing after dark. But now Augusta had to answer to Lisa, who had driven down from Portland, Ellen and Terry following a few hours behind her. She almost wished she was talking to the police instead, because the fear, anger and exhaustion in Lisa's eyes was unbearable.

"I just don't understand what you guys were doing in the middle of the night in a nature preserve."

Augusta fiddled with her cell phone. "I wanted to show Leo my favorite place. He took me to his—Castle Carver in Pale Harbor—and the ruins in the woods are mine."

Drumming her fingers on the plastic armchair, Lisa pinned her with a stare. "But in the middle of the night? That isn't like Leo, but I guess it's the kind of erratic behavior of yours he was telling me about."

Augusta winced. "Your mother will understand. She can explain everything when she gets here." But even if Ellen understood, did Augusta really want Lisa knowing the truth? She hadn't exactly gotten off on the right foot with Leo's sister, and somehow she doubted that Lisa would appreciate hearing yet another version of events, let alone one containing magic, possession and witchcraft.

Lisa's lips pressed into a tight line. "My mom. Right."

As if on cue, Ellen burst through the hospital room door, Terry following shortly behind her, and then, oh, God, was that Augusta's mother?

A flurry of hugs, reprimands and questions ensued, raised voices all talking over each other until a nurse stuck his head in to tell them that they had to be quiet or they'd be asked to leave. Everyone started whispering at once.

"Augusta Jean Podos," her mother hissed. She was dressed in her scrubs and looked like she had just come from the pediatric wing. "What is going on? You've been gone for days and no sooner do I get a call from someone named Leo saying that you're staying with him, then I get a call from Dr. Draper that you're here and the police have been questioning you." She paused, as if just noticing the unconscious man in the hospital bed for the first time. "And who is this guy? Is this the boyfriend you've supposedly been staying with?"

"That's my son," Ellen said defensively, straightening up from the bedside. She had gone right to work, tucking his blankets in tighter and examining charts. "How long has he been out? These hospital rooms are never conducive to recovery. How is a body supposed to rest with all this beeping and commotion? We should see about having him moved somewhere quieter."

It was Lisa who finally raised her voice and brought everyone to attention. "He's stable. He needed a lot of stitches and probably has a minor concussion, but they'll have to keep him a few days to make sure there's no internal bleeding that they might have missed. He should wake up anytime now."

"Thank God," Terry said, closing his eyes and sagging against the wall.

Ellen was still flipping through the charts, frowning. "What exactly happened? I still don't understand what he was doing in the middle of nowhere in a storm."

Augusta carefully shifted her gaze away. How was she supposed to tell Ellen that she had almost killed her son?

Lisa seemed to be thinking the same thing. "Dad, why don't we go get some coffees or something from the cafeteria," Lisa suggested. "Augusta," she said, narrowing her eyes, "I think you have some explaining to do to my mother."

The moment of reckoning had finally come. Augusta slid a little farther down in her seat. Ellen was the only one who even had a chance of believing her, and as for Pat, well, it was time Augusta told her mother the truth.

Lisa squeezed Leo's hand, then stood and ushered her father out. Terry looked only too grateful to have a reason to escape the room which had suddenly filled with tension. When the door had closed behind them, Augusta forced herself to square her shoulders and deliver the truth to Ellen, conscious of what her mother would think. For what felt like the hundredth time, Augusta started at the beginning, from her hallucinations to her hunt for Margaret, to the terrible moment when she'd realized that Margaret had taken possession of her body, and finally, the ceremony in the woods. Occasionally her mother would purse her lips or make a little sound of disbelief. Ellen nodded knowingly when Augusta described the ritual to bring Jack back. When she finished, she sat, staring at her hands in her lap.

"Well," Ellen said, absently twisting a turquoise ring around her finger, "I can't say that I'm surprised that Margaret would try a stunt like that, but I'm glad that you were stronger. I was knotted up with worry for you when Leo brought you back up to Pale Harbor and I realized what had happened. Then he took off so quickly…" Her words trailed off as she leaned over, gently brushing the hair out of Leo's closed eyes. "It could have been worse, so much worse."

"I can't believe this," Pat muttered. "Augusta, what has gotten into you?"

A heaviness pressed down on Augusta's chest. This was what she had been afraid of all along: that the people she loved and respected wouldn't believe her. Even her own mother—who apparently believed in family curses—thought she was lying. Leo had believed her, though. A lump formed in her throat.

"Leo will back up everything I told you when he wakes up," she said quietly.

There was no question that Leo would wake up—he was only under a mild sedative—but what if he wasn't really Leo anymore? He might still be Jack, trapped in his own body as Augusta had been. Or even worse, they could both be gone, leaving only a shell.

Ellen was the only one who seemed to share this concern, and she met Augusta's gaze over the sleeping body of her son. Even in the harsh light of the hospital room, he was beautiful, his chestnut hair damp against his temples, his full lips slightly parted.

And then, as if he sensed that he was being watched, there was a flicker of movement under his eyelids, and then his eyes were slowly opening. The doctor had warned them that he would be groggy and possibly disoriented when he woke up. Augusta held her breath, afraid that if she spoke too loudly, she might scatter his spirit away, never to return. "Leo?" she asked, her voice barely above a whisper.

At her voice, the other women broke off in their conversation. Ellen leaned forward, grasping his hand in hers.

He blinked, his gaze flitting between them until it settled on Augusta. Did he recognize her? Did he know that it was really her and not Margaret?

"It's me," she said, hesitantly placing her hand on his arm. "It's Augusta."

The steady beep of the machines and muted threads of a conversation down the hall were her only answer. He seemed to regard her with his clear gray eyes for an impossibly long time. Finally, the corner of his lips tugged upward into the world's weariest smile. "Hey," he croaked.

"Oh, thank God," Augusta said, sagging back into her seat at the same time Ellen gave a cry of relief.

"My baby," she said, leaning over and giving Leo a long kiss on the temples. "You scared us all to death."

"I'm Pat, Augusta's mother," Pat said, her arms folded. "We spoke on the phone."

Whatever Leo thought of this reunion, he was so surrounded

by the flurry of kisses and fussing that Augusta couldn't even see his face to find out.

When Ellen was finally satisfied that Leo had enough blankets, could move all his limbs, wasn't too hot or too cold, she straightened up from his bedside. "We should see if Terry and Lisa ever found that coffee. I think you two have some catching up to do. I love you, baby," she said, holding his face in her hands and planting a kiss on his forehead. "I'll be back in a little bit."

"And I have some more questions for you, young lady," Pat told Augusta, "but we'll talk later."

The door clicked shut behind them, leaving Leo and Augusta alone with the humming machines. Augusta fretted with her hospital bracelet, trying to find the right words. When Leo caught sight of her ankle in the brace and the plastic band around her wrist, his eyes went a shade darker. "What happened? Were you hurt?"

"Just a few bruises," she hurried to assure him. "I'll be fine."

His fingers curled around the blanket, and if he weren't so laid up and tired looking, Augusta would have been worried that he might try to get out of bed and inspect her himself. "And what about Margaret? Is she gone?"

That was a good question. She didn't know if Margaret would come back, if she *could* come back, but Augusta had a feeling that she was gone for good. After the fight for control on the rocks, there had been a change inside of Augusta. She had found something so deep within herself that she had never known it was there. Something strong and powerful, too strong even for Margaret to breach. It left Augusta feeling capable, self-possessed, even if she could not identify what it was.

"She's gone," Augusta said with confidence. Then she hesitated. "Leo, what do you remember?"

He closed his eyes, taking a long swallow. "Could you pass me that cup?" he asked instead of answering her.

She passed him the plastic cup and he drained it. "God, I've never been so thirsty in my life." It didn't seem like he was going to answer her, but then he spoke, his voice so quiet she had to lean closer to hear. "I remember everything. Margaret, the ceremony, Jack being in my body."

Holding her breath, Augusta waited for him to go on. Leo had been studying the cup, turning it over in his hands, but he finally put it aside and looked up, his gray eyes bright and almost mischievous. "Mostly I remember thinking that I was going to be pretty fucking mad if a one-hundred-fifty-year-old lovers' quarrel was the reason I'd never get to see you again."

His tone was light and the corner of his mouth was turned up, but there was a question in his eyes, a sliver of vulnerability.

"I would have been pretty mad, too," she agreed, finding his hand and lacing her fingers through his.

"So," he said.

"So," she agreed.

"What do you want to tell Jill and everyone at Harlowe?"

Augusta pursed her lips. She didn't want to tell the truth, she knew that much. What had happened to her felt like a secret, almost sacred. As soon as she tried to tell people what she had experienced, they would try to pick apart her story, looking for holes and ways to prove that she was making it all up. Just like her mom, who had sat there listening, her skepticism clear as day on her face. "I don't know," she said. "I can explain away some of my behavior, but not everything. Not how I know so much about Margaret's life now, and definitely not w-why I hurt you." Her breath hitched, the full force of what had almost transpired finally hitting her.

He applied the tiniest pressure to her hand. "We can figure it out later," he said. "There's no rush."

His eyelids were heavy and it looked like he might fall asleep at any moment. Though it killed her to leave him, Augusta gently removed her hand from his. "I think I better go and let you get some rest."

At this, his eyes snapped back open and he reached out and caught her hand again. "Wait. Don't go."

Caught off guard, she shook her head. "You need to rest, and I really think your mom wants to spend some more time with you."

But he didn't let go. Her mouth suddenly went dry at the intensity in his eyes.

"Do you know what I was thinking about when everything was going down?" he asked.

She shook her head.

"I was thinking," he said, gently pulling her down toward him, "that when I finally had the chance to hold you again, I was never going to let you go."

"Leo! I can't get into bed with you." Several tubes and IVs snaked from his hands, and he looked so frail and tired.

"Can't, or won't?" He gave her his old smile and she felt her resolve weaken.

"All right, but if Nurse Podos comes in, then it's your job to explain to her why her daughter is in bed with a man who only recently was sedated and stitched up. She doesn't mess around when it comes to hospital protocol."

"Done," he said, painstakingly lifting himself on his elbows and moving over so that she could curl herself into his side. "Parents love me—I'm told that I can be very charming."

"Why am I not surprised?" she said.

He yawned, and when she looked up to see if he'd heard her, his eyes were closed, his chest rising and falling, a smile on his sleeping face. As his breath steadied and deepened, his body warm against hers, she could almost understand why Margaret had done what she'd done. Almost. Because if this wasn't worth risking everything for, then what was?

When she was sure that Leo was comfortable and sleeping deeply, Augusta finally tore herself away, and went to the nurses' station down the hall.

"Could you page Nurse Podos for me, please?"

Her mom appeared a few minutes later, rubber clogs squeaking on the linoleum floor as she hurried toward Augusta. "What's wrong? Is Leo okay?"

"Yeah, he's fine. I just wanted to talk."

"We can talk later, honey," her mom said, clipping her pager back into her pocket. "I'm on shift and you're worn-out."

"Wait. Mom." Augusta caught up to her, dodging an empty gurney. Her mother turned, expectant.

Augusta wanted to be back in the room with Leo, convincing herself that he was really himself, and that he was all right. But she had things that needed to be said to her mom after their last fight, and God only knew what her mother was thinking after her disappearance.

"Listen, I'm sorry about our fight." She could see her mother already opening her mouth to say something, so she plowed on before she lost her nerve. "Let me finish. You're my family—my only family, and you should have told me everything from the start. I know things were strained between you and Dad at the end, but he was still my dad. I want to keep his memory alive, but it's hard when the only other person that knew him won't talk about him with me."

Her mother's lips had gone very tight, and Augusta braced herself for the storm. "You're right," Pat said eventually. "Here, sit down." She guided Augusta out of the traffic of the hallway to a bench overlooking a darkened window. "Things were more than just 'strained' with us. Things were ugly, and your dad wasn't always the greatest guy when it came to communicating. There were more than a couple of times when things got...when things got physical." Her mother paused to swallow some mounting emotion. "I meant it when I said I don't want to spoil his memory for you."

Maybe it was the harsh lights of the hospital, or the truth still lingering on her lips, but her mother seemed small, vulnerable.

Augusta had always looked back on the years when her parents were still together as some of the best times in her life. They had been a small family, but a happy family, or so she had thought. Sure, her dad could be distant sometimes, and he was gone a lot for work, but that was just the kind of guy he was. Old Boston stock, keeping things close to his chest.

"I understand," Augusta said at last, taking her mom's hand and giving it a squeeze. And she did understand. She had nearly fallen into the same trap with Chris, staying because it was easier, despite the warning signs. If not for Leo and Margaret, would she have eventually married Chris and found herself in a tense, unhappy marriage twenty years down the road? "Maybe sometime you can tell me more about it. I want to know the good and the bad, if you're comfortable with that." How easy it was for the past to become gilded, a shimmering memory of what once was nothing more than an ugly truth. But a tarnished memory was better than none at all, and even a clouded and cracked mirror would still shine when held to the light.

41

Augusta

THE BARE BRANCHES of January swung in the breeze outside the small third-floor window, and Augusta let the warm
smell of dust and old wood fold in around her. Downstairs she
could hear the low murmur of voices and muted footsteps as a
tour moved through the house. In the late afternoon light, the
book in her hands looked like any other historic book in the
Harlowe collection, the yellowed pages giving no hint of the
dark power they contained. She had already given Margaret's
other book to Jill and Sharon, who had promptly hailed it as
one of the most important finds in the museum to date. It was
a treasure trove of information about the women of Tynemouth
and the lives they had lived, the wrongs they had suffered. For all
that Margaret had taken from her, the book was a gift. Women
who would have otherwise been lost to time would now take
their rightful places in the annals of Tynemouth history, their

stories known. And though she couldn't bring herself to destroy Margaret's book of magic, neither could Augusta allow it to get out. The spells that she now knew it contained were too powerful, too cruel and dark. Shimmying the floorboard up, she slipped it underneath, laying it to rest for the centuries to come.

Downstairs, she slipped past the tour group, pausing to listen to the guide in the dining room. "We believe this newly restored portrait represents Margaret Harlowe, the only daughter of Jemima and Clarence. Recent research suggests that she may have been the illegitimate daughter of Jemima's sister, and was adopted by the Harlowes. If you're interested in Margaret and the stories of some of the other women who lived in Tynemouth in the nineteenth century, then you might want to mark your calendars for May, when we'll be having an exhibit in our new exhibit space…"

The tour moved around the corner and out of earshot, leaving Augusta in the dining room with only the ticking of the clock. No ghostly footsteps padded along the floor, no books were open on her desk when she returned to her office. Her hair didn't stand on end, and there were no unexplainable tugs in her chest. Wherever Margaret was, it wasn't with Augusta.

Augusta made her way to the carriage house where Reggie was busy stenciling object descriptions on the walls. When he saw her, he lifted his goggles and gave her a grin. "Hey, just the person I was hoping to see. I want to get your opinion on the color for the title text."

Augusta studied the paint chips he fanned out before her. "The pale blue is really pretty," she said. "It will be a nice contrast against the dark background." It was also the color of Jack's eyes, she realized with a pang. It was hard to shake free not just of Margaret's memories and thoughts, but also of the way she viewed the world. Maybe Augusta would always carry that with her.

"You got it," Reggie said, slipping the chips back into his jeans pocket and surveying the space. "It's coming together."

It really was. The carriage house was rapidly transforming into a state-of-the-art exhibit space, the rustic rafters soaring over the clean white walls and glass cases. It was magic to watch the exhibit come together, from nothing more than the spark of an idea, to the hours of research and coordination with different museums in the area, to helping Reggie install the cases. Sharon and Jill had lent their support and experience every step of the way, for which she was grateful, but the vision and inspiration were all Augusta's. Here was something she could call her own, something she had seen through from start to finish. Yet, at what cost had it come about? She'd like to think that she would have put together a thoughtful, cohesive exhibit regardless of her experience with Margaret. If she could go back and do it all again, would she?

Pride welled in her chest as she walked through the carriage house. They had made graphics that incorporated Margaret's portrait and excerpts of Ida's letters, and other documents from the archives were blown up and superimposed on the walls. The oral histories she'd collected from the women of Tynemouth would play when visitors stood in certain spots.

The tortoiseshell comb was mounted simply in a case in a corner of the open space. It was the one object that Augusta knew without any shadow of a doubt had belonged to Margaret, and it had felt important to include it in the exhibition. Explaining to Jill and Sharon where it had come from and how she'd known its provenience hadn't been easy, and she'd had to bend the truth a little, claiming that she had found it in storage, not in a box under her bed.

But it was Phebe Hall's beautiful shuttle, which Claudia had generously agreed to lend Harlowe House for the exhibit, that sat in pride of place. The information the shuttle provided was invaluable; not only did it illuminate the extraordinary life of one woman, but also the rich maritime history of the area and women's participation in the industry. And then there had been an extensive entry on Phebe in Margaret's book, an entry that

spoke of Phebe's vast knowledge of herbs and traditional heal-
ing, of her grace and beauty. It had ended on a note of regret,
though if Margaret had indeed possessed a conscience, little good
it did the people who were left in the wake of her destruction.

Along with the shuttle, Claudia had lent some of her own
work, her imposing driftwood sculptures gracing the entrance
to the exhibit space. In fact, the idea for an entire program had
been borne from Claudia's contribution: the Phebe Hall Fel-
lowship would pay community members to help curate rotating exhibits based on their experiences living in Tynemouth, as
well as engaging local organizations working for social justice.
It didn't erase what Margaret had done, but Augusta hoped it
would have made Phebe proud.

She was admiring Claudia's sculpture of a ship with wings,
when someone came up behind her, placing a warm hand on
the small of her back.

"It's looking great," Leo said, following her gaze. "You should
be really proud."

Lacing her arm around his waist, she leaned into him, mar-
veling at the way their bodies fit together so perfectly, as if they
had been made for each other. "I wonder what Margaret would
think of this," she said, more to herself than him. It wasn't the
second chance at life that Margaret had so desperately wanted,
but she would be remembered, and that was more than many
were granted in this world. It would have to be enough.

Leo's jaw tightened the way it always did when Margaret's
name came up. It had been almost two months, but in the same
way that Augusta would never be free of her memories, she likewise doubted that Leo would ever be free of the anger he har-
bored toward Margaret. "I honestly don't care what Margaret
would think," he said, a hard edge to his voice. Then he softened, his arm tightening around her waist. "All I care about is
right here."

He was right. Margaret would always be part of her, but Augusta didn't have to let Margaret define her, or Augusta's future. "Come on, let's go to the beach. I want to watch the waves." There was one gift Margaret had given her, whether it had been her intention or not: the gift of appreciating the present moment. She wanted to feel the cold winter sand beneath her feet, and the sun on her skin, and she wanted to do it all with Leo beside her. Fingers laced together, they left the carriage house and the relics of another time, the tortoiseshell comb winking in the late afternoon light.

EPILOGUE

GEORGE WAS GLAD to be back in Tynemouth. Boston moved too fast, and the office work was dull and draining. And while he would always have preferred to be out on the water, in Tynemouth there was at least a respect for the sea, an ever-present reminder of the world that stretched beyond the horizon.

After having patched things up with Ida, he was eager to see Margaret and tell her that she had been right, that he'd had to fight for Ida, but that it had been worth it.

But when George came downstairs the next morning, Margaret was nowhere to be found. Henry was staying at the house, as he always seemed to be these days. Why didn't Father insist on him doing something useful in the office, or at the docks? God knew there was plenty of work, but then, Henry had never been one to lend a hand.

George made himself a plate of cod cakes and eggs, then sat

down with the newspaper at the dining room table. The house was quiet with both his parents away on business in Boston, and Molly gone for her day off after her morning duties. He'd only been eating for a few minutes when Henry came staggering in, pale and red-eyed.

"Late night?" George asked, barely glancing up from his paper.

Henry started. "Didn't see you there," he mumbled as he poured himself a cup of coffee with shaking hands.

Something in his tone caused George to set aside the paper and look up properly. Henry didn't just look worse for the drink, he looked like he'd survived a shipwreck. George knew, because he'd seen shipwrecked men. They were in shock, their eyes glassy, their bodies unable to move past the trauma they had endured. Henry had that same haunted look, but unlike men who had battled the sea, he had dirt under his broken fingernails, as if he had scratched and fought against the earth.

George had never been close with his younger brother. It was not for lack of trying on his part—he'd made overtures many times—but there seemed to be an impenetrable wall around Henry. He was dark and sarcastic, restless and short-tempered. It was only Margaret whom Henry had ever confided in and let close. Truth be told, George had never been comfortable with Henry's interest in their younger sister. There was something too intense about it, and he was protective of her to the point of obsessiveness. It didn't matter that they were technically cousins; they'd all been raised as siblings, and it was understood that Margaret was one of them.

Where *was* Margaret? She was usually the first one down to breakfast, getting up before the rest of the family to work with her plants and herbs. "Have you seen Margaret this morning?" he asked Henry, who was turning his coffee cup around in his hands over and over without drinking. "She's supposed to go to town with Ida today to shop."

At George's question, Henry's head snapped up. There were dark smudges under his eyes, his face drawn and pinched. "Why would I have seen her? I just got up," Henry said, defensive. "She's probably still out in the woods. You know how she is."

Henry was probably right, but there was something in his tone that didn't exactly put George at ease. Breakfast finished, George folded up the paper and stood up. "I think I'll go for a walk. Maybe I'll cross paths with her." Henry didn't say anything, just watched George leave the room.

Outside, Shadow greeted George with a whine. George frowned. He never knew Margaret to go anywhere without her dog. A cold wind swept in off the harbor, the mournful cry of a foghorn carried with it. Something was wrong, he could feel it in his bones.

Shadow was dancing nervously, taking a few steps toward the woods, and then doubling back to George, as if inviting him to follow. With one last uneasy glance around the yard, George fell into step behind the dog. "Go on, then, boy," he said, and Shadow took off like a bullet into the woods.

Barren tree branches groaned and creaked in the breeze, a damp chill settling over the woods. Ahead of him, Shadow stopped and turned to make certain George was following before bounding off again. With every heavy step he took through the wet, dead underbrush, George's heart sank further, his unease growing.

Snow was beginning to fall in small, sharp flakes when Shadow stopped in a clearing that abutted the rocky slope to the sea, nosing the ground and whining. The earth had been recently disturbed, and a clumsy attempt had been made to strew branches and leaves over it. Without a moment's hesitation, George fell onto his knees and began digging. With an eager bark, Shadow joined him, frantically, pawing up the earth beside him.

It was her hair that he saw first, peeking up through the dirt, wet and tangled, but unmistakably hers. A cry escaped him, echoing through the still woods. Hadn't he known as soon as he'd started digging what he would find here? How could it still feel as if he'd plunged underwater, held until he could no longer breathe?

His hands were cold and numb as he continued digging, his chest empty. Carefully, he brushed the last of the earth from her, lifting her in his arms. She was light, even in her wet clothes, looking like a poorly made doll of herself. *If I had a someone worthy of such a love, I would do anything to keep them. I would cross oceans for them. I would fight battles for them, would carry them broken and cold home, tend to them and keep them safe with me always. I would not rest until they were by my side, where they belonged.*

Shadow trailed them, head down, in a solemn procession back to the house. It was well past dusk when George pushed open the back door, his back aching, his mind frighteningly clear.

Henry was in the parlor, an unread book held loosely in his hand. At George's entrance, Henry looked up, the book falling onto the floor with a thud.

"What...where did you find her?" he asked in a cracked whisper when he saw George.

"In a shallow grave bed in the woods," George answered, his voice seeming to come from somewhere far away.

Henry picked up his empty glass, put it back down again. "Perhaps she ran afoul of some crook," he said, his voice flat. "Or, maybe it was that witch woman she used to associate with. No one has seen her in some time."

His theories might have been logical, but Henry's guilt was written clear as day on the whiteness of his knuckles, the downward cast of his eyes.

"Her killer smoked," George told him. There had been a stubbed-out cheroot near the grave, Henry's brand. "Her killer was so callous, so unconcerned, that he took the time to light a cheroot and smoke it while his victim lay there."

There was no doubt in George's mind about Margaret's killer, the only question was, why? "Why did you kill the woman you adored?" he forced himself to ask. "Why did you leave her to rot in the woods like an animal?"

Henry said nothing, offered no explanation and no denial. He didn't even lift his head to meet George's eye, the coward. But as George held her cold body and gazed at her peaceful countenance, he found he had not the energy to interrogate his brother. "You're a monster," he murmured. "You have lived under this roof for all these years, and there has been a darkness festering inside of you the whole time."

"Will you report me?" Henry asked, his voice small, like that of a little boy.

George gave his brother a long, hard look. "We are Harlowes, aren't we? Justice for Margaret would mean ruin for our parents. It would mean Ida's family would revoke their blessing for the wedding. Besides, I am not sure she would get true justice in this town, not from the people that treated her so cruelly. No, I think her justice will be to see your suffering, your remorse and wretchedness. You may walk freely through the streets and go about your life, but you will be yoked to her memory for the rest of your days. She will never leave this house, and you will have to live knowing that she is here, watching you. Hating you."

Henry made a strangled sound, crumpling to his feet. "I loved her! You have no idea. I loved her, I loved her, I loved her."

George left his brother like that on the floor as he slowly staggered back down the hall and out to the back garden. How strong and convincing his words had sounded only moments ago. Was that the truth, that justice for Margaret wasn't worth risking their family, or Ida's, reputation? Or were his reasons more selfish? There had been some business with Phebe Hall, and also some angry men from town whose wives Margaret had treated. There was no doubt that there were people in this town who would have liked nothing more than to see Margaret get her comeuppance. There was no guarantee that she would receive justice in Tynemouth. But he didn't want to examine his motives too closely; he only wanted to have her nearby, forever.

She had been the lifeblood of the house, had been what made it a home. She alone had warmed the rooms with her sunny laugh, had infused wit and spirit into their dreary days. Before Ida, before the sea even, there had been Margaret. When he had been away at sea and the days seemed long and never-ending, he had known that Margaret would be there, awaiting his return.

For the second time that day, George found himself digging. And digging and digging. Above him, the gnarled branches of the apple trees watched him and each punishing stab of the shovel. Shadow regarded him, head resting on his paws, brown eyes filled with immeasurable sorrow.

He should have taken her to the cemetery at least, bury her in hallowed ground. But his sailor's heart was insistent. When a man died at sea there were two options: prepare his body, pray for fair winds, and hope for the best during a long and often hot journey home; or bury him at sea. The first option was really only for the man's family, so they could have a grave that they could visit. What sailor in his right mind wanted to be delivered, bloated and rotting, in a wooden box back to land? George, and every other sailor he would wager, would much rather be buried at sea where he belonged, and let the water take him where it may. It was the same for Margaret, except that this house was her sea, her last communion with the place she loved. If he could have buried her under the house, he would have. This was where she belonged.

George's shoulders were on fire, his hands raw and bloody when at last the grave was ready. Wrapping his coat around her, he reverently placed a kiss on her cold brow.

"Rest now, my darling," he said, gently lowering her down. "You are home now."

The first night, no animal dared to trod the disturbed ground.

George watched from his window as Shadow lay beside the grave, head between his paws. He didn't want to think about what would happen if his parents were to return home to find Margaret missing and Shadow acting strangely in the yard. As if also sensing that his vow of service was at an end, Shadow was gone the next night, returned to wherever he had come from. Every succeeding night, the dirt settled more and more, branches and twigs accumulating until it looked as innocuous as any other barren patch in the frosty garden. Gradually, winter snow blanketed the grave, deer delicately pawing it in search of sustenance. Snowdrops, peeking through the thawing mud, were the first harbingers of spring. Their roots probed downwards, drawing up the decomposing body into their white petals and weeping leaves. A hungry rabbit nibbled on the tender, green shoots before scampering away. As warmer air swept in, the white flowers died, and the grave spread over with brambles and bitter rue. A robin feasted on grubs made plump by the rich soil, bringing more back for her nestlings. Summer came and went, and with it, George, departing for an expedition that would take him thousands of miles away from the little grave in the rocky Massachusetts garden. The dry leaves of autumn danced and swirled, borne up into the sea wind and carried far away. Seasons came and went, years passed. The people who once knew Margaret Harlowe turned gray and forgetful, and then one day there was no one left who remembered the sound of her voice, the brilliance of her smile or the dark impulses that had ruled her heart. Her remains lay forgotten but for the trees and flowers she nourished, their secret laments carried on the wind and scattered to the sea, until such a time as they were called back.

★ ★ ★ ★ ★

ACKNOWLEDGMENT

Every writer should be so lucky to have an advocate, friend and colleague in an editor like Brittany Lavery. Whether she was helping to coax a cohesive story line out of a messy draft or letting me bounce ideas off her, I am incredibly grateful to have her. Thank you to an equally great team at Graydon House and Harlequin. Special thanks to my copy editor Gina Macedo for her keen eye and attention to detail, and Erin Craig for bringing my book to life with such a gorgeous cover.

Thank you to my agent, Jane Dystel, who continues to be a fierce advocate and mentor, and the rest of the team at DG&B.

Thank you to Jeannie Hilderbrand and Trish Knox for their early reading and feedback. I'm grateful to the gothic and dark fiction writers' group, Nic Eaton, Caroline Murphy, Rachel McMillan and too many others to name for their support and cheerleading.

To the book bloggers, librarians, booksellers, reviewers and bookstagrammers who read and promote my books—your work is very much appreciated, and I would not be here without you. Thank you.

A Lullaby for Witches is the culmination of my experience working in the museum field, and my sincere thanks and admiration go to the many museum workers and volunteers who are actively decolonizing the field and making museums more equitable places, both for the audiences they serve and in the stories they tell.

Lastly, all my love and thanks to Mike and Florian.